Hertfordshire with her husband and children.
Under the Ice is her first novel.

UNDER THE ICE

Rachael Blok grew up in Durham and studied Literature at Warwick University. She taught English at a London comprehensive and is now a full-time writer living in Hertfordshire with her husband and children.

RACHAEL BLOK

UNDER
THE
ICE

HEAD
ZEUS

First published in the UK in 2018 by Head of Zeus Ltd
This paperback edition published in the UK in 2019 by Head of Zeus Ltd

9 7 5 3 1 2 4 6 8

A catalogue record for this book is available from
the British Library.

ISBN (PB): 9781788548014
ISBN (E): 9781788547987

Typeset by Divaddict Publishing Solutions Ltd

Printed and bound in Great Britain by
CPI Group (UK) Ltd, Croydon CR0 4YY

Head of Zeus Ltd
First Floor East
5–8 Hardwick Street
London EC1R 4RG

WWW.HEADOFZEUS.COM

For Rob

Prologue

The frosted snowman stands in darkness as the young girl fights for her last breath. She loses, sinking deeper and deeper into the lake. The thin ice splinters with her last, feeble kick and the cracks run outwards, fracturing the frozen water. The moon watches with one eye open as the girl sinks into her final sleep.

Jenny wakes suddenly, uneasy. Has he stirred? She leans into the crib and the baby's breath, warm and milk-scented, blows against her cheek.

What was the noise that woke her? It sounded like a voice, a whisper. And the rustle – was it the wind? And the sudden cold. The chill like a sharpened blade. Phantasms of the night so real she felt sure it was not a dream at all.

She is drenched. Her dreams have left her painted in a skim of sweat. Lying back on the pillow and watching Finn breathe in and out, his tiny chest rising rhythmically, reassuringly, she is finally led back to sleep.

Hope Cottage, standing minutes from the cathedral, is quiet in the final dark hours of the deep mid-winter night. Morning will arrive soon enough, with all its demons and knives.

I

14 December

'Have we written Christmas cards for my family?' Will asks, glancing at her before turning his attention back to the M25.

Jenny watches his brow furrow. The ground will be covered in a blink and will vanish, she thinks. The lanes stretching ahead of them are wet and black, visible only in the flashing instants following the 'thwack, thwack' of the wipers.

She turns to look out of her window before speaking. 'Mmm.'

'Have we brought a cake?'

'Not this time.'

'No?' He sounds surprised. 'You always make one. Won't they think it a bit funny if we haven't brought anything? Nothing at all?'

The car running alongside them has two young children in the back. They are making faces out of the window. Jenny smiles at them and they shrink back in their seats, turtle-like, giggling at having been seen.

'No, your dad said he didn't like it last time. He said he had never tried carrot cake and he never would.' She rests her head back. Looking up and out through the window is making her feel sick. 'Vegetables? In a cake?' She can hear him now.

'You're not going to start on my dad, are you?' Will sighs. 'I could do without this today. We haven't seen my family for ages and it's a Christmas meal – just one afternoon. We're spending Christmas Day with your father.'

Jenny looks out at the rushing vehicles.

'No, not starting anything.' The heavy exhaustion is setting in, just thinking about the afternoon ahead. Jenny can feel its familiar wave swelling up inside. Her in-laws seem to survive on endless cups of coffee served up in small, delicate cups with saucers. Their immobile precision awaits her like a straitjacket.

She had thought of her mother last night. Slivers of a memory had laced themselves before her lids as sleep fell: Jenny's fingers knotted in her mother's, resting on the bed, the feel of her black hair as Jenny brushed it out, sticking it with clips of all colours. Since having Finn, the loss is cavernous. She had been so young, the grief had been for a figure, a picture – for what she had not known. Memories for years had held themselves like postcards on a board, sepia, inflexible. The ache a faded bruise. But since becoming a mother, questions shaped themselves in her mouth before she remembered not to spit them out. When Finn was coming, deep in the birth pool, she was sure she had heard her mother's voice call out, '*Jenny*.' It had fallen in the pool with her, the sound landing lightly as she heaved up to clench against the surges, arriving slowly then quickly.

She is tired a lot. She knows Will thinks she has gone a bit mad. Maybe she has. She had been so *capable* before. Now, trying to do one thing a day takes all her will and might.

4

Some days pass and she realises she has forgotten to clean her teeth until bedtime. Will is Will, but busier. She worries she has become someone else. Motherhood has taken her by surprise; it has taken root and possessed her.

The snow falls, and she loses herself in the rush of flakes, remembering: day, night, day... morning, and then Finn. The gift. She has been wholly changed.

It had begun with excitement. A throb. An ache below her stomach, and she had leant forward on the sofa, placing her hand across the band of her trousers, wondering.

Will had hurried in from the kitchen, nervous, laughing, asking her all the questions at once. This first stage might take a while: 'Don't call until they're four minutes apart, until talking is tricky.' So, they had watched a film and held hands. Jenny had looked at his fingers, interlaced with hers and felt thankful she had chosen him.

Later, the pain was so much more than an ache. It had taken her to a place where she had felt entirely alone, working in isolation on breathing, straining, pushing. She couldn't remember the point at which she had taken her hand away from his and needed it for herself, or even if they had been pulled apart by other demands: calling the hospital, arranging a taxi. Later, she had not wanted his hands on her or near her, his touch peripheral. She hadn't slept and couldn't eat. She had sunk intermittently beneath the surface of the birthing pool, to disappear.

The murky, confused minutes ticked by. Will appeared, dressed in a surgical gown, topped with a blue hat, pulling his hair back from his forehead and leaving him shorn and strange. His chin was bristly and without his hair bouncing upwards he had looked younger, vulnerable. For a brief moment, she had not recognised him. His had been a familiar face, but she couldn't place it amongst the many faces vanishing, reappearing.

It had been hot; time had not been linear. Things happened in waves and bursts. They had made her sign a consent form for a C-section. She had grasped the pen and moved it in circles, only partly aware of what was being asked, absolutely unable to construct anything resembling her name. She was writing in code: red, warm circles that had clenched her and held her, and wrapped her up with this tiny baby.

The movement towards the theatre seemed to have spurred Finn on and when he appeared she had been too tired to weep. When they placed him on her chest he had been so tiny, defenceless. She had navigated the birth and now she was in charge. Finn. She had been entrusted with something remarkable.

Some part of her had quietly left, and something else had crept in.

Jenny looks across at Will's hands now, holding the steering wheel. They grip tightly as he tuts: another car pulls in front. Will brakes hard in response and Finn wakes in the back. A shrill, desperate wail goes up and Jenny can feel the familiar tightening in her chest.

At the mercy of his cries, the pounding inside will not stop until she can pick him up and soothe him. Like a kinetic watch, the engine beneath her chest feels as though it will fail her if she sits still.

The cries fill the car and she glances at Will. He says nothing, staring determinedly at the road ahead.

She turns and picks up a toy from her bag, then waves the animal face with a bell for a nose wildly in Finn's direction and smiles brightly.

'It's OK, darling, nearly there,' she sings out.

The crying continues for minutes, stretching like hours. His fragile face has become red and wet, he is squirmed up and hot. She can see him in the mirror they have positioned on the back of the seat. Reflected back at them, he seems so far away. One of the books (she has read many, many books) has said babies need to be picked up within two minutes of crying in order not to feel abandoned, and she believes it. Her body screams *Climb in the back*. She can't continue like this. The bubble of panic is rising, and it will escape in a bang if she doesn't let it out gently, bit by bit.

'We're going to have to stop,' she says, tensed against his response.

'Where? Where do we stop, Jenny?' Will's voice is tight.

He isn't deliberately trying to obstruct her but it is no good. She can't sit here for another twenty minutes, as a witness to the tears.

'Please,' she says.

She looks up at him. His jaw is set.

Minutes pass.

Without speaking, Will flicks the indicator and she exhales, unaware she has been holding her breath. The car slows in a lay-by.

Her seatbelt is undone before the car stops moving and she climbs in the back. Finn is latched and feeding as Will slams the door and climbs outside. She doesn't know where he is going, but she doesn't care. The warm of calm slowly softens her stiff frame. She watches his face, smooth and intent as he drinks.

Will's voice floats through the car window.

'... probably about twenty minutes late... Yes... No, Finn's hungry. We thought he'd sleep... back on the road soon. God yes, traffic rubbish… No, not the A34… Yes, I know you said it might be better…'

Slipping her little finger in his mouth to break the latch after ten minutes, she straps him back into his car seat and watches his tiny body, fast asleep. His face her entire world.

Fastening her belt, she doesn't immediately look at Will as he opens the door. The moment of quiet is loud with something.

'It's OK,' he says, turning the key and looking at the road before looking at her. 'It's hard for me to listen to his cries too, but if we're on a motorway we've got to be sensible. I don't think it would hurt him to cry for a bit. For fuck's sake, Jen, he's four months now.'

'I can't let him cry. I just can't. You know that. I told you it was the wrong time to travel, that he would be hungry.'

'We can't dictate every action around his feed pattern!'

Another pause.

It didn't used to be like this.

Jenny adjusts her top, as Will checks his mirrors.

She knows Will loves him, but she also knows, every fibre of her body knows: Finn needs her. Not Will, not yet. Not grandparents, not yet. Just her. She is Finn's mum, and that's it; it is all she can manage.

'They're here!'

The call from behind the door disappears in the ice wind as Jenny waits outside the big stone house; Will follows behind carrying presents, crunching frosty gravel. The large wooden door, decorated with an elaborate wreath, swings open without Jenny needing to ring the bell.

'My darling boy,' Felicity announces, swooping in and picking Finn out of Jenny's arms, kissing him loudly on the cheek. A waft of expensive perfume drifts out of the doorway.

Jenny first understood Felicity through scent: perfume, coffee, sherry, leather gloves, mints, talcum powder. She enters rooms smiling. Today the musk is warm and expensive, with undertones of mulled wine by the fire.

Finn squirms and writhes under the embrace. Felicity adjusts her hold so he is more comfortable, and he grasps her finger, staring upwards intently. His blue eyes are serious.

'Hello, Felicity. Lovely to see you. Sorry we're late,' Jenny says, as she climbs in over the step, shivering involuntarily. 'He woke and needed feeding. I know Will wanted us to push through but I couldn't leave him to cry.'

'Of course you couldn't. I remember what it's like. William used to scream like a wailing banshee whenever we went anywhere in the car.'

'Really?' Jenny is surprised. 'How did you cope?'

'We wound the windows down, dear, to let the noise out. Henry was determined we weren't letting ourselves be ruled by a little one. That's what one did back then. All different nowadays, I think. None of the "teach them disappointment" attitude we grew up with. There was lots of disappointment when we were young so I don't think we knew how to do it any differently.'

Shoes and coats come off, and the clatter of disrobing and unpeeling fills the usual expectant pause by the shoe rack. Henry doesn't like muddy footprints.

Floral stuffed sofas sit around a low coffee table, scattered with house interior magazines, tilted precisely.

Felicity lowers herself into a chair, and looking at Finn, not Jenny, asks, 'Coffee, dear? How's little Finn's reflux doing?'

'How is she? Coping any better?' Jenny can hear the loud, shouted whispers from Henry coming in from the hall with Will.

'Jenny. How lovely to see you,' he says, entering the room, his large frame hiding Will from view.

'Lovely to see you too, Henry. How are you?'

'Oh well, struggling on. Now tell me about this terrible business...'

'Henry, let them settle,' interrupts Felicity with a frown.

'Sorry, dear. Coffee?' he says, picking up the pot from the tray and pouring it into the arranged coffee cups, waiting expectantly for their fill with an unblinking eye. The liquid splashes in obediently.

Felicity asks if her father caught his flight on time and Henry says, 'Now what do you make of...' and carries on uninterrupted.

Jenny allows the warmth of the room to relax her. Time ticks on. Will rolls into home mode, detailing work successes, nodding appropriately. She feels her eyes closing and her head lolling forward, and she jerks it upright, pulling herself awake. She catches the end of something.

'... clear what's going on, with this trouble up your neck of the woods.'

'Sorry?' Will asks. 'The office?'

'No, no, St Albans. They found a girl's body in the lake this morning, I saw. Only a teenager. You haven't heard?'

Jenny has been popped. The air whooshes out of her; she deflates, like a sagging balloon, suckered to the sofa.

'Really, in St Albans?' Will asks, sitting up straighter.

Henry picks up the iPad. 'Let me get the story up.' He flicks his fingers over the screen.

'I can't believe it! We were walking at the lake only yesterday,' says Will.

'Poor girl.' Jenny tries to speak, but she has no voice.

'Here, have a look,' Henry says to Will.

Jenny leans forward, gripping her cup. The handle is hard and cold in her hands. She looks over at Finn and opens her mouth, fish-like.

'How old was she?' asks Felicity.

Will is reading. 'Mmm, they don't give her age. Either she's not been identified, or they're not saying yet.'

Jenny's throat closes in, gripped by something, gently squeezing each breath. Trying to ask questions, to ask for help, nothing will come. Everything swims around her, and she feels herself begin to sink beneath the surface. Fluid, heavy, her head bobs down. Darkness closes in. The cold, like a knife.

Henry's face contorts. His lips are moving, but she has sunk so far, she can't hear him.

'Your coffee!' Henry half calls and half shouts.

With effort, she glances down. Warm liquid is seeping into her jumper. She feels a wetness against her chest. The brown stain on the soft cotton is bleeding into a formless wound.

'For Christ's sake, it's dripping on the carpet!'

Will looks up and sees tears on Jenny's face.

'Dad, leave it. I'll get a cloth. She's upset. Jen, it's OK. Fuck, it's terrible. It's really sad,' he says, standing up and pulling her up into a hug.

She falls against his chest and gasps for air. The suddenness of her lungs filling makes her woozy.

'Henry, get the cake and the cloth,' Felicity begins. 'No, not now,' she says to him, silencing whatever he has been about to say. 'I think we all need some cake and I can't move because Finn has fallen asleep. I'll sit right here until he wakes up and Jenny can have a rest. Would you like to go and have a little sleep, dear? The spare bed is all made up.'

Prising open her mouth, Jenny can't think of what to say. She puts out her hand to Will, an anchor, unbalanced by a sudden gratitude. Felicity is usually welcoming, but this is kind.

'Well…'

'Go on. No one will mind. If he wakes I'll come and get you,' Will says and smiles at her. 'He's pretty much slept all day and all those books you read say you need to sleep when he does.'

His arm is still around her. It's unusual – he isn't demonstrative in the presence of his parents. It makes her feel like crying again; his sense of familiarity, missing for weeks, makes her giddy.

She tries hard not to look at Henry. She knows he will be watching to check for coffee on the furniture or the carpet. She doesn't want to dislike him.

'OK then,' she says. And quickly, before she can allow herself to change her mind, she leaves the room and navigates the wide, elegant wooden staircase.

2

Dredging the lake is cold work. Bodies, bent and busy, fill the park: camera flashes, phones, police tape. The air vibrates.

The trees, covered in frost, hang jewelled in a shaft of sunlight ending in front of Maarten's boots. Now the snow has arrived, this English winter finally feels real. Last year had been only damp and cold, and he had hankered after the frosty canals of home and stretches of white fields that lie out flat to the horizon, like a solid sea.

Pausing, he allows a brief reprieve. The sky has been grey so far, this morning. Taking a breath, he pulls his shoulders back and looks upwards, judging the likelihood of more snow, wondering if the search will make headway today.

The shaft disappears as a cloud passes overhead, and the colour of the morning darkens. The grey light erases the shine from the snow and frost. Shouts fill the air nearby as something is found and demands a crowd of detail seekers.

'Here you go, sir.'

He takes gloves from a member of his team, and he nods thanks, pulling them on and flexing his stiff fingers.

'And you'll need this,' says Imogen. She appears quietly to his left, passing a steamy coffee cup into his hands.

He smiles.

'When did you get time for that?' He takes a sip. '*Kak*, this one's yours.'

They switch. 'Always time for coffee. Seb drove me – I nipped out at the lights. First one for today, and looks like we might need it if we're going to get anywhere here.' Taking a last pull on a metal cigarette, she pockets it and reties her scarf.

'Have you caught up?' He notices the scarf is pale blue, like the blue of a baby's room.

She nods.

Maarten scans the scene. Mud and ice make for a murky ground. The cold takes tiny bites out of his face as he unsticks his feet with effort and slides over frozen puddles, unbalanced.

The last few months here have been uneventful: drunks, domestics, pre-Christmas busyness. Today, adrenalin snakes the air.

Aching, his fingers warm through as feeling floods back in. Liv had been talking him through the Christmas timetable when the car had arrived. There are twelve days left before Christmas and the calendar on the wall at home is awash with nativity dates, in-law visits, drinks with friends and office parties. Christmas looms as a to-do list. He'd been scribbling in his diary and wondering quietly what to get her for Christmas. A kitchen mixer? It's dangerous ground, buying kitchen items for Christmas. Does it constitute a present or a house thing? He wanted a new bike, and had considered getting her one too, so they could ride out together with the kids, but that would definitely be a gift more for him than her. She had mentioned that the boiler was playing up, and he made a note to check it; he had watched her cross things off the lists, and then he had left his gloves on the table, distracted.

The letter sat on the table. He doesn't have long left to respond. She still won't talk about it. 'I'm leaving it to you. You decide what you want to do first and then we will discuss it. Don't mention it to the girls yet.'

And he doesn't know. Not yet. Rotterdam. The smell of the city, the trains: their efficiency, graffiti. The port with its open arms; its sea that leans outwards. The architecture: balls, curves, soaring towers. Its pull is physical. He can smell the city, even by this lake. But this is Liv's home. And the girls have moved so much. English is their first language. Nic would manage, she'd lived there until she was three, but to Sanne it isn't her home, just a place that is other.

Moving deftly around the edge of the lake, slightly hunched, listening to the crime scene breakdown from his staff, Maarten thinks again of the face of the girl. Young, her features bloated by water, her eyes told them nothing, except she had now vanished. He interrupts his staff with questions, and stores others to run through later. Like Liv, he relies on lists. The A–Z of procedure his map to the truth.

Imogen is beneath the trees on the far side, her red hair falling over her face, staring at something, not touching.

'Anything?' he shouts.

'Not sure. It's a wallet; it's covered in snow. It's been photographed, but hopefully some fingerprints are on there.'

The call had come that morning to say a body had been discovered. His first assumption had been that someone had fallen in. The ice made the pathways around the lake lethal.

If someone toppled in, after a few drinks, then that would be that.

But then in came a report of a missing girl. Her parents had checked on her when she hadn't come down to breakfast, venturing upstairs to discover her room hadn't been slept in. She was too young to wander off without permission, and it was completely out of character. Moreover, when her mother had tried to contact her, the mobile phone had been switched off. She had never been known to turn her phone off, even when asked.

'She would never stay at a friend's without letting us know. Never,' the mother had said, holding back the tears, when he'd phoned to ask for a photo.

It had been the father who had come down to the station to make a report. Her mother had wanted to stay at home, near the house phone. Just in case.

'She's a good girl,' the dark-haired man had said. He had spoken clearly, making a visible effort to keep himself in check. A fading northern accent pulled at the edge of his vowels. Maarten made a study of the English accent, with all its connotations of education, wealth, class waiting to be decoded syllable by syllable.

He had made reassuring noises, without making any promises: the cars were already heading to the lake to look at a body.

It did indeed appear to be Leigh Hoarde. Aged fourteen, a pupil at one of the local comprehensives. Now drowned. The official identification yet to take place, but the picture her father had brought down that morning indicated it was merely a formality. Unlike the face he had seen that morning, the photo had burst out at him like many similar snaps: taken on a holiday somewhere, a smile, white teeth, guileless. The shards of broken youth, mourned by a nation the moment the photo is out, and Leigh Hoarde will be frozen for ever in the split-second frame.

In his boots and by this still lake, he is cold and nervous. Facts are his bible, not instinct; however, a sepulchral feeling sits heavily at the bottom of his stomach. He waits for evidence, but inevitably so. She didn't simply slip on snowflakes.

'Sir!'

A shout comes from further down the pathway, near an overhanging willow, standing winter bare.

He moves forwards, glancing around.

'Imogen?'

She steps alongside. Her breath clouds before her.

There are three police officers in a cluster, around the ground. They are bent low and are moving carefully. The photographs have finished and the tape is in place.

'Here,' one calls out, and another moves over with a notepad, scribbling as the first one speaks.

'What have we got?' Maarten asks. He can taste the answer on his lips and closes his mouth. He will be told, rather than ask the question, no need to encourage such news.

'Footprints, sir,' the officer nearest to him says.

'Yes.' The second one stands up. Maarten struggles to remember her name, Adrika? She's quite new.

'They're moving away from the lake,' she continues. 'They're quite fresh and we've found some clothing too. It looks as though it's been dropped. It's marked with what looks like fresh blood.'

'What is it?'

They look down. It looks a pale purple; drenched, it drips as it's raised. Dark patches scatter the front.

'A jacket. Looks like she put up a fight, if it's hers. Not sure there's enough blood to be the cause of death. I'll let you know what comes back from Forensics.'

Footprints and blood. Moving away from the lake, past the bushes, where tiny icicles hang over the top of branches like jewelled tiaras.

'Good job. Confirmation on a suspicious death, then.' He thrusts his gloved hands back into his pocket, where he can feel the buzz of his mobile.

'Imogen?'

'Yes, sir, I'll call in and get going.' She turns and walks away, her phone rising to her mouth. 'Can you let the CSM know we've looked at…'

He avoids looking at the body again. The post-mortem will come soon enough. Observing the treads, running away from the point where the girl has been found, he rocks with a brief flash of apprehension. Its force is fleeting, but it sinks within him, a curdled viscous drink.

His phone rumbles again in his hand and this time he pulls off a glove and turns back to the path. He answers without looking at the caller ID.

'Yes?'

'Maart? Are you busy?'

Liv.

Oh God, he thinks. He will be late tonight, and she's got this dinner planned with the parents of their daughter's best friend.

'Maart? Can you hear me? I heard they found a body, a young girl. Is that right? Are you busy with it?'

'Yes, love. I'm at the site now. There's no real evidence to say what has happened, and we've not gone public with it yet. But yes, it's a young girl, drowned in the lake.'

There is a moment's pause.

'Looks suspicious,' he says. 'Probably be quite busy today.'

'Shall I tell the girls, in case they see the news? Nic's got Becky Dorrington here – they're making their party invitations and then Becky's sleeping over. Remember her parents are here for dinner tonight – perhaps I should wait for them before I break the news to Becky? God, such horrible news,' she says. Her voice is tight. He can imagine her fingernails tapping the table as she speaks, bold with the orange varnish she'd painted on in quick long stripes, for her design meeting tomorrow.

Fuck it. He doesn't know. He needs to call Rotterdam later too, and he'd been hoping to talk to her. To balance out his thoughts.

'I won't say anything to them yet.' Her voice is clear, cutting into the crime scene, taking him briefly back home.

Neither of them speak and he hears a shout from further down the riverbank.

'Look, *liefje*, I've got to go. I'll try not to be late. Kiss the girls for me. Don't say anything. But keep the TV off. I'll try and let you know about dinner.'

'OK, Maart. Try your best though please. I really want to meet the Dorringtons before the girls share their party.'

He puts the phone away and moves heavily down the muddy track, skirting the roped off area, the flash of photographs and forensic collection. Each boot sinks deeper into the sodden ground. His large print is grey on the white snow.

3

'Could've gone worse,' Will had said, when getting into the car.

Jenny had not answered, instead, she had curled against her rolled up coat and closed her eyes, waking only as they entered the edges of the tiny city, the darkness folding them like a blanket, watching the blackness and the silence. They pass no more than a handful of cars, crawling back through the whitened, Sunday evening roads.

It is still so new, she thinks. Its criss-crossed streets, small and cobbled, are wrapped like a present waiting to be opened, if she can just find the right piece of string. The two months they've lived here have seemed longer. St Albans skirts the brow of Zone 6, a breath above London. Its train route pumps into the heart of the city, taking Will under an hour to his desk.

Fleeing their home in London, which burst like an over-packed suitcase after Finn arrived, Jenny remembers she had loved it immediately. She had been swept to a standstill with déjà vu – she had felt at home, a burst of the familiar and unfamiliar as she had stood at the heart of the park. The city, the lake, had felt like slipping on a forgotten coat, found buried in a wardrobe. She had caught her breath.

To move quickly, they had rented out their flat and signed a lease on Hope Cottage: a chocolate box three bed set back off a tiny, winding lane leading up from the park.

The narrow streets are slippery.

'Bugger, I'm going to have to leave it,' Will mutters, as the wheels whir beneath them. They are at the top of their narrow, cobbled lane.

'Do you think you can walk from here?' he says.

He vanishes out of the car into the dark carrying the bags and Jenny jumps out. The icy air is biting but still against her cheek; there is no wind. She doesn't bother waiting for Will to return, and climbs out, slipping as she closes the door and Finn stirs. She steadies herself against the car, waiting for him to settle, and then opens his door carefully, releasing his seat belt through his travel sleeping bag. She counts to three in her head, lifting him on the third and pulling him to her chest. The change of air makes him squirm, but his eyes stay closed, and she picks her way carefully down the hill. Will has put the lights on in the front room and the bathroom, but left the stairs and bedroom dark. She can hear him unloading the bags in the kitchen.

Carrying her heart in her hands, his breath is warm against her neck. She places him gently in his crib, holding his hand, watching him settle.

A blast of cold air, tunnelling through the house, makes her shiver as she heads downstairs. The clock in the front room shows just after nine p.m. Sitting on their battered leather sofa, she opens a note found on the doormat. It's from the police, asking them to call. Jenny thinks again of the girl in the lake and before going to turn on the kettle, she dials the number.

'Hello? I'm Jenny Brennan, I live in Hope Cottage on Lake Lane. We've got a note asking us to call... Yes, of course I'll hold.'

Will enters the room as she waits for the desk to connect her to the officer concerned. He raises his eyebrows and she passes him the note.

'I'll go and make coffee,' he whispers. 'And bring biscuits.'

As he leaves the room, she smiles, the frustration she felt with him earlier dissipates. She wishes she could call her dad, to let off steam about the day, but at sea there is a patchy signal at best and it will be even later over there; tomorrow will be better. She taps out a text anyway: *Hope you're having fun in the sun. Much to tell you. Love J xx*

The line clicks and a male voice takes over.

'Hello? Mrs Brennan? Thank you so much for calling us back. I'm Detective Chief Inspector Jansen. We were down your way this afternoon interviewing everyone who lives on The Lanes. We're anxious to make some headway quickly. Sorry, I'm just assuming you've heard...'

'Yes, we heard,' Jenny says, not wanting to be told again.

'I know it's late, but would you mind if we came out to run through a few things with you? It wouldn't take long.'

'Yes, that's fine,' Jenny says. 'They want to come out now,' she mouths at Will, as he enters with drinks.

He shrugs. 'I don't think we'll be any help. It's bloody late.'

She nods at Will as DCI Jansen explains the station is only a few minutes away. But what with the snow...

'Yes, fine. Goodbye,' Jenny says.

'They said they should be done by ten,' she says, taking a biscuit out of the tin.

'Well, I might go and open some wine before they get here,' Will says. 'They probably won't want a drink but I do after that journey. The car will need digging out tomorrow. I can't see the trains running either, so I think it will be a working from home day.'

Jenny smiles. It is better with someone around. The snow has been bad recently and she's struggled to get the buggy out. Aside from a few coffees, she's spent too long inside. The house has felt tight. Ill-fitting.

Being in the house for too long is a challenge. Some moments, life's jewels, she's incapacitated with the love. But feeding Finn and changing nappies can swallow a day. It is wonderful and lonely. The rooms have shrunk. Having someone around, just to talk to, helps. Some mornings, when Will leaves for lunch hours and drinks after work, she hates him. Viscerally.

They each hold a glass of wine when the knock comes. Will answers the door.

A man and a woman enter the room, both in plain clothes.

'Hello, no, please don't get up,' says the man to Jenny, as he follows Will in. 'I was just saying to your husband, I'm DCI Jansen and this is Detective Inspector Deacon.'

The DI nods and smiles at Jenny and Will, shaking her head at the offer of coffee.

Standing anyway, Jenny observes the DCI is much younger than she would have expected. Roughly forty, his tall frame seems amplified in the cottage room. Wearing dark, thick-rimmed glasses, she can imagine him on an adult scooter, in pop-up restaurants, paying a fortune for a tiny plate and talking tech. His hand, extended to shake, isn't calloused, but smooth like stone: desk hands. He doesn't fit with murder. He seems untouched.

'I believe you've heard the news?' DCI Jansen begins. That accent, a soft lilt she can't place.

They both nod.

'Well, I'm not sure what you've heard, but the body of a young girl was pulled out of the lake at about nine thirty this morning, and we believe she was taken down Lake Lane at around two a.m. We are anxious to interview you because we've had a sighting of her in The Lanes.'

Jenny bites a sliver of frustration. It's slick, this delivery. 'Taken' can't be the right word. The girl must have been screaming for her life. Out loud she says, 'Really? Outside our house?'

The DCI nods and smiles again. Will indicates to the sofa and they all sit, sinking into the nearest chair, holding themselves upright. A tea party.

'We don't really have a clear picture of what took place. It would help a great deal if you could just run through what you were doing yesterday, any details you can think of, no matter how insignificant.'

Jenny glances at Will, who catches her eye.

'I don't think we can be much help, I'm afraid. We were in bed by about ten. We watched something on TV and then Finn, our son, woke for a feed. Jenny looked after him and I cleared up; then we both went to bed.'

'And earlier in the evening, sir?' Imogen Deacon is speaking now, her legs cross, smoothly. 'Did you happen to walk down to the lake at any point?'

Jenny watches her movements, controlled, elegant.

'Not in the evening. We took a walk by the lake in the afternoon, then I went for a run, but back about four-ish?' Will looks again at Jenny.

'Yes,' says Jenny. She speaks to the DI. 'We had dinner. It

was cold outside, and with a baby we don't do much in the evenings.'

'No, I can imagine not,' says DCI Jansen. The smile again. Bland, slippy.

Jenny wonders if it is a real smile. It has a practised air. His accent is a mix of German and South African. She almost asks him, but holds back. The meeting feels awkward. The body could be in the room and someone may comment on the weather, or compliment the curtains.

'Any chance you saw any vehicles driving down the lane yesterday at any point?'

'Not that I know,' Jenny says, eventually.

Will takes a minute longer, his brow furrows in earnest. 'Actually, I might have done – I went to the car when we got back from the lake to put some blankets, shovel, et cetera, in there. We were planning to drive down to my parents first thing and I was worried about getting stuck with the snow. There was a black car. It was going quite fast for the icy road, and I jumped out of its way.'

'Did you see who was driving?' asks DCI Jansen.

Jenny catches his quick glance to the DI.

'No, I don't think so. I looked at the driver's window, but I didn't really see him.'

'You say "him"?' asks Imogen Deacon.

'Yes, it was a man, I think… assumed,' Will says. 'Roughly our age? Maybe because of the car he was driving – it was a grown-up car – something driven by a professional, not a teenager. I think it was a BMW. But other than that, I really didn't see much. The sun was quite bright and reflected off the windows.'

'Was there anyone else in the car, sir?' asks Jansen.

Will sits a little straighter. 'You mean it might have been the girl? I'm not sure. I think there might have been someone in the passenger seat... I don't know. It was only for a second.'

'Any chance you remembered the number plate, sir?' asks the DI.

'Sorry. I didn't even look. I jumped up onto the pavement, in case he slid into me, and then he was gone. Do you really think that might have been them?'

'You say about four p.m.?'

Will nods. Like a boy scout. Pleasing the nice policemen, thinks Jenny.

'Well, at this stage everything counts. We need to build a complete picture of events. It would be helpful if you could come down to the station to give us a statement? Either now, or in the morning?'

'Now is fine, I think.' Will looks at Jenny. 'Jen?'

'Yes, of course.' She doesn't want to sit in on her own and think of a murderer driving down the lane outside, but she wants to help. There is a tightness around her chest that hasn't fully disappeared since she heard the news.

'Can I leave you my card?' DCI Jansen stands up. 'If you think of anything, we'd really appreciate it if you could give us a call.'

Jenny looks at the card. Usually a card is a signal for a handshake. She hasn't stood up and feels compelled to do so. She takes the card, but he's already started moving away before she can pocket it. His poise wrong-foots her.

'Thank you both so much for your time.'

'Of course,' Will says.

'How old was she?' Jenny asks, unable to help herself. It comes out in a blurt.

'She was fourteen.' DCI Jansen speaks. He stops to turn and meet her eye. This time there's no smile. Her frustration turns cold. His dark eyes are unreadable. Her ears fill with the noise a seashell makes when held to the ear: the hollow sound of the swoosh of water, washing overhead.

The room blurs before her and she makes no move to follow the police to the hall. She hears Will say he's forgotten something. He comes in and hugs her.

'I know,' he says. 'I won't be long. Go to bed – I'll clear up when I come in.'

Tears spill.

Will pulls away and gently helps her sit down, topping up her wine glass.

'If anything like that... ever...'

'Well it won't,' Will says. 'We're going to make sure it doesn't. He's upstairs, fast asleep. Come on... I'd better go.'

Later, fetching a glass of water, she glances through the window, looking out over the park. There are snowmen of all shapes scattered around the sloping hill. Someone has built a snowgirl: she wears a pink woolly hat and a necklace made out of twigs, pasta shells, pebbles. Instead of lumps of coal for a mouth, she's decorated with a grin of red berries. A flower sits in her hand and she smiles glaringly through the falling snow, lit by the moonbeams. Just as the sky becomes heavy with clouds, the moon sends out a lighthouse beam. The berries dare to stand out, demanding to be noticed, bright scarlet in the soft light. Garish. Violent.

4

15 December

'How long until you have post-mortem details?'

'Any word on whether this is linked to Sunderland?'

'Have there been other deaths in the lake?'

'Over here, please, over here!'

Maarten leans forward into the microphone, catching the full glare of the media's blinding, obliterating eye.

'As I said, we will be taking questions later. I thank you for respecting the privacy and grief of the family at this time.'

'Over here, over here!'

It doesn't stop. He pushes out of the room quickly, disorientated, striding for firmer ground and the solidity of detail-seeking. He nods at the superintendent as he passes.

'I need to speak to you, Maarten,' the super says.

Maarten nods again, making his way upstairs, unwilling to stop. The paperwork requesting references will have arrived. He can't avoid talking about it. He's been dodging it at work, not wanting to start the process. He hasn't spoken to Liv since last night.

Footsteps sound behind him and he turns.

'I know you're busy, Maarten.' The super has followed him.

'Yes, sir. I'm just on my way to speak with the parents before they go home.'

'Yes, can't imagine what they're going through. Look...' Standing a head shorter than Maarten and lower still now as he stands a few stairs down, Maarten fights the urge to step down to his level. It will only prolong the exchange.

'Look, about this job offer you've had.'

'I haven't done anything about it yet, sir. It only came through a week or so ago and we've been busy.'

'I know, but I just wanted to say that, obviously, I won't stand in your way, but I do want you to know that we'd be sorry to see you leave. You've made a great start here.'

Nodding, Maarten thinks of how to say little, not to commit himself. The urge to reassure is pointless. He's going to consider it. Is considering it. 'Thank you.'

'You go. Think about it, though. You've a very strong future here. Particularly if you can get this case cleared up. The chief super is here later; she is taking an interest... with all this press...'

'I know, sir. The team are working hard.'

Watching him walk down the stairs, out of sight, Maarten hears the footsteps become lighter before disappearing. Slight, greying, it would be a mistake to dismiss him. Neither a kind nor an unkind man – Maarten knows kindness doesn't come into it at all. It's about the law, and how the law is perceived. The gentle warning, gentle incentive, was loud in the brief exchange.

Striding up the steel stairs, he pushes open the heavy door and takes out his phone. It has been ringing all morning. About sixty emails have come in since he stood outside in the cold, before heading into the conference room.

It is a crazed public event. The national news channels have picked it up and the press are crowded like ants over a rotten apple, swarming in their armies for nibbles. He glances out of the window and watches them, clustering outside. The British – reserved on so many occasions – have, at times, the capacity to dangerously overspill.

The public display over, he pauses before pushing the door to where the parents sit. The press ordeal has been bad for him. For them? He envisions the room: tea, biscuits, drenched tissues, waiting for him to enter. Coming to terms with the press conference, waiting to be told whoever has done this has been caught and that some sort of reckoning is just around the corner.

His eyes ache. He didn't sleep well and the day stretches ahead like a marathon. The phone buzzes again in his hand: Liv. He doesn't open the text, despite the urge to ground himself, to reach out to her. He needs to call Rotterdam by tonight, and he needs to speak with her, but first this.

There is nothing they have yet that will offer any sort of resolution for the parents. Not yet. Undigested rage tastes like bile. Tea and biscuits can do little to temper that. They wait for information he doesn't yet have.

'Hello,' he says. The heavy door clicks closed behind him; the hush envelops.

It is bare and softly lit: the victim room. Imogen sits quietly at the corner of the table. Her expression of sympathy is fixed. She looks up at him and it doesn't waver, just a flicker in her eyes, as his meet hers.

'Is it true?' Tessa, the mother asks. Her voice is quiet and high. Her throat sounds raw. Her pale face, lined with vivid pain. Her coat is pulled tightly around her, despite the close heat of the windowless room.

'Which bit?' he asks, forcing himself to smile gently when he speaks. He sits down opposite so that he can lean towards her, look directly at her.

'You said you would catch whoever has done it. Whoever did it, to Leigh. Leigh,' she cries quietly. 'Our Leigh.'

John, the father, cloaks his arm around her and she turns her face to his shoulder. She melts against him, bending like warm candle wax. The intimacy in the gesture is compelling, and Maarten averts his gaze briefly: a very private grief.

'You will, won't you?' John asks. 'When I think of her... calling for us. Screaming, needing us... I can't shake it from my head. Every time I close my eyes... our little girl...' His voice, barely above a mutter. 'Sorry, like.' His gaze drops to the table. 'She's our little girl. I should've looked after her. When I think...'

Maarten shakes his head gently in response, and Tessa says, 'John,' only just audible, the effort of speaking exhausting her.

Nodding a reply to Tessa, Maarten says, 'Yes, yes we will.' But he's irritated with himself for promising. 'We'll find them. I'm sorry we haven't caught whoever did this yet. I wish that we had.'

'That was pretty rough outside. Tessa, are you OK?' Imogen asks. Maarten watches her exclude the father. She has a tendency to assume the worst of fathers. John hasn't been ruled out yet, but looking at his face, the trembling – Maarten's mind wends to other avenues, to further suspects.

Maarten leans forward to echo her words, speak to both of them. 'Have you any questions about what happened, or about the media?'

She shakes her head.

'John, how about you?'

The man is heavyset and tall, hair cropped close, and beneath his blue shirt he wears a chain. His wrist has some dates drawn in tattoo ink, with initials. Maarten doesn't stare, but he guesses the dates and initials include Leigh's.

'I heard them ask something about Sunderland; what was that about, like? Is there something we should know? I'm from Newcastle.'

Maarten had guessed the north-east. The vowels are flat, more pronounced today than he heard yesterday.

'No, nothing to do with you. There was a murder in Sunderland last August: another young girl, but older than Leigh, a student. A drowning.'

'Might it be the same man?' Tessa asks.

'No. An arrest was made; an ex-boyfriend who had had too much to drink. They're linking it because they're looking for anything, and because I worked up there.' He looks up as the tea enters the room, pushed on a trolley. They pause as it's poured.

The silence kills him and he makes small talk as they stir sugar into cups.

Maarten doesn't need to mention that the press are searching for any link, digging into the Hoarde family, the brother in jail; the assumptions, that everyone would search for connections – the microscope they would find themselves under.

Tessa's shoulders sink and she begins to sob.

John's voice is harsh. 'I just keep thinking about why she left the house, about why I didn't ask her where she was going; why nobody stopped her – what if...?' He dips his head, his hand pulling roughly down over his face. 'When I think back, I bloody wish I'd stayed up later that night...'

Tessa's weeping gathers pace, softly. Imogen passes her a tissue.

'What if I was too busy to see if there was something wrong? I've been rammed with work… making a bit extra to pay for Christmas. What didn't I see?'

His voice cracks, and his words slow. Gravel and sandpaper, Maarten thinks, as he listens to the voice wind down.

Did this man kill his daughter? They need to cross him off. The innocence seems clear writ: his hands tremble, his eyes red, and the tattoo ink calligraphy… But there's an anger in there. There's something. Imogen's eyes are clear and dry as she watches his distress.

John begins again, more slowly. 'Who would do this? What kind of sick… fuck…'

The words rasp from within, and it's time to end the session. To leave them to their naked grief. Each syllable, spoken and unspoken, bare.

'I found this.' Tessa, tentative, introduces a notebook, which she holds above the table. She doesn't place it down, and its cover – backed with pictures of a boyband Maarten recognises but doesn't know the name of – has scribbles over the front. Sharpie doodles, with a teenage hand.

John places his hand on Tessa's, and teases the book from hers. 'Tessa wants you to have this – we want you to have this. We want you to catch him. But… well, we only found it this morning. And we haven't read it yet – couldn't.' He places it on the table, and Maarten reads the title upside down, as the book is laid flat: *Leigh's notebook.*

'There's not much in there, she didn't keep a diary as such; we couldn't read it – it was too… raw. But you have to promise you will look after it.' John leans, and the rasp is there again. It's a voice about to break, or scream. 'We've got nothing left now. Nothing of her.'

Maarten nods. But John isn't finished.

'Look at us, at her, at Leigh. Too late to change our minds about anything now. Too bloody late. If I could go back... protect her. She was a tiny wee thing when she was born – almost fitted into the palm of me hand. Our little girl. Our bairn...'

Imogen glances his way, and Maarten speaks gently. 'I will have a car brought to the front for you. When the post-mortem is finished... we will come as soon as we hear anything.' He watches them both shaking: rage, dolour... It's contained in this room. It will be unleashed later.

'Too late.' John speaks, without looking at Maarten, without any acknowledgement of the others. He looks away at the wall, and rubs his again face with his hand, pulling his large palm downwards over his eyes and to his chin. 'Too fuckin' late.'

5

Hollyhocks is rammed. The morning is crisp outside, but all the wet clothes and boots have turned the warm air in the café moist. It's like a humid greenhouse. Jenny has Finn strapped to her chest and she wilts once through the door.

'Got you a latte,' mouths Sam, or shouts, from her table at the far end. Her words are gathered up and dispersed long before they reach Jenny.

The noise is like a cocktail party in full swing.

Will is working from home, trying to concentrate, so out she has come. She needs air too. The house has felt even smaller today. She has roamed rooms putting away clothes, pacing a cage. The lounge door has taken to swinging closed on its own and banging loudly if she forgets to push in the doorstop. It has created a tiny pulse in her head that has hammered into her calm all morning.

The relief of the walk to the café has pushed outwards her ever-decreasing circles.

Making her way through the throng of people towards Sam takes time. People are dressed in suits with briefcases and laptops scattered on tables; unwilling table-sharing is a necessity. There are about six cafés in the centre of town and on a Monday morning there is always space to meet. Not today. With the trains down due to the weather, frantic workers are out escaping houses full to the brim with children on school holidays and from schools shut with the snow, bursting with all their toys and desire to run.

And the press: beanie hats pulled down, winter coats, feather-down gilets, collecting coffees to clutch as they stand outside waiting for news. The press conference that morning has swamped the town. Jenny had skimmed the edges of it on her way in.

Climbing over a briefcase, Jenny flinches as its owner shouts into his phone. The slam of metal on the counter is loud as the barista bangs the foaming milk jugs, making coffee for the snaking queue, and the door knocks behind her intermittently, opening and closing with busyness.

'Mad, isn't it,' says Sam, rising and kissing Jenny on the cheek. 'Happy Christmas, my lovely, only ten days to go now. How was yesterday? I want all the details. How was the wicked overlord?' Rosie is asleep across Sam's shoulder and barely moves.

They had met in hospital: Jenny sobbing in St George's postnatal ward; Sam with tissues, swearing loudly in her northern Irish lilt about being lied to by all women who'd ever had a baby: 'a fucking burning candle?', 'a bit of breathing?', 'no effing antidote to childbirth', 'ripped in half!'. Jenny wasn't sure she could have made it through the first bit without her; and then Sam had already been in the process of a move to St Albans with Ben and Rosie, giving Jenny and Will the idea to look. The affordable familial home, the perfect commute.

'Not so bad, all things considered. Bit uncomfortable.' She pauses, thinking of the drowning sensation, of feeling airless and panicked, trapped.

A bang behind her is loud; she jumps.

'Uncomfortable?' asks Sam. 'It's pretty uncomfortable here. Something wrong with all these suits so close to Christmas!'

'Yes.' Jenny glances over her shoulder at the crowds. 'And I can't believe this, the murder. Christ.' She settles Finn out of his BabyBjörn and onto her knee as she speaks, pulling a teether out of her bag and shaking it for him with one hand and reaching for the latte with the other. She cranes her neck away from Finn so that if he flings his arm up the large white mug won't spill its contents on his head.

Sipping the coffee with one hand, she feels Finn curl his fingers around the thumb on the other. 'How are you?'

'Same. I can't believe it. I saw this morning they've identified her: Leigh Hoarde; she's only fourteen years old. Was, only fourteen. Horrible,' Sam says, shaking her head. 'They're appealing for witnesses, anyone who's seen this black BMW. Same as Will. Did he actually see the girl?'

'No. Didn't really see the driver, it didn't really register. To be honest I don't think he would have remembered seeing the car if he hadn't had to jump out of its way.'

'Have you heard if she was… raped?' The word comes out in a whisper.

They stare at each other.

'Shit, I don't know. I hadn't thought about that,' Jenny says. 'Will didn't mention anything after his interview…'

'Can you move in?' says a man, behind them. 'There's not much room in here.'

Jenny looks but she has no more room. Finn will be squashed. 'Sorry, not really,' she says.

The man puffs loudly, pulling his table further out into the aisle, the screech of the chair's metal feet on the stone floor stark. The legs of the table move into the path of a photographer, carrying coffee and a camera round his neck. He trips and coffee spills over the man, who screams, 'For fuck's sake! What the fuck!'

Jenny leans in, trying to help, passing the photographer a handful of napkins that sit on their table.

'Oh, bloody hell!' says the man in the suit, and he stands, pulling his bags and banging his chair.

The photographer smiles in thanks to Jenny, grimacing comically, saying loudly, 'Fucking cock.'

Both move away.

Sam rolls her eyes and whispers, 'Honestly, all this business that won't stop, not for a holiday, not for a death. I popped into the library to return a book earlier and besides the usual pensioners, it's rammed full of about thirty toddlers singing "Twinkle Twinkle" in Rhyme Time, and another twenty people all trying to plug their laptops into the same power point and complaining about the internet speed. I heard multimillion-pound deals discussed to the background of "Wheels on the Bus".'

'What about just going out sledging instead?' says Jenny, watching the chaos of the table behind them as two groups simultaneously tried to occupy the newly free chairs.

'I know. Let's hope the trains are back up tomorrow.'

'God, I don't. I love having Will off – an extra pair of hands at bedtime,' Jenny says.

'Getting on a bit better then?'

Jenny sighs. Were they? She'd lost her handle on who he was recently. 'Yes, yes and no. I had a bit of... I don't know, a panic attack yesterday? He was great.'

'A panic attack? What happened?'

'I don't really know. I heard about the drowned girl, and then I felt ice cold and started gasping for air. Will thinks I'm still a bit "overly emotional". He gives me a metaphorical pat on the head, and then we move on. Looking forward to having Dad back.'

'He doesn't bloody get it, Jen. I don't think any of them do. I cry at the drop of a hat. I want to have sex as much as I want to grate my nipples against sandpaper and yet still Ben gets into bed with a sparkle in his bloody eye. They'll have to learn.'

'I hope so. I felt like someone was squeezing the air out of me. Can you imagine me telling Will that? He'd have a fit. This girl...'

'Scary to think that it could be someone we've seen around town,' Sam says. 'Did you see her picture?'

Jenny shakes her head.

'Hang on...' Sam plunges her hand into the large bag hanging over the back of the chair. After a few false starts, pulling out nappy bags and toys, she produces the folded local paper. 'It came through the door just as I was leaving this morning. Here, can you open it?'

Jenny stretches it open, smoothing out the front page, and they both stare at the picture of a young girl, whose large eyes smile out at them from the black and white page.

'Shit,' says Sam. 'She's really familiar.'

They stare for a few more minutes.

'It's Tessa's daughter, isn't it? It is her, isn't it?' says Jenny. She turns the paper towards her and reads the text quickly.

The girl's face floats in her memory: it's the girl who had been helping at their baby singing class. They only met her once, last week. Tessa's daughter. She had made a fuss of Finn and Rosie, cooing at them and smiling shyly at Jenny and Sam. She'd worn mainly black, and Sam had joked about Rosie: pink dresses to EMO black in about ten years' time. She couldn't be dead?

'Leigh. She was at singing. I thought she was younger than fourteen? Can it really be her?' Sam says, looking up at Jenny.

Jenny opens her mouth to reply but nothing comes out. She had barely exchanged more than a couple of sentences with the girl last week. She had not even really registered her beyond a quick smile.

'She can't be dead?' Her throat is raw.

'I know… It's unbelievable. God, poor Tessa.'

Jenny takes a sip of her drink, but struggles to swallow. She feels sick.

Sam's face is white. Rosie wakes up suddenly and begins bawling, quickly red with the effort of screaming.

'OK, OK,' coos Sam. 'Hungry, pickle?' She begins feeding Rosie, hoisting her up onto her knee and resting her in the crook of her arm.

Jenny looks down at Finn, happy with his teether. He will be tired soon. She picks up the coffee mug distractedly; the latte is gone.

'I'm so bloody tired.' Jenny stretches her head out to the side and then rolls it back round slowly, leaning the other way.

'Another one?' she offers, hoping Sam will say no. She has lost the energy to sit here, and she longs to be outside, moving away. She wants to go home.

'Tomorrow, after playgroup?' replies Sam.

Jenny lifts her head and glances at the clock on the wall. The dense air is thicker. It tastes of plastic: acrid in her mouth.

Finn needs a nap; she needs to move. The room swims slightly. The business suits surround her like a phalanx.

'I'll call you later,' she says to Sam. Even to herself, her voice sounds dry and reedy.

'Let's send a card. It's the least we can do. I can't imagine how she feels but I'm sure Tessa will want to know people are thinking of her.'

'Yes.' Jenny nods, her head spinning. 'God, we don't even know her; we've only been to about four of her classes, and only met her daughter once. Why am I this upset?'

'It's horrible.' Sam is pulling Rosie into her snowsuit. 'I'll call the others. We could maybe send some flowers from the class.'

They make their way outside and say goodbye, hugging on the slushy pavement.

Jenny steps through the tiny streams of muddy water, running from the banks of dirty snow lying against buildings; the pavements have been cleared in the city's losing battle to stay moving. The sky is dark; gone is the crisp start to the day.

Finn rides up against Jenny's chest dozily as she hunches and wraps her arms around him. At the top of Lake Lane, she ducks from the trees on the narrow pathway. Bare branches loom and an uneasy breath blows up from the frozen lake.

Her mind blooms with a long-buried memory of her mother taking her hand, damp, warm... She slips her hands together around Finn, pressing her fingers together: a burst of grief.

Quickening her pace, she could swear she can feel something pushing her forward, out of the cold and into the warmth.

6

'The parents, background on them?'

'Yes, almost there, enough to make a start.'

'And friends? Boyfriend? Teachers? Local groups?'

'Working on it, sir.'

Words fly, bouncing off the walls of the grey room, rimmed with a stainless-steel quality. It's a clean look, thinks Maarten, and it ricochets the energy – nothing lost – but it can be bloody difficult to hear with nothing to soak up the noise. Long, open-plan desks, usually clear of paperwork, are filled with the activity of investigation. Maarten feels the bite of adrenalin.

'So, who are we putting at the top right now?' he says.

'John Hoarde, father. Originally from Newcastle. An electrician. Speeding tickets and one drink-driving charge, but so far nothing to indicate anything suspicious. Some family problems up in Newcastle – his brother's in prison and has been for a few years. But we need to start with the parents – standard practice. Tessa's up there as well. There is no real alibi – they both stand for the other.' Imogen talks as she writes his name on the board at the front.

'And?'

'Adrika? You've got the list of teachers?' Imogen says.

'Yes, we've run through them, and from talks with her friends so far, there is one possible, nothing concrete. "Creepy", bit overly friendly with sixth formers. Some mention of him in her notebook: dates for music after school, et cetera, but it's sketchy at best.' She glances at Maarten. 'The headmaster's coming in this morning to go over his statement. He highlighted that she was a victim of bullying. The friends were reluctant to talk much about it.'

'Right, once this is over, you and Sunny go and reinterview the friends. All the usual, but make sure you get the low-down on this teacher and also find about the bullying – names, details. Push for it. Assure them of confidentiality.' Maarten taps his pen against his knee.

Adrika nods.

'Right, headmaster, teacher. What else – boyfriend?'

'He's been away. Family left for a Christmas holiday in Australia over a week ago – but we're trying to locate them to arrange a phone interview, see if there's anything he can add. Nothing's come up so far,' Sunny says, checking his notes.

'I had a bit more luck just now, actually, sir,' Adrika says. 'I spoke to the mother – she's fairly fierce. Worried about her son being upset, and also about us dragging him into this. But there's nothing that he's said to her that she thinks will be any use. He's very upset.'

'Can we talk to him directly?'

'Yes, we can Skype him with his parents. They're willing to do it later today – their morning, our evening.'

'Right, I'll come back after the vigil tonight and speak to them.' Maarten taps his iPad, making a note.

'We need to push on with friends too. Probe. Don't let them get away with keeping anything from you. If you suspect there's anything they know, press hard.'

'What about evidence from the lake? Any word back on the clothing?'

'So far, there were three sets of DNA found. One was Leigh's, and two others. Blood and semen. We're cross-checking DNA with the wider family, but nothing conclusive, early days. Looks as though one might be the father's but if it's her jacket that's tentative evidence to work on.'

'Wasn't there a wallet found at the scene too? Anything there?'

'Not yet. Cash only inside; it's a Velcro one. The kind runners sometimes use. Nothing back so far,' Imogen says.

'Shall I chase that up?' Sunny says.

'Yes, thanks, Sunny. Now tell me about that notebook.'

'There wasn't a lot in there, but there was a date covered in hearts and question marks. And the date was the thirteenth of December.'

'So we can work on the theory that she knew her killer. We'll have to ask the boyfriend if she had met any other boys lately.' Maarten speaks as Imogen turns to the team. Finished with writing on the board, she picks up the notes nearby.

'OK, friends' interviews, background on father and who's doing the neighbours?' Maarten glances down at his iPad.

Imogen reads out from the list, tasks pinned, allotted. Chatter, details. The office group disperses; noise spreads around the room like spilled popping candy.

Maarten checks his emails as Adrika passes a box of muffins round the office. Maarten takes one, chewing as he reads.

'They're good,' he says. 'Who brought them in? Is it someone's birthday?'

'I think it's DI Deacon's,' Adrika says. 'Her husband just dropped them off.' She indicates to the far side of the room. 'He said we'd probably need a bit of sugar today, given this morning. I'm not arguing.' She grins, her mouth full of cake.

Maarten looks over and catches Seb's eye and waves. He hasn't seen him for a few weeks and he owes him a pint.

'Maarten!' Seb crosses the room and the two shake hands.

'Kind of you, Seb,' Maarten says. 'Wish I'd had a heads up – I've not got a card signed or anything. She kept that quiet.'

'You know Imogen – she hates her birthday. Not too much celebrating when she was young. Hey ho. We're heading to dinner later, as long as she's out on time.'

Maarten smiles. 'Will do my best.' His phone beeps, and he picks it up. 'Sorry, got to go – pint soon with Liv and Imo?'

They shake hands. As always, Maarten notes the fluidity of his movements – his grace. Seb, he thinks, again, is born out of time. He should have been a benevolent lord, or a poet, dark-haired and writing in the pitted night; ink-stained fingers and a mouth bloodied with red wine.

Watching him kiss Imogen on the way out, her head tilting upwards, Maarten thinks of a Christmas card picture – then thinks of Christmas, coming apace; the undone tasks will have to wait.

Sunny shouts, 'Sir, headmaster's downstairs. They've put him in room six.'

'Right, thanks.' Maarten climbs from the desk on which he's perched, swinging his feet forward, fired by momentum: sparks of coffee and the crackle of the investigation.

'Imogen!' he calls, as he swings his jacket over his shoulder and pushes open the double doors that lead down to the station interview rooms.

The click-clack of heels sounds on the stairs.

Pulling his arms through his jacket sleeves, Maarten pauses and stands back, to allow her in first.

The headmaster rises as they enter, and Maarten leans over to offer his hand.

'DCI Jansen,' he says.

'Alex Craven, headmaster of Rolyhill School.'

The man wears an expensive tie, pastel and sharp, and his top button is undone. His hair is styled. Very styled, Maarten thinks. He's overdone in this drab room. Maybe he would slot into a school better, against walls filled with artwork, certificates, bustle. But why so dressed today? A photo opportunity?

'How can I help?' Craven tips back slightly, fingers touch in a pyramid.

Lifting the statement that has been taken by one of his officers, Maarten skims it.

'You mentioned some bullying when you gave a statement to our officers. You've said low level. Maybe we could start with that?'

'Yes, of course. Well, Leigh is, was, a lovely girl.' He takes a drink of water that sits by him, sleeve riding up, expensive cufflinks flashing, catching the strip light. 'I can't quite believe it. Such a shock. She was fairly popular, fairly good academically – solid B grades. But last year she was a victim of some bullying by a group of older girls, aged about sixteen, so a couple of years older.'

'How did it start?' Imogen asks.

'Some WhatsApp, Facebook and Snapchat trolling, late at night – all these kids have phones; they tripped her up on the way out of school – they flushed her school bag down the loo and flooded the toilets.'

'And did you manage to stop it?'

'Well, it was the toilets that helped us spot it. That was when we found out, and we dealt with it once we knew. There are policies in place for bullying and we're rigorous about following them. We brought in a counsellor to speak to Leigh for a few sessions, to reinforce her confidence.'

'A counsellor?' Maarten asks. 'Can we have the name? Did the sessions take place in school?'

'Yes – we referred her through the CAMHS programme, I think, but I'll need to check. You know I worried, when I first heard, before they said murder, I worried we'd missed something and she'd... you know. Well, bullying can have repercussions...'

He drinks again, his swallow loud.

Maarten watches him. Each time he said the word 'bullying', he had dropped his 'g': bullyin', bullyin', bullyin'. The stiff suit incongruous with the language, and with the wobble of the hand. He wonders where the strength of leadership lies.

Craven's tone softens, and Maarten reflects on the evident grief, the shock.

'Anyway, no. We got her parents involved too. A bit of trouble there, but then nothing since, I don't think. I mentioned it in case it's of any help. It was the most contact I had with her; she didn't really raise her head much. I had to tell her off once, send her home because she came in with blue stripes in her hair – I didn't mind, but we obviously can't allow it in school.' Shakes his head. 'God, I wish I'd just let that go, now. Rules, though.' He shrugs his shoulders.

'And the trouble with the parents?' Maarten says.

'Yes – it blew over, but I think Leigh's father, Mr Hoarde, became a bit of a victim himself of one of the fathers. It happened on school premises, well after all the children had gone home. We'd finished a meeting about the bullying, and a row began in my office. It escalated once they were leaving, walking through the building. The father of the girl who began the bullying is not the easiest of men – quick with his fists, by all accounts.'

'You say a fight?' Imogen says.

'Yes. I think, and I'll need to check, but it was Mr Hoarde who took a good whack. Two teachers nearby pulled the father off him. It was a split lip, not a broken arm. Nothing came of it – he didn't press charges. I think Mr and Mrs Hoarde just wanted it all to stop. Leigh had been through enough.'

'Can we have the names of the other family?' Maarten asks.

Imogen is nodding, making notes. 'What about Leigh's relationships with her teachers?'

'Again, nothing much to report. Her English teacher really liked her, thought she had a spark...'

'What about...' Maarten checks his notes, 'a Mr Pickles?'

Alex Craven's eyebrows rise, and his mouth purses, tight.

'Tim Pickles wasn't one of Leigh's teachers,' he says, and Maarten sees the authority.

'What about discos, after-school activities?'

'I can't say right now. I'll need to check what shifts he's covered at after-school clubs or discos. They're more PTA events than teacher-led, but I know teachers sometimes help out. I'm going to be honest with you.' He looks flustered – irritated. Maarten watches as he flexes his fingers then leans forward. He places both palms flat on the table. An element of self-justification chimes. 'Ideally, he's not going to be with the school much longer. We've had a few reports about him being seen in clubs with sixth formers... But nothing else. I would imagine it's inappropriate, rather than criminal, but I can't give you any link right now to Leigh. The school is keen to discourage any fraternising between teachers and pupils.'

A knock on the door is followed by a uniformed officer. 'Post-mortem's in, sir.'

Turning back to Craven, Maarten sees the headmaster wince, and his face is now ashen. He feels a flicker of sympathy for the man. Dressed up, in costume only.

'I'm going to leave you with DI Deacon, to take the various details down and finish off here.' He rises. 'Thanks for coming in.'

Alex Craven rises too, and they briefly shake hands. Craven shakes firmly, making eye contact, yet Maarten can feel his palm, cold and clammy.

'If you had to call it, to guess who might have done this, and why, is there anyone else we're not discussing? Is there anything else you think we need to know?'

Alex Craven shakes his head. 'No, nothing. I wish I could tell you that there was. But there is nothing. Nothing and no one.'

7

Will's text beeps: *Met Connor on train. They've invited us out for dinner. Can we get babysitter? Or they come round?*

A babysitter? They don't have 'a babysitter'. His parents every now and again, but too late to ask about tonight. And she can't leave a grouchy, sleepless baby with a stranger: Finn, on his own, needing her, while she drinks wine and makes small talk. Will encourages her, but has never managed to produce anyone. It will fall to her to find someone. And to her to make peace with it.

On impulse she tries her father's number again. Its ring tone is broken, distant. 'Dad? It's Jenny.'

The static is loud. 'Jenny? Jenny? Sorry, pet. The line's not good. How are you?'

'Dad... something's happened. Something's happened here...' In spite of herself, she starts to cry.

'Jenny? Is Finn OK? Is it Will?'

'No...' The white noise blasts down the line. She has to pull the phone away from her ear. 'No, it's not that, there's been a death in the city.'

'Jenny, can you say again? Is Finn all right? Are you OK?'

She shakes her head, her tears slowing. He is on his cruise. It is only for ten nights. Away with his golfing friends. Mainly widowers. What is she doing, upsetting him?

The last time she'd seen him, they'd walked in the park, after hot chocolate at the Waterwheel Café. They'd followed the path of the river that runs from the café to the park, feeding the lake by the willow tree. The lake, in its loose outline of an eight, had been thronging with people: model boats, swans and scooters. He'd stopped by the lake. 'The water...' he'd said, and he'd stalled. 'Your mum...'

He'd looked older, grey. His voice had cracked with emotion. He needs this break. She knows he wishes her mum was here now, to share this time with them.

'No, it's OK. We're all fine, Dad. It's just something that's happened in St Albans. Nothing has happened to us.'

'As long as everything is all right? I'll see you next week – you can tell me all about it. Jenny... Jenny, are you still there? This line is awful.'

'Enjoy your day!' she finishes off as breezily as she can manage. She can't ruin his holiday. And nothing has actually happened to her – how to articulate this sense of dread? This sense of...

Jenny walks up the stairs. Finn's due a nappy change. He grizzles.

Will is out late a lot. Not always drinks, but meetings that run late, work dinners. His law firm hands out big deals with big names: *Titan, Platinum, Zeus*.

'It is work,' he says. 'I'd rather be at home, Jen.' He falls into bed late and details the close of the deal: 'They rolled over in the end. I knew they would'; 'I held out, got it...' His pleasure with the work, his performance, covers his tiredness like a band-aid.

She remembers it: the sense of achievement at work, of pride, of success. Its buoyancy a life force. People saying, 'Well done.'

And the drinks after work, playing squash. She hasn't been to the gym for such a long time. Even taking the tube to work with a book was something she took for granted. A stretch of time where steps, escalators and busy commuters didn't seem like deliberately placed obstacles.

Finn whimpers as she lays him down.

The walls, a gentle grey, darken as the light from the window clouds over. The snow is back. Fat flakes begin to fall.

A breath of draught whispers through the window. It reminds her of... something.

She jumps, and moves away quickly. Her head feels thick this morning – echoes reverberate.

Being inside in this weather is driving her mad. She had mentioned to Sam she might seek someone out, speak to someone... Just to talk.

Washing her hands, her arms are leaden. Finn is squirming.

The whisper sounds again around the empty rooms. Familiar.

Downstairs waits for her. She could go out, but the buggy will be hard to move in the snow.

Connor and Erin can come to them. She's not ready for a babysitter.

The snow swallows things whole. If she wanted to escape, to leave a trail of breadcrumbs to tell of the way back, it is not the season.

8

Sunny is banging gloved hands together and stamping in the car park when Maarten drives up to the school entrance. The dark of night is coming in early: navy and a hint of violet.

Imogen had put her head round the door earlier: 'Hi, we've finished with the friends, first round anyway. Two things have come out of the interviews: Leigh had mentioned to friends that her boyfriend was worried about something going on with someone else, and the teacher, Tim Pickles – apparently, he was due to give her a lift to a pantomime the afternoon she went missing. Sunny's heading over to the school now.'

He stands straighter as Maarten gets out of the car.

'He's still inside, sir. He was going in for marking or something when I spoke to him earlier. I said we just needed a chat.'

'Thanks, Sunny. Come in on this one, will you? Chip in when you want.'

Pushing open the door, the school is ghostly. A cleaner opens the glass door that sits beyond reception when Sunny knocks and holds up his ID. Maarten enters, imagining it swamped with children. Empty now, the grey stairs that lead up out of the hall seem huge, and a cavernous assembly hall can be glimpsed on the left. The school reception desk lies to the right-hand side, on which a coffee mug sits, half-filled with an old drink that has turned white and grows a film of something on the top.

The hall, a mix of paint and decay, displays a damp patch and large pieces of artwork, with children's names and year groups printed underneath, pinned above chipped skirting boards. The stair rails gleam shiny black.

'Gives me the willies, this place,' Sunny says.

'Here?'

'Where I went, didn't I. Five long years. Pleased to get out of it, I can tell you. Not over-keen on coming back.'

Maarten smiles and steps aside. 'Well, you can lead the way then, Sunny.'

The art room door swings open, and Tim Pickles sits at the desk, at the front of the classroom. Blond hair, a hint of wax, an expensive sweatshirt emblazoned with A and F. Maarten recognises the brand from a shop his daughter tried to drag him into, with a half-naked male model outside, music blaring from within. He had left her to it, visiting the Apple store instead.

Sitting down on a red plastic chair, Maarten watches the man start shifting in his seat, eyes Bambi-like. Fingers long and thin, he picks up and fidgets with his phone. He doesn't look, Maarten thinks, surprised to see them.

Maarten gives Sunny a small nod.

'Tim Pickles? I am Detective Constable Atkinson, and this is DCI Jansen.'

'Yes?'

'We'd like to talk to you about Leigh Hoarde. Can we start with the nature of your relationship with her?' Sunny sits on a chair. Its four legs are slightly uneven, shifting his weight front to back.

'I didn't have a relationship with her.' Pickles hasn't really moved. He sits still, like a rock. He hasn't stood up to shake hands.

'No? We've had reports of you two talking, of the offer of a lift to the pantomime on the day she went missing? That she didn't turn up?'

'I said a few of the kids from the school could have a lift. I don't remember if she was one of them – it was a casual thing. I was driving from the school that morning.'

Sunny tries again. 'Well, maybe you could tell us your whereabouts on the evening of the thirteenth of December, and into the early hours of the morning of the fourteenth?'

'I was at home. I finished at the pantomime and then I went home.'

'On your own?'

'Yes.'

'Any telephone conversations? Any takeaway deliveries?'

'No, I don't think so. My housemate was out that night. Why, what have you been told? Has Craven been badmouthing me?'

'If you could just answer, sir,' Maarten says.

'Look.' Pickles puts down the pen he is holding, and looks at Maarten, ignoring Sunny. 'I'm friends with some of the kids at the school. That doesn't make me a criminal. Some of them have fairly crap lives: chaotic families, domestic violence, no encouragement. I'm nice to them. I don't try and hurt them.'

As his arms fold, Maarten can feel him bristling, closing up. The voice is clear, well-educated, with long clean vowels. Expensive, like his sweatshirt.

'You went to boarding school?' Maarten says, thinking of the file he'd read.

'Yes, a small one in Oxfordshire.' Tim Pickles' eyes narrow. 'How have you found working here?'

'It's fine. Great. I like it.'

Sunny crosses his legs and leans back in his chair. It wobbles again, and he sits up. 'An odd choice, for a privately educated teacher? Why not something you're more familiar with?'

'A girl has died and you want to know why I chose to work in a comp?'

'Maybe you could just answer the question, sir,' Maarten says, smiling.

His shoulders drop a notch, and he looks, Maarten thinks, much younger when the fear leaves his face. Can't be more than twenty-three. 'I left Bristol, went travelling, and came back to teach. I chose a comprehensive because I decided I wanted to make a difference. You know teachers often think about it as a vocation, rather than a job? They don't always work just for the money. Well, at least, not to start with.'

'Why here?' Sunny says.

'I was seeing a girl at the time who worked in London. St Albans is great for a commute. We moved in together, but it didn't work out. So now I live in the house and she's gone travelling, bitten by the bug. South America this time. To find herself – again.'

The hard edge has disappeared a little, rubbed away. Maarten leans back in. 'And I bet they like you, the pupils. Young, good-looking, dresses well... I bet you're popular.'

'I am popular. But not just because I'm young; I get stuck in. Once, teachers led clubs, trained kids in sport... Now, with more than thirty in some of my classes, and the curriculum changing all the time, I can see the jaded looks on their faces here. I was taught in a class of twelve. Now? I'm lucky if I get more than twelve books out of thirty marked in my lunch break. But still, I tutor the choir; I run school trips. I give them lifts to school events. I help out at PTA stuff, when none of the other teachers do. That display in reception? That's my work with the kids.'

The phone on Pickles' desk lights up, and he quickly turns it to face down on the desk.

'Craven doesn't care about them; he cares about his statistics, his record. This is his fourth school in ten years – he bounces around like he's playing career ping-pong.'

Maarten watches his face begin to heighten in colour: pink, puce. The tone is defensive. Even if this man is not a killer, he is hiding something. His speech on the behalf of the defence continues. Gains volume.

'Leigh came from a brilliant family, but she was bullied at school. It was me she told first, and because I asked – found her crying after class. No one else asked her... Thirty kids in the class, a bit of bullying gets overlooked. Yes, I offered her a few lifts... No more to her than to any of the others.'

The phone on his desk vibrates and Pickles swipes it up and pockets it. Maarten looks around the room, back at Pickles. He taps the car keys on the desk in front of him, the large chrome key extended and bright.

'If you could think carefully, sir, about anyone who might have seen you on that evening, it would help us out a great deal.'

Pickles leans forward. His eyes bright with intent. 'I did *not* kill her.'

No one speaks. Maarten places the car key on the table, and glances at Sunny.

'I want a lawyer. I'm not saying anything else until I have a lawyer.'

They stand; the small plastic chairs scrape on the floor and Sunny bangs the door on the way out. Maarten touches his elbow and shakes his head as Sunny opens his mouth to speak. Nodding his head to the right, Maarten walks down the corridor and stands beyond the turn. He holds his finger to his lips.

'Sir?' Sunny whispers.

Maarten shakes his head again and glances at his watch, counting one minute. Gesturing, he turns and retraces his steps. Pushing the door open quickly, he re-enters the classroom.

'Dropped the car key,' Maarten says.

Pickles, who is talking on the phone, leaps in the air, his hand waves as though carrying a hot coal. He stumbles backwards, dropping the phone, and as Maarten strolls towards the desk, Pickles bends quickly, scrabbling on the floor.

'Tim? Tim? Are you there? Is it the police again? We won't say anything...' A voice, a young female voice, rings out loudly. Speakerphone has been inadvertently activated.

Pickles' face is beet-red. Flaming skin touches the edges of his hair, and Maarten can see a vein pulsing in his neck. Caught in the headlights, lit by fear, Maarten watches the face colour by numbers. He had expected Pickles to get straight on the phone; his itchy fingers had been twitching during their interview only minutes ago.

'Do you need to get that?' Maarten asks.

Standing, phone in hand now, Pickles shakes his head.

'Ah, here it is.' Maarten bends to pick up the car key, lying on the desk that sits between him and the teacher.

Pickles twitches.

'Who was on the phone, sir?'

'What?'

'The phone, who were you speaking to?'

'I don't have to tell you that. I've told you… I'm not bloody talking any more.'

'You don't. You're right. But I can request your phone records. This is a murder case. It might be simpler for you to just tell me now. I'd be interested to know how many pupils' numbers you do have on your phone. And how frequently you contact them.'

Maarten watches as sweat collects on the man's brow. His eyebrows lift and fall. Eventually, he shakes his head.

'Was it a pupil? Just answer me that.'

'I'm going to call my lawyer.' He rubs his brow with the inside of his wrist, hand still holding the phone. 'Yes, it was a pupil, but it's not what you think. *I'm* not what you think!'

Maarten nods his head and turns to leave.

'We'll expect you at the station in an hour. If your lawyer isn't with you, then you'll be welcome to wait with us until he arrives.'

9

Sam indicates to an empty pew. They duck in, carrying Finn and Rosie. Jenny sits at the end, nervous, but unsure why.

'Busy, isn't it?' Sam says, looking round.

The cathedral is ethereal, lit by candles and a shimmer of grief. Full and still filling, the chatter doesn't rise above a discreet stir, a mumble. Sadness is thick.

Arranged quickly in memoriam of Leigh Hoarde, the small city has turned out to pay its respects.

Will had not been able to get home in time, and guiltily, Jenny is pleased. Sam is easier; she will not be watching. Will has been even more jumpy around her since the in-laws' visit. Since the news.

The dark head at the end of the row in front of them is familiar. Staring, she realises who it is, and nudges Sam. 'That's the detective,' Jenny says, nodding to the end of the row. She can see his DI is there too, a few rows further ahead, straight-backed, respectful.

'The really tall one?' Sam asks.

Jenny nods. It must be his wife with him, and two daughters.

The youngest sits on his wife's knee, and the detective is pointing something out to the eldest. Her eyes are bright, despite the mood. He loops his arm around her shoulders and she leans in to him, following the sketch of his hand as he indicates to the huge coloured windows.

As he gestures to her side of the cathedral, he catches Jenny's eye. She's embarrassed, caught looking at him, and she waves. He nods in response, but she's not sure he recognises her. His daughter waves back, with an open friendliness, and points out Finn to her father. Jenny takes Finn's hand and gives a little wave back, and the girl giggles. She doesn't like him more, but seeing him with his daughter makes him seem at least human. His coldness the day before... she shudders. If it weren't so stupid, she would believe she is afraid of him.

Organ music swells. The congregation stands.

Sam reaches out and takes Jenny's hand.

'*Abide with me...*'

Finn stirs, and Jenny lowers him from her shoulder to her chest, pulling him close. Fighting tears for a second, she allows them, and they overwhelm her. She cries into the folds of his stripy Babygro, breathing, trying to regain self-control.

'*The darkness deepens...*'

Beside her, Sam sings and also wipes a tear. Jenny's eyes are flooded and flowing. She fights for discretion, opening her mouth to join the singing.

'*Change and decay in all around I see;*'

The breath comes, and she joins with the final verse. The singing is loud. Someone nearby is clearly trained and his deep voice booms; someone else equally enthusiastic yet off-key. She looks up at the stonework, arches and curves lift and soar.

The hymn has always been evocative, and yet she hasn't thought of it for years. Her memories often feel as though they begin with the death of her mother: the hospital, the funeral. This song. There are only patchy snatches before that. Her mother's green eyes close to hers if she'd fallen, and the feel of her mother's lips on her forehead – the chocolate buttons she'd slip her after a bump. The sound of her voice, reading a bedtime story, different characters all with different voices. And yet she's not crying for her mother, who, after all, she didn't really know. These tears are different. They swallow her. They drown her.

'*Shine through the gloom, and point me to the skies,*
… morning breaks, and earth's vain shadows flee…'

As the final line approaches, the horizon of control approaches, is within grasp. Her grief is disproportionate; she instinctively needs to hide it. It is sad, but why is she *this* sad? Why *this* girl?

From behind her, from the aisle, where there is no one, like a fridge opening at the corner of her ear, a frosty breath makes her cling to Finn so hard he whimpers. The voice is faint, a brush against her arm, the whisper crystal: '*Save her.*'

It is a female voice. Light, like a bell. A tiny chime.

The room stands around her, and Jenny feels as though she is pinpointed, the axis on which the city rotates. The bustle: organ music, grief, singing, candles… They move round her. The spot on which she stands is still like stone. Darkness begins to press. She daren't turn. Daren't breathe – even the movement of an eyelid feels as though the balance of this world might collapse. '*Save her.*'

And then the breath vanishes. The fridge door closes. The darkness recedes. She knows, without looking, without listening, that whatever had been there has now gone.

The chorus swells to the finish. The hymn is still playing and Jenny, crying no more, still dare not open her mouth. Beside her Sam sings:

'*In life, in death, O Lord, abide with me.*'

10

'I'll try not to be late,' Maarten says, kissing Liv and the girls.

They stand at the top of the park, down from the great wooden doors of the cathedral that preside over the sloping hill. The shadows of the nights are long. Snow falls softly, but only visible in the yellow circle around the old iron street lamp that lights the path leading down to the lake.

'Bye, Papa!' Sanne throws her arms around his neck.

Nic is more subdued. Maarten kneels, looking at her from her level.

'You OK, *schatje*?'

She nods, but doesn't speak. He glances up at Liv, a bright blue beanie hat failing to contain her curls, and she shakes her head.

'Why don't we go home for a hot chocolate and a Christmas film? I'll make popcorn.' She scoops up Sanne in one arm and takes Nic's hand in the other. 'Shall we keep some for Papa, or eat it all?'

The girls laugh, and Maarten wishes he could follow them, as they turn to walk towards the car. The outline of the three of them blends into the crowd of the city as the cathedral empties. He owes it to Leigh Hoarde to go back and try to unpick this mess.

People cluster and throng. St Albans is a grieving huddle. They deserve his full attention.

'Want a lift, Maarten?'

He turns; Imogen and Seb stand behind him, layered with hats and scarves.

'We're heading out for a late birthday drink after the interview, so Seb is driving me to the station to wait.' Imogen shivers as she speaks, hooking her scarf up her face with her nose.

'Even one drink is better than nothing. Even tonight. Especially tonight,' says Seb.

Maarten nods, and they head down the dark, curved path, weaving through the graveyard amongst the crowds, finding their way back to town.

'Think he was in there?' Imogen asks, stepping alongside Maarten as they walk out of the scope of the lights of the cathedral doors.

'I'd be surprised if he wasn't,' Maarten says. 'I'd put money on him watching, creeping. Either that or he's fled – far away.'

'No Pickles,' Imogen says.

'I looked too.' Maarten watches the backs of the throng of people as they enter the cobbled street that leads up towards the centre of the market square. 'But he wouldn't show his face, not after this evening. He's not got the swagger.'

Seb pulls out a key, and the lights flash on the car that is parked at the edge of the sweeping curve of the cathedral road.

Maarten ducks his head to get into the passenger seat.

'I think—' Imogen begins, but there is a shout from further up the street.

'What's that?' Maarten climbs out, and sees the throng up ahead on the narrow street collect to a mass. A congregation. He strides up past the tiny shops, where windows wink and blink their Christmas lights.

'Why were they there then, if it wasn't one of your staff, Craven?' The shout from the crowd is loud, and Maarten can see the headmaster, not physically flattened, but surrounded, pinned by the crowd. He stands up against a gift shop, and a white porcelain reindeer head peers out of the display window, watching.

'God, it's a mob,' Seb mutters.

'Do you know? Do you know if it was someone from your school?' someone shouts, and there are mutters floating down the street, to where Maarten stands: 'He must know...', '... someone capable of that working there...', '... doing their checks properly?'

Imogen walks into the crowd. 'Police, move aside please. DI Deacon. I'm not sure what is going on here, but it's time to get going.'

Some glance around, and see Imogen and Maarten. A few fall back immediately, and a small path opens to where Craven stands. Seb moves aside to let Maarten walk ahead, and he skirts round the back of the crowd, behind where Imogen stands; he searches the mob.

'Was it someone at the school? We heard you were there today!' The shout is loud, as eyes swivel. Maarten wonders for a second if they need to call for backup, but it's only seven p.m., no one is drunk here.

'Anyone can walk into that school... sign your name Mickey Mouse and you're in!' Another shout. 'Must be someone at your school!'

'Yeah, falls at your feet, doesn't it, Craven?'

Maarten tenses but, scanning, is reassured; it's a mild-mannered group: a grieving crowd rather than an angry mob. And he doesn't blame them. The death of a child can stir up the sleepiest of towns.

'It's time to head home, or on to your destination. This is not the time or the place.' Maarten uses his full height to look down upon them, and more scatter, stand back.

'What about the family – have you checked them?' Another shout, but this is met with some dissent: 'Leave them alone!', 'What they're going through…'

And Maarten can feel a return of the rising tension.

'Well, if it wasn't them, why weren't they keeping a better eye on her?'

There's a flash from the side, and Maarten closes his eyes against the light. As he opens them he sees what looks to be a cluster of press gathering, and he sees Seb step forward so that his back is up against the cameras, shielding Maarten and Imogen. Here for the vigil, Maarten thinks, like sharks.

'She was only fourteen!' Another shout, but the press have thrown the group, and more have scattered; the sting has left the throng; some heads dip, and they begin moving slowly up the winding lane, towards the centre of the tiny city.

Imogen takes out her badge and flashes it at a few of the aggressors, walking towards them. Maarten sees Seb raise his hand in front of another camera, as it points towards them.

Slowly, it ebbs away. They are left with a handful of people, who look shaken, and duck their heads.

'Thank you,' Craven says, approaching Maarten, and Imogen joins them. He is flustered, and his hands shake.

'No problem. Do call us if you are bothered again.'

'This isn't going to blow over, is it?'

Maarten shakes his head. Shadows from the street lamps fall across the narrow lane, and the snow comes once more, as Craven tucks his hands deep into his coat pockets, hunching, turning away.

It will get ugly soon.

The sound of a car engine hums behind them, and Seb, who must have ducked out early, calls out from the driver's window. 'Come on, I've got the heat on. I'll buy you both a drink when you've finished tonight. Doubles.'

11

'Hello, can you hear me?'

The image, of a family, unresponsive, waiting to begin, appears before Maarten. The room is bright with the Australian sun, and their faces are rosy-brown, like builders' tea, Maarten thinks. The boy's face – and he only looks about twelve, younger than his years – in contrast, has a pallor beneath the glow; starling scared; mock-turtle sad. There are no tears on his face, but they wait in his eyes, like a drop at the end of a tap waiting to splash.

The mother, composed for battle, is devoid of expression. She has a notepad before her and her shoulders sit high, tense.

'Hello, can you hear me?' He tries again.

The screen goes black then lights again, and the image opens to full screen, with sound booming. 'Hello? Hello? Is it on?'

The father comes into view and sits down next to his son, and the mother leans forward. Engages.

'DCI Jansen?'

'Hello, yes. It's good of you to organise the time. I realise this must be difficult for you. Arjun, for you in particular.'

The boy nods, and the tears begin to fall. His father puts his arm around his shoulders; the mother winces.

'I won't keep you long, but I know that you've heard about Leigh and I just wanted to ask you if you had any information that might help us. I have a couple of questions, and I'll just jump straight in – try not to keep you.'

They nod again. Maarten begins. 'Firstly, can I just ask about Leigh? Is there anyone she has mentioned recently, who you think it is worth telling us about? Anyone who she was scared of, or excited about meeting? Anything unusual?'

The boy, Arjun, looks to his mother before answering, and she nods, encouraging.

His voice, high and newly breaking, trembles. 'No, she didn't mention anyone. Not really.'

'What do you mean, not really?' Maarten asks. He stops himself leaning forward, looking interested.

'Well, nothing. It's just… well, she took a few calls, on her phone. And…' He cries, leaning forward and his shoulders shake. The mother looks to the father and tilts her head, juts her chin to the left, indicating to the screen. Maarten watches it from across the world, and feels impatient. He hasn't got long. This woman is not going to let him have much more time with her son like this.

'Detective Chief Inspector, my son…' The father's voice is reluctant, pushed on by his wife.

'This really won't take long at all,' Maarten says, leaning forward now, trying to look into the eyes of the boy, to hold his attention.

'Who was it on her phone, did you see?'

Arjun shakes his head. 'No, and when I did look...' he looks embarrassed, 'I did look once at her phone, when she had left the room. I thought maybe it was Max Davies from year twelve who was calling – but there was no name. It was just a number. And it wasn't...'

He looks nervous now, Maarten thinks. The glance to his mother – this is something he wonders if he should have already said, or should not be saying.

'Well, it wasn't her usual phone. Her normal one has a green cover, with stickers, but this was an old one. A Nokia or something – I don't really know the make. It only has a small screen.'

'She had two phones?' Maarten asks.

'I asked her where she got it. She was really casual, like it didn't matter, but she said someone gave it to her. I thought it probably wasn't Max Davies then, because if he was going to ask her out, he'd just do it. He wouldn't think I would stop him. And I wouldn't of, couldn't of. But I did think it was really crazy, that someone would give her a phone to just make calls to her.'

'Arjun, who do you think it might have been? Who do you think might have given her the phone?'

This time, when he cries, his shoulders pulse, brittle. Only a fledgling. And the mother looks directly at Maarten, placing her hand on her son's. 'It's enough, DCI Jansen. That's enough. He's only fourteen.' The strength in her face is melting. She too looks as though she may cry. Maarten moves quickly.

'Arjun, do you have any idea?' he pushes. He only has a few seconds.

'It was something a grown-up would choose. No one else would buy a crap phone like that – it wouldn't be a good present. I wondered if it was Mr Pickles. He was always nice

71

to her, and always nicer to the girls than the boys. I wish I had said something. Mum, I'm so sorry.'

Maarten watches the mother, her arms scooping up her son, say, 'Turn it off.'

'Thank you, Mr and Mrs Asante. Thank you, Arjun.' And he hopes they heard his thanks as the screen goes dark. The strength of the Antipodean sun vanishing like a light switch turning off. Black.

12

'... and this murder.' Erin takes a swig of wine. 'Fuck, I can't get my head round it.'

The dressed wooden table, the wine, light from the dimmed lamps and candles; the hiss of the cooking pot every now and again gently answering scrapes from chairs as they settle in and settle down.

'How did we get so wet, only coming from next door!' Erin had said, her blonde hair dancing out of its grips.

Friends for only the two months since moving in. 'We're so lucky!' they'd exclaimed, discovering people roughly their age, as neighbours, able to socialise without arranging babysitters. Will had met Erin before at work – different firms, but same job.

'Tell us about the interview, Will. I haven't had the details. Did they tape it, and get you a lawyer in? Bet it was funny being on the other side for a change,' Connor says. He grins. 'Were there doughnuts on the table?'

'He's not a bloody suspect, Connor!' Erin waves her hand.

'Anyway, he might not want to talk about it, and they might have asked him not to.'

'Oh God, Erin, you deal with mergers and acquisitions; I bet you've never set foot in a police station. You're not the kind of lawyer I want to hear about. Come on, Will, tell us what it's like at the dirty end.'

Will shakes his head. 'Nothing to tell, really. I told them what I'd seen. They wrote it down, I read it and signed it. That's it. You didn't see anything?'

'We were away,' Erin says, topping up her glass. 'I was at a spa thing and Connor was playing boozy golf with some friends. I couldn't believe it when I got back. Connor was being interviewed by the police on our doorstep. I thought he'd been done for drink-driving. Again.'

'You know, I thought you were in for some reason. Oh shit, is that dinner?' Will glances up as the top of the pot lifts with the steam, banging down hard.

He glances at Jenny. 'Anyway, let's not go on about it.'

'It's pretty hard not to think about it. It happened outside our door,' Erin says.

'I know.' Jenny had picked up the olives but puts them down again, untouched. 'I know. I can't stop thinking about her. It almost feels wrong, somehow, to carry on with Christmas when it's all so... so up in the air.'

'Well, we can't do anything about it,' says Will, eyeing Jenny carefully.

Jenny sees Will watching her. He has urged her to relax, and not to 'dwell' on things. She has been doing too much dwelling, it seems. She is to enjoy tonight – it had been a gentle instruction. She had not told him about the voice she thought she had heard earlier. She had laughed it off to Sam, but her hands had trembled all through bathtime with Finn.

She had not told him how much she was missing her mother. That splashing water on Finn had made her voice, calling her name, ring in her ears: '*Jenny! Jenny!*' Her hand had stalled for a second, to catch the last falling syllable. She couldn't place the memory, but it was new, lurking, ready to peek through. It had caught her unawares and the halcyon glimmer had held until Finn had splashed, and the drops had brought her round.

'What are you doing for Christmas? Still off to your parents, Connor?' Will changes the subject.

The couple exchange a look and Erin pauses before answering.

'We're not sure now. Connor's not been feeling too well so he's decided we should spend this one at home and head up for New Year.'

'Cold getting to you, Connor?' says Will. 'Getting a bit soft in your old age?'

'Ha ha,' says Connor, taking a drink. 'I just need a restorative beer. Erin's been trying to make me cut back. Wrong season for that!'

He looks quickly at Erin, and Jenny watches his smile not quite reach his eyes: dark anyway, they are like coal tonight. His chin, fashionable with stubble, is thick with shadow, a walking advert for the creative agency where he works: designer beers, expensive jeans, boys' toys. A dark tattoo creeps from under the sleeve of his T-shirt, like a snake.

Maternity leave has provided a welcome break from the shiny world of advertising – she misses the independence, but not the job.

The pot lid bangs again, and Will leaps up to the hob which has started to hiss and fizzle. Rivulets of stew run down to the flames below the pot. The smell of the stock on the metal wafts around the kitchen.

'Ready! Jenny, plates?'

Jenny stands up to help serve. As she loads the plates and turns to hand them out, she catches the end of a hiss from Connor in Erin's direction. She pauses for a second, allowing them to finish whatever they had started.

'No, I won't be quiet, not if you're going to tell me to be,' she hears Erin say as she takes a step towards the table.

Erin finishes the wine in her glass in one swallow and then picks up the bottle. Connor's expression changes swiftly from a frown to a smile as he sees Jenny approaching.

'Wow, this looks great! You been working hard this afternoon, Jen?'

'No, it was all Will. He likes to cook.'

Jenny glances over to Will, to see if he has noticed anything, but he is bringing over the salt and pepper. Instead of the traditional shakers, these tall, sleek-looking devices shed their loads quickly and discreetly at the press of a button. Jenny prefers the traditional wooden curved shapes, but these too had been a wedding gift. They would make good weapons, she thinks, and her mind balloons with an image of Erin hurling them at Connor's head, one of them lodging, sticking out... the damage they could do.

'Jenny? Ready?' Will asks, looking up.

She realises she is still standing and holding the plates which have been warmed in the oven, suddenly hot in her hands. She bangs them down and blows on her fingers, glancing at Erin, whose eyes are fixed defiantly on Connor. Whatever is going on has gathered pace in the last few minutes.

She pours more wine for Erin, then holds out the plate. 'Here we go.'

'This looks lovely, thank you. I'm planning an Indian takeaway for the big Christmas feast. I think we only eat home-made food when we come to you.'

Laughter softens the tone and they begin to eat. Will describes their search for a house, now that they are thinking of staying in St Albans. Jenny observes the couple carefully but the sudden rancour appears to have quietened. Erin drinks quickly. She speaks loudly and laughs brightly, louder and brighter as the evening wears on.

Every time Jenny looks at her, she seems more and more like a figure from a child's comic: every gesture exaggerated, words floating up from her mouth in speech bubbles, complete with exclamation marks. She holds her nose defiantly, as though she were balancing a book on her head; it rarely falls below a deliberate and sustained level, like a striped pole on a horse jump. Her hair bounces up and down on her back as she shakes her head, betraying her attempt at control, having now fully escaped its grips of earlier.

The evening passes with chatter about work, the snow, the murder, the snow.

The air gradually warms, and Jenny can feel the beginning of a headache.

The soft chimes of eleven sound, and Jenny glances at the clock with a yawn. Finn will be up at some point for a feed. There is something overdrawn and bloated about the evening now. She wants to strip down and curl under the covers. The smile she wears is heavy and sags the corners of her mouth.

Erin suddenly lets loose a baying howl of laughter and Jenny flinches, knocking over her wine glass. It flies off the table in a perfect arc and lands in the centre of the room, smashing, crystal slivers scattering.

'Jenny!' Will says, jumping up. His chair protests as it flings back. 'No, don't move; don't worry, I'll clean it.'

'Too much wine, eh?' Connor grins at her.

Jenny suddenly feels sick and dizzy. Connor's face is wolfish and large. What big teeth you have, she thinks.

'Let me help,' she says and she stands to move towards Will, anxious to be further from the table. But as she takes a step forward, she swoons to the right, and falls against the wooden kitchen unit.

'Jenny!' Will speaks again.

She can feel him by her side, pulling her arm over his.

'How much have you had to drink?' he asks.

She opens her mouth to reply that she hasn't had more than two glasses, but he has picked up the bottle from the centre of the table – empty – and gestures to the other bottles, awaiting removal to the recycling.

'Bloody hell, Jen. You've put away a fair bit.'

She feels admonished, like a naughty schoolgirl, and to reply, 'But it wasn't me, it was Erin,' will only compound the impression, so she says nothing. Her limbs are heavy and pull hard, a curious weight, encouraging her to lie down on the kitchen floor and curl up, close her eyes.

Looking at Will, to plead with him silently to end the evening, she is drawn to a movement behind his head. At the window, out of the darkness of the velvet night, appears a young girl's face, pressing up against the glass.

The skin on her face is taut over her cheekbones and she has hollows under her eyes. The mouth is curled in an O shape, with her lips parted, stretched. Her dark hair sticks to her face, wet and clinging.

The green eyes are compelling: pools that swim up with an invitation to dive in.

The face pushes up against the window. The most terrible thing is not that she is there, but that Jenny is sure she is there to look for her. The girl she had heard in the cathedral. The icy whisper.

The noise of a waterfall – cascading, crashing – is deafening as she feels the scream release from inside of her throat. It stabs the soft tissue below the tongue, like pins into a cushion.

The sound of her cry: loud, crystal in the air.

The face vanishes into the dark air. She tries to raise her hand to point. Her limbs feel as they do in a dream: heavy and unreal. She isn't sure if she has managed to raise her arm at all.

'A girl; there's a girl outside…' Her voice is parched.

Things happen around her. She can feel a sudden flurry of looking. The draught that enters the kitchen tells her that someone has opened and closed the door. At some point, Connor and Erin empty from the room, and she can hear words spoken, but she can't make them out. They come from far away. She remains fixed upon the window, which now looks out onto nothing but blackness: the light from inside obscuring everything beyond the glass.

As her head begins to clear, she sits in her chair, with a pillow under her neck. The tall back of the wooden dining chair is bearing her weight, but threatening to spill her sideways.

The room clarifies around her; the dizziness passes. She feels as she did: tired, but sober and in charge of her body. Her top is wet – she has spilt something and her wrist aches. She can't remember banging it.

'Better?' asks Will, looming over her. 'I've cleared up the kitchen. You've been a bit out of it for the last five minutes. Are you OK?'

She nods. His brow uncreases. Recreases.

'Connor and Erin have gone – who knows what they thought. One minute you were fine, and the next practically passing out. And that scream – did you think you had seen a ghost? There was no one outside. I think you just caught your reflection in the window. You drank too much.'

'Does it matter? Was I awful?' she asks. She tries to raise her head to look him in the eye, but her neck aches.

Yes, she thinks to herself, that's what it must have been. I've seen a ghost.

'What? Does what matter?' He crosses his arms, then uncrosses them and crouches to her level.

'Does it matter what they thought?' she asks again. 'Was I so very awful? Erin was drunk – she put away most of the wine. There was something going on. I don't want to have ruined their night, but they were having a row about something.'

'I honestly don't know what you're talking about.' He kneels before her. 'Babes, I can't be doing with much more of this. Can you not just get it together a bit?' He reaches out his hand and takes hers.

The room is silent.

'I do, Will, you know.'

He eyes her with suspicion.

'What? You do what?'

'Think I might have seen a ghost,' she says.

He rocks back on his heels. His hand slips.

A silence stands up and demands to be taken notice of. They observe it, obediently and a tiny bit fearfully. It is difficult to look over its head, or peer around its side. It stands between them, and Jenny doesn't have the energy to wait it out.

'Let's go to bed,' she says, not looking up at him as she rises from the chair and heads towards the stairs.

The clock ticks their way out: step, lift, step, lift.

Cleaning her teeth, Jenny feels the sweep of the toothbrush over her gums and teeth, toothpaste foaming under her tongue. Her reflection in the mirror is misted. She can't quite make herself out. She wipes it with her hand.

Holding her toothbrush aloft, she turns to Will. 'I'm sorry,' she says. She's unsure why she's apologising, but he hasn't spoken to her now for about fifteen minutes and she's tired.

Will dries his face and hands and turns. 'You're fine, Jen. I'm sorry too. I think you just need to get a handle on things. And try not to drink so much; cut back a bit. A few glasses of wine and your imagination... Well, just because a girl's been killed...'

'Just because?' She looks at him quickly. 'Just because?'

'You know what I mean. The girl dying is shitty, but it's not really anything to do with us. It might have happened nearby, but it's a world away...'

'I don't know how you can say that. I *knew* her, Will. I didn't know her well, but I had met her and I *knew* her. And now she's dead. If it can happen that easily, then yes, it's got something to do with us.'

'I didn't fucking mean—'

'I know what you didn't mean.' It wasn't going well. She had felt contrite. And now she felt like hitting him. 'There's evil around.'

'Evil?' Will rolls his eyes. 'Oh, for fuck's sake, Jen. You're talking like some Harry Potter rip-off. We can't go mad with worry over everything that happens outside or we'll never set foot out of the door! You've just had a few drinks. Calm down. This isn't about your mum, is it?'

His voice has risen slightly, in anger or exasperation, and Finn lets out a cry. There's something sharp in the air. She winces, ignoring Will. She feels a pang, regret that she can't speak to her own mother, about the enormity of this role – had she felt it too?

'A few drinks? Didn't you listen to me?' she seethes, not speaking the words that fill her mouth like marbles: cold, hard, glass. If she does speak, it will be to provoke. They will spit out, hitting hard and wounding.

She listens; there is nothing else. Finn must have settled.

'Come to bed, babes. Come on. We'll have an early start in the morning.'

She leans forward, rinses and puts the toothbrush carefully back in its mug, forcing herself to calm. It isn't Will's fault the girl has died. She knows that. Whatever she has seen – thinks she has seen? – at the window is probably down to exhaustion.

'OK,' she says. And she follows him into the bedroom, pulling the cord behind her to turn off the light; the click sounds sharply in the silence of darkness.

Her head aches as she rolls over onto her side and stares at the shadows on the wall. Will snuggles up behind her and pulls her into him, his arm lying heavy over her stomach. In seconds, he is snoring. Jenny feels his breath blowing onto her cheek as she listens to the raspy expelling of air. She doesn't mind the snoring; she isn't ready for sleep just yet. Despite all the reason that Will speaks, the shadows and the shades of night-time are vividly louder. The marbles are in her mouth and she's afraid of choking.

13

'One more?' Seb offers, and Maarten shakes his head.

'Not for me,' he says. He's already drunk more than he needed, on an empty stomach. Thinking about it, he can't remember the last time he ate anything. Breakfast? He remembers Liv handing him some toast as he was leaving.

'So the phone comment is interesting from the boyfriend, then?' Imogen says.

Seb tops her drink up from the bottle on the table. His dark head rests back against the glass panes, set in the deep oak panels.

The roof is low, the air warm, the draught beer heavy. Maarten is starting to feel sleepy. He drops his shoulders, non-committal. 'It is, but finding the phone, that's the next step.' Lifting his pint, he takes a swallow, and glances out of the frosted window. The black sky looks clear and cold; an easy walk home now, once he can force himself to stand up.

'I'll set another call up, sir,' Imogen says. 'Give them a chance to recover – it must be a shock, and he might think of something.'

'Yes.' Maarten stretches. The quick drink to wind down had run late, and his eyelids are falling. It won't do to sit in the pub and theorise about the case.

'Points to Pickles though, doesn't it?' Imogen finishes her drink. The white wine has been depleted, and her eyes are red. Maarten isn't sure if it's that, or the exhaustion kicking in, if she feels as weary as him.

'The phone, that's going to be our key. For sure. Let's hit it hard and early tomorrow.' Maarten has less than half a pint left. He doesn't want to talk about the case any more. 'Sorry for the shop talk, Seb. What are you two doing for Christmas?'

Imogen and Seb glance at each other, and too late Maarten remembers that neither have family, that it's just them. It's one of the times Liv would usually recover the conversation for him, but then again, it is what it is.

'A quiet one for us,' Seb says.

Imogen nods. 'Lucky for us, we get to escape all that forced family fun that you all complain about. A fire, a film, a few bottles of wine.'

'We thought about going away, but with all this...' Seb shrugs as he knocks back the rest of his driver's Coke. 'And you're going to be busier than ever, now there's the phone.'

'Yes.' Maarten nods. 'We were lucky with the lead.' He starts pulling on his coat. It's late. 'But, it might be almost impossible to trace it. If it was bought with cash, and loaded up with credit for Leigh to use, then we will have to have luck on our side. But we'll go round the local phone shops that sell the make that Arjun mentioned, trace records, check CCTV...' Looking outside, it's started snowing again. He pulls his coat collar up. 'I'm off. Have a good night.'

'No, hang on; I've only had the one, so I'll drive you back.' Seb picks up his keys and steps forward. 'If we head back now we can have one glass at home. What do you say, birthday girl?'

Imogen smiles, and Seb pulls her to her feet. Maarten thinks of their quiet Christmas, no family banging on the door, lying in bed, unwinding. It's appealing, but he'd trade none of it for Nic and Sanne. He will be up before dawn Christmas morning to deal with stockings, and he smiles.

'Maart, is that you?' says Liv, her words thick and sticky with sleep.

'*Ja*, who were you expecting?' he says, gruff with beer, and he kisses her before stripping down and falling into bed beside her. He fumbles with the duvet, pulling if off her before managing to pull it over himself.

She tugs the duvet back. 'I thought you might be Nic – she's not sleeping so well – is it late?'

'It's gone midnight. *Kak*. What a shit end to the day. We're loaded with suspects and no closer to a killer. Had a beer afterwards. Sorry I'm late.'

'It's no problem. You need to speak to the girls tomorrow though. Sanne's too young to get it, but Becky and Nic were getting each other worked up about Leigh after the vigil. The idea of being a victim; it's a lot for young girls to take in.'

'Nic doesn't know Leigh though? It's scary when the world is suddenly not what it seems.' He thinks briefly of the knock at his grandparents' door. He'd been ten. The way the world can flip; and quickly it's too dark to see which way is up and which is down. And the darkness can make it hard to care.

He would stand in front of anything to hold that back from his girls.

'I don't know; she seemed fine after the vigil, but then when we got home she had a huge meltdown. She won't talk about it; she clammed up tight once the tears stopped, but she's been into our bed once tonight already.'

She is already rolling back over, eyes closing.

'Liv,' he whispers, his hand snaking out.

'Night, Maart,' she says, already gone.

14

Jenny runs. Her heart beats, pumping the adrenalin so hard, close to being paralysed by panic.

She's felt this way before; her muscles remember – thrashing, tight with frenzy. Her brain is working too fast to place it, but the fear and the damp are familiar, powering forward, lying in wait.

The lake lies behind her. Glancing over her shoulder she holds back a cry. The silver surface, tilting at the corner near the willow tree, flashes under the moon and blood pounds in her ears. It was the willow tree that had woken her. Its long fingers stroking her arms. A whisper on the wind: '*Save her.*' Before then, she had been sure she was asleep, dreaming.

She's holding a phone: a strange phone, a damp phone. She holds it outstretched, not daring to drop it but not wanting to pull it too close. She remembers picking it up, but she can't remember coming here. Or leaving the house to go into the park. At night. In the dark. Only that something had called her here.

She swallows the fear like it's food and runs again. Home.

The cold, iced wind like a competitor, outpacing her. Threatening to undo her, to unlace her.

'*Save her.*'

She runs.

It's hard underfoot. Compacted snow, earth, stones… She's not wearing shoes.

Halfway up the bank, the cathedral hangs in the distance, looming larger as she runs. Her breath stabs, a lesion, and she can see the top of the lanes.

The air is dry, the sky clear. She's not wet, just freezing.

The gate bangs behind her as she flees to the door, and her fingers fumble with the catch.

Standing in their kitchen, her heart races, her breath tight. And yet the table still holds the wine glasses from earlier. Will's coat is slung over the chair. There are still four walls and nobody seems to have been disturbed. The house will not come crashing down.

Waiting for her heart to slow, to calm, she looks down at the phone. Its wetness, its heaviness consolidating, concrete. But where did she find it? She puts the phone in her handbag, hanging over the back of a chair.

A sip of water and then bed. She will wake in the morning. This must be a dream.

15

16 December

The post-mortem had spoken of terror, ending in murder: no way for anyone to make an exit, least of all a fourteen-year-old girl. The smell clings to his nose, the back of his throat. Clinical, but not clean. The coldness of the room takes a while to shake off. The memory of the bruises, the thought of the blood, turns his stomach.

The psychological report had hypothesised that this was a first offence. The blows were random, flailing, but not a fatal force behind them. They were on the back of the head, as though the victim had been running away. Death had been caused by drowning. The bruises had come first. There was blood. The victim had fought back.

And there had likely been assault of some kind. Semen was found on the jacket, though not anywhere in her body. Hair pulled from the back of her head. Her bra had been ripped but she had not been undressed. Did he try to rape her? Did he kill her because she fought back? Maarten closes his eyes. His profession is a window into the darker side of human behaviour; into the acts that people are capable of after rejection. The violence, the rage. He shudders.

First offence. It felt like a first offence. But who?

Sneezing, repeatedly, Maarten leans back in his chair, picking up his hand gel and rubbing it in.

The weather is affecting every aspect of the town, but St Albans won't begin to recover if they don't manage to work through the case. Snow or no snow, the city is at an impasse.

'We're missing something,' he says, walking out of his office and looking at the board. 'It's right under our noses.'

Imogen moves close to him after pinning on another photo of another interviewed schoolgirl: more information, no leads.

'Are you going to charge Pickles?'

'Don't have enough. Sunny is going through his phone records, looking for Leigh's number. And Adrika found a mention in her notebook a few weeks earlier, mentioning the lift to the pantomime. It seems the boyfriend wasn't too happy she said she would go with Pickles, but there's not much there.'

Imogen shakes her head. 'It's enough for a start, maybe? Sunny didn't like him.'

'Well, hopefully the interview today will turn something up. I thought about keeping him overnight, but no point. I told him to expect a car at one. Need to speak to the Hoarde family first.' He checks his phone; there's an email in from Rotterdam.

The notes from the post-mortem results have been added to the board. He skims again:

Death from drowning. Some hair pulled from head, suggesting struggle, and bruises around the head and wrist area. Attempted sexual assault but no signs of penetration. DNA from the blood and semen unconfirmed due to chemical contamination from the river water. Bruises and injuries to her body indicate she was physically restrained, possibly tied up for a few hours, as well as indicating resistance.

Imogen reads the summary of notes ready for the team briefing: 'She'd told her parents she was going to meet a friend at around two o'clock on the afternoon of the thirteenth of December and never returned. A possible sighting in a black BMW at four o'clock. The date of the thirteenth of December is in her notebook, surrounded by hearts and question marks. The identity of the friend is unknown, no leads to the identity of the driver. Witness reports indicate that a girl of her age was seen in a black BMW being driven by a man. We have no licence plate.'

'Good work,' he says, thinking the opposite. They feel no further forward. They stare at the board, silent.

'Anything turn up with the counsellor?'

Imogen shakes her head. 'We checked with the school office and they had some records. It was a Dr Bhatti – he worked part-time out of a local clinic. The clinic had offered some free hours to local schools if the CAMHS wait list was too long.'

'CAMHS?'

'The NHS mental health service for children, sir. Overworked and stretched.'

'How many sessions did she have?'

'The school have a record of three. Looks like they were effective. I phoned his clinic but it seems he moved to Hong Kong about six months ago. They've passed on his details.'

'Have we managed to speak to him?'

'Not yet. Adrika is doing the follow-up calls. With the time difference it's tricky, but she's left a message with his office over there.'

'Let me know. He might have some further info. What about the boyfriend?'

'We're following up. The mother says her son is still very upset, but she said we can speak to him again tomorrow if we need to. She's trying to be helpful.'

'Well, he's no suspect but again it will be good to hear if he's got any further thoughts. The mention of the phone is the best new lead we've got.'

Imogen shrugs and picks up her bag. 'How is Liv? I haven't seen her since our summer barbecue – it was so lovely to catch up properly with her. I only seem to speak to her when I can't get you on the phone.'

Looking out of the window, Maarten thinks briefly about Liv. He had got home last night to an efficiently wrapped pile of presents hidden in their cupboard. Christmas was happening without him.

He'd been late, again. After they had met for the vigil and he had gone back to the office. Her kiss had pressed hard against his mouth this morning. It rests on his lips now, dry. Home is no place of refuge right now; it's a guilt pit.

Putting his fingers up to his mouth, there is a bitter taste. The smell of the autopsy hits him and his hand moves back to the desk, holding it firmly.

'She's fine. You'll see her at the Christmas drinks, if we get there. It would be good to get together soon. Liv always asks after you both.'

The perfume Imogen is wearing smells different. He thinks of commenting but stops himself. It smells fresh. She's only a few inches away.

'Come to us for drinks if the work thing doesn't pan out. Seb is difficult at the moment. I feel like he's hovering around me. I wanted to collapse yesterday, but he's trying to look after me, asking about the day... trying to give me dinner later today.' Her phone on the desk buzzes and she reads the screen.

'Liv's the same. They care, Imo.'

'I know. I could function entirely on my own at times like this. I think it's the upbringing – bad foster home after bad foster home, until the last one – which was brilliant; like a home should be.'

'But I thought that's how you two started talking? Didn't you meet at a support group for people in care? Surely he understands.'

'I got lucky. He didn't. Things are different now, a closer watch on the people in charge. Seb was in two homes. Imagine the stereotype of the worst-case scenario for a young child in care...' She shrugs. 'No physical scars for him, just the deeper ones.'

Maarten glances at her. His parents had died in a car crash when he'd been ten, but his grandparents had taken him in. No money to spare, but a lot of love.

'The team are on their way now. I need a fag,' she says. 'I'll nip out, before they all get back.'

'You're smoking again? But it's been, what, at least six months – seven?'

'Nine.' Her face twists in rue.

'What are you thinking, Imo? You were a nightmare. Have I got to go through that again?'

'Nah... it's just a blip. A quick one-off. A Christmas blip. We're all allowed one of those.'

As she exits, the phone rings, and he answers. 'There's a Mrs Jenny Brennan down here, sir. She'd like to speak with you.'

He'd been thinking of joining Imogen, not to smoke, but to soak up the smell: erase the mortuary through the seeping, clinging smell of the tobacco. He stands to make his way downstairs to see the visitor.

The snow begins to fall.

'Inspector Jansen?'

He doesn't correct her use of his title, as he sits down. The desk sergeant had shown her into the interview room, and she holds something in a plastic bag, which lies on the table. Her face is familiar, as are her movements: jumpy, ill at ease.

'How are you, Mrs Brennan?'

'I'm fine. I have something. I wanted to give it to you, and not the front desk...'

He waits, as she pauses, but she doesn't complete the sentence. Reaching for the bag, he opens his hand. 'May I?'

She pushes it towards him, but doesn't let go immediately.

He glances at the clock on the wall. They had to get going to the Hoardes'.

Inside the bag is a mobile phone. The battery is dead and it's damp. The screen is small, and it looks similar to an old Nokia. He stares at it, heavy in his hand. Could this be the phone? Could it be this easy?

'I'm sorry, I don't quite understand.'

'I found it, in the park, near the lake. I thought it might be important.' She turns from him as she speaks. There is a buggy next to her, and there are snuffles coming from under the hood. She leans to check, then turns back to him. 'I found it in the park, when I was... walking. And I thought... well, I wondered if it was important. You know, to do with the case. With Leigh.'

Maarten wraps the bag closed, for evidence. 'You found this, when?'

'Yesterday.'

She looks at the floor as she speaks. She's withholding something. Lying? She doesn't seem the type. It's more something she's not saying, rather than speaking an untruth.

'Well, thanks for bringing it in. I'll hand it to our forensic team, and we'll be in touch if it's important.' He stands. It will be checked. But from her point of view, an abandoned phone, found in that huge park, doesn't seem to warrant the private room, the call for him. She still seems unfinished, as though there's something to say.

But could it? Could this be the phone they want? His pulse picks up pace. But how could she have found it? It's surely too much of a coincidence.

'Is there anything else, Mrs Brennan?' He sits again, slowly, giving her time. He needs to get going, but she seems to want him to peel something away.

'Jenny, please.'

'Is there anything else, Jenny?'

Her hands rub together; her palms meeting and parting in a clutch and a twist.

'No, nothing else.' She stands this time, and he follows her. Moving to the door as she wheels the buggy round.

Shaking her head as he holds the door open for her, he watches her pause at the display of leaflets near the door, then disappear out of sight. He shivers in the corridor. She had something to say, and the ghost of it hangs in the empty hall.

16

It's just after ten as Jenny finally manages to leave the house, after nipping back after the station.

Lifting Finn, she kisses his cheek, and he giggles, blowing bubbles. 'Shall we go out, my gorgeous?'

There's some shopping she needs, and playgroup before lunch with Sam. Get out of the house. Will is due home early this afternoon for the appointment. She had picked a name – Klaber – from a brochure of local counsellors that had been on display at the police station, and it had jumped out at her – solid and clinical-sounding. She'd called first thing and there hadn't been any appointments, but the secretary had put her through to Dr Klaber himself – she must have sounded upset, as tense as she feels. When she explained that living so close to the murder was taking a heavy emotional toll, he had relented: 'I'm pretty much closed down for the holidays, but this is an exceptional situation. Come in this afternoon. And if you'd like to bring your husband, he's welcome too.'

And when she had phoned Will, he said he would. He'd left that morning before she'd woken, but there'd been a cup of tea next to the bed, which is a first. Peace offering. Or tending to the infirm. Making an effort.

Finn smiles with his mouth open, waving his arms, fat in his snowsuit, and gurgles.

'Let's go and count the snowmen, little man,' she says, as she manoeuvres the buggy backwards through the doorframe, and lifts it down the doorstep.

The lock bangs from next door, rattling back out again as the catch doesn't take.

'For fuck's sake…' Erin says, turning on her heel to try again.

'Morning, Erin,' Jenny says. She can't ignore her, but her face flushes hot when she thinks of last night.

'Jenny!' Erin turns and smiles, and does it so brightly Jenny realises she'd been trying to avoid the hello.

'Look… I'm sorry about last night…' Jenny starts, feeling stupid. Not sure what she's supposed to say.

'Last night? What have you got to feel sorry for?' Erin's face clouds in confusion. 'You fainted! God, I'm not surprised… it was really hot and you're not sleeping much. It was late and we overstayed our welcome. You're OK? I was worried you'd stood on some of that broken glass.'

'Yes, I'm fine thanks…' Will had made it sound much worse. His attunement to public shame must be turned all the way up.

'If anything, I should be apologising to you,' Erin says, dropping her head an inch.

'Why on earth would you need to do that?'

'God, you must have thought Connor and I were so rude… squabbling like children. And I drank so much; I feel like shit this morning.' She raises her hand to her cheek.

Jenny can make out a red mark, faint now, lying beneath the make-up.

'No, not at all,' Jenny says, remembering the hissed whispers, the snipes from Connor. 'Everything OK?' She looks again at Erin's cheek. 'Did you... Has Connor...'

'Oh, that! I bumped against the door last night. Just the wine.' She shakes her head. 'Is everything OK? Yes... no... We're having a... tough time. We're,' Erin looks at Finn and smiles, 'we're trying for a baby at the moment. I haven't really wanted to talk about it, but it's not happening as quickly as we'd hoped. I'm trying to get Connor to eat a bit better, cut back on the booze. But maybe I'm trying too hard.'

'Oh, Erin, I'm sorry. It's not uncommon. I've got friends that it's taken a year or so...'

'Jenny, we've been trying for well over two years now.' Erin begins to cry, but shakes her head and wipes the tears away from under her lids with the tips of her splayed fingers, preventing any mascara from running. 'Anyway, we're being positive. I'm having tests and going to start a round of IVF. The pressure of the year has been quite intense. I'm so bored with weeing on those sticks that tell you when it's time, and then weeing on the sticks to tell me if it's worked...'

'Look, do you want to have a coffee? Have a talk?'

Erin takes a step backwards. 'No, no...' She checks her watch. 'I've got to go. I've got to be at work. I'm running late this morning. I felt so crap from the wine I had an extra hour in bed. And Connor has lost his wallet, so I've got to meet him in town to lend him my credit card.' Another backwards step, lifting her chin a little higher, smile in place. 'I'm fine. Anyway, it was lovely to see you both. Let's have a drink again soon.'

Jenny nods. Glancing with a hot heart at Finn, before watching Erin stride away, Mulberry handbag firmly in the crook of her arm.

17

The phone buzzes and Maarten answers. It's Liv. He pauses before the double doors that lead outside, on his way to the car.

'Maart, you need to speak to Nic.'

'I haven't got time…' he begins. Her voice disappears.

'Papa?'

'Nic, *schatje*, how goes it?' He leans against the wall, letting the door he'd started to push open fall closed.

'Papa, I'm worried about the girl. I'm so worried – I had a dream last night… Papa, I'm scared. But Mama said you will find out what happened. You can stop it happening again?'

Maarten closes his eyes. He flashes to a memory of Nic crying when she'd been three, because grey bunny had fallen under the bed. And all he'd had to do was lift him back up. 'I will do my best, Nic. I will do my very best. Now tell me what you're doing today.'

'I'm planning my party with Becky; you remember we're sharing our birthdays? What do you think about a painting pottery party? Becky really likes *Star Wars* but I don't, so we can paint whatever we like and it doesn't matter.'

'Sounds great. Make sure you plan lots of balloons. You know how good Papa is with balloons.'

'Ten's a bit old for balloon animals!' She laughs.

The sound of her laugh takes some of the sting away. And he looks at his watch. He has to get going.

'OK, *schatje*, well, you sign me up for any job you like. And I promise you have nothing to worry about.'

'I love you, Papa.'

'Love you too.'

God, what they must be going through. The worry. Every noise, shadow.

'You're only ten once so have a think about what present you'd like. Put me back on the phone to Mama and I will try to get back early tonight, for a story at bedtime.'

He blows his kisses down the phone. Nic's birthday is less than a month away. He is hoping to feel like celebrating before then. Christmas is counting down: nine days to go.

18

The corner before Hollyhocks is slippery. Hanging onto the buggy handle Jenny only just manages to stay upright.

'Fuck it! I'm sorry!'

She feels a sharp pain in her right ankle, and the ground disappears beneath her in a whoosh.

'Ow!'

'Fuck, I'm so, so sorry. Shit, here, let me help.'

'The buggy!'

Jenny watches as the buggy rolls forwards and bumps gently into the wall, threatening to bounce out and disappear round the corner.

A man on the ground next to her is pulling himself up. He lurches forward and grabs the wheel, to stop it moving further and slipping out of view.

'It's OK, I've got it,' he says.

She scrambles up, but buckles slightly as she stands.

'Sorry, sorry! I just slipped,' he says, panting with the effort of his lurch. 'The fucking ice with these cobbles is lethal. Where's the grit, eh?'

He rights himself, brushing his jacket before turning to her with a face full of concern.

'Did I hurt you? I kicked you as my legs went.' He pauses. 'Here.' He holds out his hand, and she takes it, righting herself.

Jenny looks quickly at Finn, who doesn't appear to have noticed a thing; her heart pounds. He is chewing on his toy giraffe and looking at the man with interest. She takes a breath, calming herself. The man looks familiar, but she can't place him.

'Hang on, didn't we meet recently?' He looks confused, and then his face clears. 'Some idiot in a café pulled his chair out and I spilt coffee over him. You passed me tissues. Yesterday.'

She remembers now. He had been undeterred by the aggression of the man in the suit.

'Yes, I think so.'

'I'm Matt. What an idiot. I should have been going more fucking carefully.'

'Didn't you have a camera with you last time?' She feels a bit steadier. Nothing seems to have been hurt, but her ankle still throbs. She places a hand against the wall for support as she picks up the bag she's dropped. She leaves Matt holding the buggy.

'Yeah. I'm covering this case. You know, the murder.'

He's about her age, or maybe younger. His clothes are put together, considered.

'Jenny,' she says, following his introduction.

'It's a big story. Not sure we'll be staying much longer though. Not much headway.'

She takes the buggy handle, and he bends to collect a few bits that have spilled from his pockets.

'No. I wish they would catch him,' she says. Then adds, 'My husband saw the car, he thinks, near our house. I hate that it happened so close.'

She shifts her weight onto the ankle she has been holding gingerly, and she flinches.

'Oh fuck, look, I've hurt you.'

'No, honestly. It'll be fine in a second.'

'Were you heading inside? I was – can I buy you a coffee?'

Jenny is taken aback. 'Well…'

'Please, let me. You're obviously heading inside and it's the least I can do. Fucking idiot that I am. You don't have to sit with me if you don't want to.' He grins.

She walks slowly, leaning against the buggy. The café is half empty.

Finn is chattering when Matt comes back with drinks and muffins.

'Thanks,' she says, picking one up.

'So, your husband saw the car?'

'Hmm. We live near the lake. It might not have been "the" car.'

'Bet it was. I've heard of the sighting – they think it's the real deal.'

Jenny chews. He's got dark hair; he wears a silver chain round his neck, and he's got one earring at the top of his ear lobe. Will would rather slice off his ear.

'It's a right old fucking mess.' He slings his coat over the back of his chair.

'Do they have any leads? Do they think they know who it might be?'

'Nah. No leads, as far as I know. Loads of suspicion. The father has been checked out. Got a brother in jail, been arrested himself before for something minor. But murder? Different ball game. Jury's out there.'

'The father? God, it can't have been Tessa's husband. I've met him.'

Matt looks at her, one eyebrow skirting an upwards curve. 'You knew them?'

'No, I didn't know them, not properly. She took a class in town that I went to a few times.' Jenny gestures at Finn. 'A baby one. He came in once to collect her and the stuff for the class.' She thinks back. She had vaguely recognised him when she'd seen him on TV. It had been Sam who had reminded her where they'd met.

'Small fucking town, this one.' Matt gulps his coffee, the mug spilling as he bangs it back down.

'You live in London?'

'Yeah, we've all been commuting up here, but I reckon today will be the last day, or maybe tomorrow. If nothing else comes up. It's a nice place. Really pretty – quaint. But fucking cold.'

'Let's hope not all the time,' she says, and smiles. 'I suppose you know quite a bit about the investigation, then?'

'A bit. So, there's this teacher at her school they've been grilling. "Down with the kids" type. A right posh, sweaty tosser, by all accounts. Been seen hanging round clubs with the sixth formers. On all their Facebook pages. Not sure if he did it but he'll get the sack before Christmas.'

'Really?'

'Yeah, plus the dad, and there's a bloke from her school, in year ten, who she's been out with a few times, a boyfriend. He's definitely higher up on the list for motive, I reckon. But it's so fucking planned – if it was a straightforward fight or something – but the car, the lake… it's got all the marks of someone older. Some fucked up nutter.'

The faceless figure Jenny has held in her head twists and morphs.

'Have you met Jansen? The copper?'

She nods.

'He's a bit of an odd one. New down here. He's from Rotterdam, but moved over to the Met for a few years and then worked up north for a bit, then he was out for a while – suspended. All cleared in the end, but not sure if he's got the goods to sort this out.'

'Really?' Jenny says again. 'What did he do?'

'Can't remember. But I can find out. Want me to let you know?'

He's smiling at her. She likes him. It's interesting to talk about the case. To be able to talk about it with someone who thinks of it as a job. And not a horror story.

'Yes please.' She thinks of Jansen, of the instinctive recoil she felt, still feels. His plastered smile and his sharpness; his shiny intellect that seemed so transparent and flimsy in the face of the death. 'I didn't know what to make of him.'

Matt glances at his watch. It's brightly coloured – lime green with a huge square screen. 'Look I've got to get going. There's another press conference this morning and then we're heading back down to London this afternoon. Here, give me your number and I can let you know about Jansen, if you like? And maybe I can give you a call, and find out if your husband remembers anything else?'

Jenny scribbles it down, and seconds later her phone has beeped with a missed call.

'There's mine,' Matt says. 'Really sorry I hurt you. You're OK to get home?'

She had forgotten about her ankle. 'Yes, it's fine. Honestly, don't worry about it.'

'I'll be more fucking careful next time,' he says. And he's off.

19

The car pulls through the snowy lanes. The roads have been cleared but the grey sky is lying low, threatening to open its jaws, hurling down hail upon the slushy roads. Imogen drives the car carefully and Maarten stares out of the window, watching the snow banks darken as the car sprays up muck from the wet, black roads. He taps his foot quietly and impatiently, but doesn't allow himself to urge her to drive faster.

They are moving out from St Albans to Abbey-Ville, the optimistically named suburban village where Leigh lived. It lies on the outskirts of the city and Maarten watches the landscape turn from a littering of picturesque churches to built-up housing estates, put in place for those who have been slowly squeezed out of the increasingly expensive city. They are only about five miles away but the journey is taking longer than expected, as cars move cautiously through the countryside.

Maarten doesn't mind taking longer to arrive. He is in no rush to tell the family of the murdered girl how she died. It's always like the first time. His hands are warmer than usual, his mouth a fraction drier. It is always and never the same.

They pull up outside the house, which looks much like any other on the street. Empty bins are covered with snow, waiting to be moved back to where they belong now the bin men have left. Lights are blinking in the gloom from across the street, where life-sized reindeer stand on the lawn, flashing on and off. Santa on his sleigh, drawn out in multicoloured lights and wire, sits on the roof next door. Dull Christmas music plays out; the drone of a department store lift, jarring at festivity.

As they knock on the door, the sound rings sharply into the frosty air, as it would have done a month ago. And yet, as the door opens, Maarten can see the signs of a home so fractured that the peal of the doorbell shivers; bricks may crumble.

He hesitates as he steps onto the doormat. Such vivid grief has the ability to paralyse, and he is determined not to stall, or forget his words.

'Come in, officers. Please.'

The hollow eyes of the family gather quickly around them. Tea is made and pressed into their hands. There is a grandmother, from which side no one mentions, and someone's sister is there too, along with friends or neighbours. The house isn't huge, and the expectant faces fill the room.

Maarten watches the older family members eye him with suspicion, looking his long, dark, expensive coat up and down, and two young children nudge each other, pointing at his glasses. His discomfort with groups, his inability to make small talk, presses on him.

He says nothing, until there is something to say.

A man stands next to John's seated figure. He is bending as Maarten enters the room, and rises as Maarten nods a hello. The look is cold, appraising. His hand lingers on John's shoulder, and he steps away, glancing back at John. 'Think on,' he says quietly, and Maarten watches John's face flitter from anguish to anger, to anguish. Traffic-light grief.

'Have you found him yet?' asks John. He hasn't shaved and his eyes are red. Maarten watches the fingers of his fists uncurl and then curl again.

'John, let the inspector speak,' says Tessa, sitting next to him. She too has red eyes, and her face is a pale grey. She doesn't fidget; she sits as though she is reeling from a punch, occasionally wilting to one side, and then pulling herself upright. She holds a cup of tea that has been administered by one of the relatives in the room. Maarten holds the same. Both are untouched.

'We have Leigh's post-mortem results,' he says.

The room is hushed. Even the small children, who will not understand what he has just said, are stilled.

Maarten, his voice neutral, nods to the children. 'I wonder if maybe Tessa and John might like to listen alone, and certainly the children might be better off playing in another part of the house?'

There is a flurry of activity, and a woman, looking very similar to Tessa, her sister he guesses, drips tears over John and Tessa as she hugs them, marking a watery, salty trail as she leaves the room. The man Maarten assumes is her husband pulls her away. He is broad, and he leans once again to John, and mutters something in his ear. Maarten watches as John's fists, curling and uncurling, firm up and lock. Huge and weighty.

Beginning, Maarten allows his voice to drop a decibel. The facts are clear, and he doesn't falter over the words 'attempted sexual assault', but waits for a moment, to allow for a reaction.

Tessa, Leigh's mother, whimpers at the term. Her tea remains upright in her hands, but her eyes close.

'What did that bastard do to her?' demands John. The rage in his voice vibrates.

Maarten glances at Imogen. She has been sitting to the right of him throughout.

She leans forward and looks gently at the parents. Her red hair tied back, professional; brown eyes sympathetic.

'What did he do?' he demands, this time of Imogen.

She explains it all: assault, restraint, blows. She explains that Leigh fought back. That she might not have been conscious or in distress when she died, there is no way of knowing. It is likely she was unaware.

Maarten resists the urge to offer sympathy, to lean forward and put his arms around the mother. There are people better placed in the house for that, but he never gets over the feeling that to pass on such bald news, without offering comfort, feels inadequate. Her eyes remain closed for a good few minutes.

They discuss the case. Maarten answers questions, Imogen reassures; and it's time for them to leave. Grief is spilling over.

On their way to the car, parked down the street, Maarten stills, hearing a scuffle. It comes from further up the street, outside the house they have just left.

'John, no!' It is Tessa, screaming into the street, arms outstretched and being held up by the sister. The two men, John and the brother-in-law from the room, jump into a car, and the doors slam as the engine revs. The tyres screech on the black road as the car pulls out of the street. It veers dangerously to the right, skidding on the ice, but recovers, and tears away. Another couple of men also jump into another car, and Maarten runs towards the house as the blue exhaust fumes kick out, dirty and noxious. He runs through the stench of burning tyres and old engines.

'Where are they going? What's happening?'

His strides are long, and he allows his height to rear up over the heads of a group of the younger men, aged about twenty, who kick their toes into the snow and don't want to answer him, mute with defiance and belligerence.

'Where are they going?' Maarten says. This time he raises his voice, and the boys quake, eyeing each other and unsure of what to say.

'They're going to see that perv,' one of them says. He carries a can of Red Bull and a cigarette in the other hand. His knuckles are carved with a single letter tattoo on each rise.

'What?' Maarten says, taming the roar he can sense in his throat.

'You know, that fucking perv, Pickles. We know you're talking to him. We know it was him. Fucking cunt.' He spits. 'Fucking foreign coppers,' he mutters to his kicking toes. Loud enough for his mates to hear, but quiet enough to not dare to provoke.

Spinning on his heel, Maarten runs back to the car.

'Get backup out to Tim Pickles' address,' he shouts.

Imogen jumps into the passenger seat, pulling out her phone.

Maarten powers the car and the heavy tyres, expensive and with a traction that can equal the weather, whirl and plunge forward. His grandfather owned a farm just outside Rotterdam. These streets have nothing on the snow in rural Holland.

Imogen speaks into the phone. '... we're en route, we believe two cars are headed to the home address. I need that address now.'

'Turn left,' she says, as the car surges out of the housing estate. 'We're heading back to St Albans. North – near The Field.'

Maarten changes gear quickly, steering past a lorry that is stuck, and as the car begins to skid he turns the wheels into the skid and they pull out of it, opening up onto the long open country lane that connects the village to the town. Snow begins falling.

'Sir!' Imogen screams, as the car spins too wide around a corner.

He ignores her. The car is holding up well.

The Field is another suburb, but this time built with money to meet the rising demand of housing for young professionals. People flock here. They aren't pushed. This landscape is different to the last: expensive cars, smarter gardens, smaller, boxy new-build houses. Lights decorate trees but there are no life-size Santas.

Entering the street, as Imogen shouts the final direction, Maarten skids the car to a halt and runs towards the house. It is clear to where they should run. Both cars from the Hoardes' house are parked, doors left open in the snow, abandoned in the cul-de-sac turn, and the four men are piled, fists flailing, on the lawn of a small, smart house. A few neighbours stand worriedly around, one or two on phones. Someone is shouting, 'Call 999!' as Maarten reaches the men.

It is only just possible to make out Tim Pickles beneath the fists and feet, and Maarten dives straight in. These men are strong but he is tall, lithe. He can't beat them, but he can lever them away.

'Police! Stop! Get off!' he commands, pulling at the arm of one and spinning him away. The snow is compacted underfoot, and he slips, his foot sliding beneath him with the force of pushing.

Maarten feels a sharp blow to his head, but can't see from where it comes. It makes him reel but he needs to keep moving or he will become a punchbag. He ducks under the arm, striking out after a recoil, and pushes the soft-bellied body backwards. The man falls, and Maarten sees colours flash in his vision as he turns to stand and face the last men.

'Stay out of this, copper!' It is John.

'John! Stop!'

Maarten manages to pull the arm of one of the men behind them, and holds him steady. Imogen has appeared to his left, and she snaps handcuffs on his wrists, allowing Maarten to step between John and Tim Pickles. The fourth man goes back in for a lunge, and Maarten sees Imogen sidestep him, using the thrust of his lunge to spill him forward, tumbling head over heels. She stands over him, reading him his rights, refusing to allow him to rise and rejoin the fray.

'John, stop!'

The fist of the giant man is raised high. Maarten stands over Tim Pickles, and if John releases his blow it will land on him, hard and heavy. Maarten is taller, but John is broad and angry. There is an implacability in his stance, and Maarten doubts that he can halt him.

Sirens scream into the street, and there are footsteps, running towards them.

'He fucking killed my girl!' John's face is wrenched in rage. His fist has blood on it and his T-shirt, once white, is spattered red. He stands in the cold but the heat of his rage vibrates.

'He killed my girl!' he repeats. This time the edge is a fraction dulled.

'We don't know that. It's not the right way, John. Trust me.'
Maarten watches his eyes, waiting for a change.

John's shoulder drops a millimetre as police officers pile on him from behind. He is felled, and Maarten suddenly feels incredibly sorry.

'Ambulance, to 46 Rosewell Avenue.'

He hears Imogen making the call.

Dropping to his knees, he speaks to the mashed body on the white lawn. His face is awash with blood. 'Sir, can you hear me, sir? Tim? Can you hear me?'

There is no response, and he checks his breathing.

'Leave him, don't move him,' he says as a police officer runs up.

'It's me, Sunny. Sir, you're bleeding. Christ, your head!'

Maarten looks up to face Sunny, and as he does so, a trickle of blood lands in his eye. He takes his glasses off to wipe them, and sees that the lens is fractured on one side. The arm on that side is bent in the middle. He sways, and feels a pound in his temple.

'We need to get you to hospital. Can I get some help here?' Sunny shouts loudly, but it seems to come from far away.

Looking at the lawn, as the snow and street spins, Maarten watches two uniformed police officers run towards him. He can see from their faces that he must look bad. But the pounding is just making him sleepy. He's so tired. He could just close his eyes.

Eyelids drooping, he watches another officer pull John up. He is hunched and sobbing.

They all fall down.

20

The door to the office is imposing. The waiting room is empty: magazines, water cooler, carpets. Therapy isn't cheap, and this room is gently expensive.

'Feeling OK?'

Will's half glance, fidgeting hands, reassuring smile, are beginning to grate on her. 'You're sure you don't want to see a woman?' he asks again.

But she doesn't. It isn't about gender; it is about distance, about the dispassionate feel... And also something calming about the name, something compelling; it had lifted off the clean, white page.

'Mrs Brennan?' a tall man says, smiling. 'Come in.'

He has dark hair, not much older than her. He looks like she imagines a doctor to look: expensive-looking glasses, professional, polished, unflappable; and he speaks to Finn before she has a chance to say hello.

Sitting, handshakes done, she sits upright in the chair. After introductions and a faltering start from Will, Klaber turns to her.

'And how have you found it? Having a baby can be a shock to the system.'

Unaccountably, Jenny begins to cry.

Will leans forward and lifts Finn out of her arms, offering her a tissue and speaking for her.

'Jenny's struggling a bit, doctor. She's not normally someone who struggles... she has found the last few months difficult.'

Jenny's skin prickles.

'Yes?' Dr Klaber replies, speaking to Jenny but looking at Will too. 'I bet it's been hard for both of you. Professionals in their thirties often are hit harder than younger parents. They're used to being in control, to being organised. And reflux, I see from the notes; possibly affecting sleep?'

'Yes,' says Will. 'Finn can be up a lot at night still. He needs to be held upright after feeding.'

The hum of the air conditioning is gentle. The seat in which Jenny sits is leather, and it swings, right and left. She tries not to move too much, to sit into it. But any shifting seems to produce momentum. She's nervous.

'What about eating, sleeping? Broken sleep can be hard. Are you lying awake at night?' Dr Klaber looks at Jenny. He ignores the tears, and they slow.

She manages to shake her head. Sleep, when available, is usually instant.

'Jenny, before we go any further I just want to reassure you. I'm here for you to talk to, because sometimes talking helps, but crying is normal. Being tired is normal. Worrying about your baby is normal.'

'It's more than that.' Jenny can hear the apology in Will's voice. Whether it is to the doctor or to her she can't be sure. 'Jenny has been tired, but more than just lack of sleep... she's seen a face in the window late at night... It's becoming a bit like... an obsession. She's obsessing about a murdered girl...'

Nodding slowly, as though Will is describing failing mechanics in a car, Klaber takes a sip of water, and pours two more glasses. He offers the first to Jenny, saying, 'Jenny, would you like to tell me?'

Wishing for a wave to wash her away, she opens her mouth to speak but no words come. They are caught in her throat, bloated and bulbous. The marbles.

'Well, you must have heard about the murdered girl...' She can hear Will stalling.

'Yes. That happened near you, did it?' Dr Klaber glances down at the file before him. 'Oh yes, I see. I know that area. I've done Parkrun there a few times, and my wife works near there.'

'Yes, well the lake is minutes from our house. Since then, Jenny's been thinking about it; too much really. And the other night she thought she saw a face at the window...'

A pause. She knows Will has finished. He is worried and he has tried, but saying it aloud has diminished it. There is nothing to really make sense of. It is a jumble of stories about someone who Will doesn't recognise. He doesn't know what to do. That is the sum of it. He is terrified. The fear resonates, pings, in his voice.

Klaber leans forward, handing Jenny a tissue. He looks from one to the other, waiting.

Neither speaks.

'You know, as a couple with a new baby, it would be strange if you felt unaffected by the death of a child near your home. Even feeling the impact strongly. Given your sleep disruption, the change in your lives... small changes can unsettle us, but a murder is anything but small.'

Jenny meets his eyes. The tears have stopped. His voice has a hum to it.

'What about the faces at the window? What about those?' It's Will's last stand.

'Seeing things in the dark? If I told you I thought I'd seen someone out of the corner of my eye, but a tree had moved, or a light had flashed, you wouldn't think that odd. Possibly a distorted reflection in the dark, against glass?'

Will is out of bullets. He takes Jenny's hand; she sees his sideways glance. They have told a professional and he has said it is fine. It's Will's balm.

Realising what she wants to say, the words shape in her head. They are stored, boxed, unwilling to enter aloud, but they fizzle gently: *I feel alone.*

'I'm fine,' she says (*I miss my dad; I miss my mum*). 'Really I am. But Will is right, I am tense, and maybe talking would help.' It doesn't matter if she believes it or not. This concession to Will is easy. She does feel more solid. Less likely to dissolve and leak.

Will's phone buzzes and he offers his thanks and pulls out of the room.

'Call me, if you like. My secretary can make your appointment, or you can talk to me over the phone. I'm not busy at the moment,' Klaber says, handing her his card.

As he places a hand on her arm, as the other hand holds the card, she wants to tell him that she's sure something isn't right. Part of her wants to scream, to shake his arm. The urge to open her mouth, to tell him of the whisper, the voice, the face of the girl... the night-walking, the park, the cold, the dreams...

'Thank you,' she manages, her arm warm where he holds it.

'Is there something else, Jenny?'

'I found a phone,' she begins, in a blurt.

His eyebrows rise, and he smiles. 'Sorry, you found a phone? Your phone?'

'No,' and the words come with urgency. An urgency which suddenly presses, out of nowhere. Like a confession. 'I found a phone in the dark, in the park... I walked there...'

'You took a walk in the dark?'

She has begun. It's like rolling a ball down a hill. She can't stop it. It must come out. It's driven out of her. 'I walked, I think sleepwalked, to the lake. And I found a phone. Cold. Wet. And I...' Her eyes close. *Save her.* What had that meant? What does it mean? 'I've given it to the police. But why did I find it? Why was I there?'

Will walks back in, phone call finished, and picks up Finn in the car seat.

With a tiny shake of her head at Klaber, and the panic in her hiding, finding somewhere to crawl, she manages to drop his hand. She has been gripping it throughout.

'Give me a call.' He smiles. 'Why don't you make another appointment?'

Finn sleeps in the car on the way home, and Will has bought some coffees from the hospital café. Jenny sips the hot frothy liquid, letting it warm her from the inside as the car is battered with fresh snowfall. The huge wet flakes come at the windscreen quickly, clinging, before being pummelled by the wipers and disappearing. The warmth of the carpeted room stays with her.

She thinks about seeing Dr Klaber again: if she will be able to speak, to articulate the muddled sense of unease.

'Well, he seemed quite good. Feel any better?' Will says, his sideways glance anxious.

He is always nervous after a public crying fit. It is as though crying in public means that she is much more upset than when she does it at home. She, on the other hand, finds that her tears are indiscriminate. They simply arrive, demonstrating no awareness of place or occasion.

'Much,' she replies, trying hard. 'I liked him.'

'Takeaway tonight? I'll brave the arctic conditions and hunt and gather you a lamb pasanda with Peshwari naan? Me Will, you Jenny?'

She laughs at his bestial grunting and when Finn wakes they are at the house. The day is already darkening, and after Finn's feed Will lifts him out of Jenny's arms.

'Go and pour some wine. I'll put him in pjs and bring him in to you to take upstairs.'

Jenny resists the urge to remind him where the clean pyjamas are. He will call to ask in a minute, but if she tells him in advance he feels reprimanded.

Feeling calmer than she has in weeks, the moment of solitude is a gift.

She thinks of his hand on her arm; someone to rationalise her disquiet. The words had loosened the knot in her insides.

'Babes, where are the clean pyjamas?' Will shouts from the bedroom.

Turning on the tap to rinse out dishes from earlier, the water stutters. Jenny turns the tap on and off three times before the pipes grunt, growl. The water follows in a belch and a burst. A shout. Jenny flinches. The pipes must be freezing in the cold. She'll have to get Will to check them – the house is old, and they can't go without water. She places her hand in the flow, to feel its temperature. Its coolness runs against her skin.

Her hand becomes numb. Its feel familiar – there's a stab in her stomach – the sound of a voice.

Slowly, she pulls it backwards, reluctant. The creeping sensation of the coldness of the water is magnetic.

21

It's cold. The wind blows like ice. Feet wet, she stumbles. The hill dips and the ground crunches beneath her feet like glass, sharp, stabbing.

It's not far now. She's running, and the lake appears. This time it's snowing and she's wet.

The suddenness of arriving shocks like a blow. What is she doing? How did she get here?

In the stillness of the night, she pauses, tries to think. There had been a voice?

'Who's there?' she calls, but the words float out, and the cold of the air freezes them before her.

'Why am I back here?' Her whisper lands on the ground, unanswered. Fighting tears, she turns as a shadow falls across the moonlit path: it's the willow again, waving, dancing.

'Save her.' The whisper is close, and it makes her run. She runs and she runs. Along the lake, turning past the old pub and up the hill.

She must get back to Finn. What if he's crying? She needs to get back to Will, before he wakes and finds her gone. She's not running from him. Is she?

22

17 December

The hospital's corridor is empty, and the smell is interlaced for Maarten with the birth of Sanne, number two daughter. Nic had been born in Holland, where home births were more common, and by the second they had moved to England, living in London. He had sat hot and hungry, holding Liv's hand, as she strained out the tiny baby. The vivid sense of exhaustion and elation is wrapped up in this odour of disinfectant and the unwell – sterile blood. Apprehension and happiness, with each breath. Her tiny hands, waving and fragile.

'How's the war wound?' asks Imogen, sitting down beside him.

Jolted back, reaching up, he touches where the glue holds the cut together, held under a dressing to keep it dry.

'Not too bad. *Kak*, not too great.'

'What time did you get home?'

'Can't remember. Liv picked me up. Before the sun.'

He had passed out when he'd arrived in the hospital. They had scanned him, watched him, wanted to keep him in, and all he had wanted to do was to flee. The mess and the chaos of the emergency room had been oppressive, impossible to unpick. He couldn't have recovered in there. His memory of the night is faint. Liv had come. Liv. His mouth had been full of cotton wool. His lips cracked as he spoke, and his eyes had only partly opened: the bandage that keeps the wound tight pulled his eyelids forward, just a chink of light.

'Are you sure you want to come home now? It's four a.m... they said you were adamant?' She had leaned over him and her scent was a relief, a warmth. Her hand had reached for his and her touch was all he needed to muster the strength.

'Yes.'

Voice parched, scratched, he'd barely managed to speak, and she'd got him out.

'Nice glasses,' Imogen says.

The spare pair has a red rim, and are too bold for a murder investigation, but he's got no choice today, as the others are being fixed. 'Liv's going to collect mine for me later. How's he doing?' He gestures to the room, where Tim Pickles is linked to machines that monitor in beeps and blinks on the screen.

'Not great, but I think he'll be OK. The doctor's heading over in a second. What will we do about the interview, sir?'

'Well, it will have to wait. Has there been anything else? Are his phone records in yet?'

'Yes. He's called a number of sixth formers but we've got nothing that links him to Leigh. He has, however, had a visitor.'

Maarten glances at Imogen; her eyebrows are raised.

'Young?'

'Seventeen. She came in yesterday evening. The hospital wouldn't let her see him, but Sunny was outside the room so he managed to speak to her briefly. She didn't say much, and ran away when he told her who he was. He did manage to get out of her that she was worried about him, and he got the impression that she might have been at the other end of his call. She answered a few questions: Pickles has loads of their numbers, from what I can gather. Smokes with them sometimes, gets drunk. Been to a couple of house parties when parents have been away. She said nothing to link him to Leigh – the girl looked as though Sunny was mad when he suggested it.'

'Have you identified her?'

'Yes, Sunny's got her name and she's coming in later with her parents so we can check her out then. We'll keep digging.'

'Good work.'

He glances down at Imogen's wrist, wrapped in a white bandage. 'What happened? Were you hurt too?'

'Not really – I think I sprained it putting the cuffs on. Seb made me get it checked out this morning – he's driven me in. Gone to get coffees. He's getting you one too.' She glances down the corridor. 'Here he is.'

'Maarten,' Seb says, his long stride halting as he passes out a coffee, face filled with sympathy. 'Shocking news – how are you?'

'OK.' The room spins. Holding the coffee close he breathes in – he can't drink, his mouth feels too raw, but the bitter smell rises and takes the edge off the hospital aroma. 'Tired. Looking forward to the end of the day.'

'Pay attention to what they told you, Maarten. Head injuries are no joke, and I know what you and Imogen are like.'

Liv had handed him a bottle of something this morning. She had been angry he was going in after so little sleep. 'Whatever you do, don't get behind the wheel. You're likely to collapse at any moment. Honestly, it's a job, Maarten, there are other people…' Her brow had creased in concern; her hands had been covered in glitter. The girls had woken early and been decorating the party invites. Her cheeks were dusted with it and it made him blink.

He could see two of things, if he blinked quickly.

Steps sound on the hard floor.

'This is the doctor.' Imogen gestures to a woman in a white coat heading down the corridor. 'I came back last night, once the paperwork for the men was finished, to relieve Sunny.'

They stand as the doctor shakes their hands. She is short anyway, but Maarten towers over her, looking down at her pale white face, forcing her to look high up in the direction of the strip lighting, and she rubs her eyes at the glare.

'He's been fairly lucky, all things considered. Nothing serious, we think, to his brain. Concussion, a dislocation and a bleed into a joint, but the minor surgery has gone well, and we're hoping he will wake up later today. Fractured cheek. There shouldn't be any long-term consequences, hopefully.'

'Are his family here?' Maarten asks.

'No. He's got a housemate, who came in last night. He said he would call the family, but so far we haven't heard anything.'

Maarten looks through the door. Pickles lies immobile. A lot rests on his regaining consciousness.

'We need to interview him when he comes round. Can I leave someone here?'

'It's up to you. You can leave an officer sitting in the corridor, if you like? But he needs rest.'

'Yes, I'll do that. I'll call someone in now.'

They move to walk down the corridor, Seb falling behind, and as they turn, a beep begins to sound from Pickles' room. It turns quickly to the squeal of an alarm.

The doctor runs into the room and nurses appear from all directions.

Maarten steps back to let them in, and he can hear the whirr of the emergency team in action, but from where he stands it's like a cloud of confusion. His head still aches. There is shouting and someone wheels a cart past him. Flurry, dash. The room spins.

'Oh shit,' Imogen says, to his left.

Seb moves to her and puts his arm around her shoulders. 'Don't worry – they've got this.'

It's frantic and furious. There is some shouting, and then it calms a little. The silence is powerful. More people run down the corridor. Someone pushes a bed.

'Should we go?' Imogen is jumpy beside him.

'No, let's wait. We'll give it five minutes.' The outcome of this could impact the case from all different directions. Threads will tangle.

The beeping slows, nurses file out and the doctor steps back out. Her face shines with sweat.

Maarten steps forward.

'Alive. He was fitting. We will need to keep a close eye on him. It's likely that he has an underlying condition we're not aware of; he could have epilepsy or it could be the fever. The injuries he sustained yesterday have placed stress on his body. We'll need to run a few tests.' The tiredness on the doctor's face ages her – ten years in the last five minutes.

'I'll have an officer here in half an hour.' Maarten tips his head an inch in Imogen's direction and she turns to make the call.

'I know I shouldn't ask,' the doctor says, 'but did he do it?'

★

Pushing the door open to Interview Room One, Adrika and Sunny sit opposite John Hoarde's brother-in-law. Maarten recognises him from earlier, one of the larger ones from the attack, but not the one who hit him.

Back in the station, he wants to show his injuries to the men, give them a glimpse of what they may be prosecuted for: lend weight to his officers' questioning. His plan is to ask for a quiet word with Adrika, and then exit, but his entrance causes a snicker.

Surprised, Maarten catches his eye. The man is wearing police issue clothing because his clothing had been covered with bloodstains, now evidence of the assault.

'Who the fuck do you think you are?' The aggression stirs, the tone lazy, slow.

Maarten doesn't speak, but holds the man's gaze. His head is still throbbing and the night in hospital has upped his exhaustion, nerves newly stretched.

'Really, you come in here, dressed like you're in fucking costume, with your black suit and your red glasses. You've got your people talking to us in here, holding us for beating up a cunting kiddie-fiddler, a murderer!' The man, shouting now, lunges forward. The speed is a surprise. His chair spins behind him.

Sunny throws himself between the two men. Maarten holds his position.

'Help in here!' shouts Sunny.

Officers run through the door and wrestle the man backwards, holding him by his arms and cuffing him, locking his hands behind his back.

'I pay your effing wages! And you're wasting my time! Go and catch the fucking killer, you fucking foreign ponce!'

A glob of spit lands at Maarten's feet. With one last look, he leaves.

Back at his desk, Imogen comes running up. He can hear her footsteps outside the office. She knocks quickly before entering. She carries a coffee.

'Sir! Are you OK? I just heard.'

Placing the coffee down before him, she sits opposite. 'You know you shouldn't even be in today. Shall I phone Liv? I can drop you back now, or if you'd prefer I can ask if she wants to come and get you. I don't think you should drive...'

'Oh, it's fine. Don't fuss.' He opens the packet of pills, and knocks two back with the coffee. 'I would imagine we've found our charge for incitement, if nothing else.'

Imogen sits back and scratches the back of her hand. 'I've got something for you.'

'Yes?'

'One possible, actually. We took a statement from one of the inhabitants of Lake Lane. Their alibi didn't check out. The statement came in half an hour ago. He said he was away golfing, but no one at the club remembers seeing him. We can't pin him down, and the car passed right outside his house: one of the last sightings of Leigh.'

'Anything else?'

'Well, we did some background checks and his place of work, a creative agency in London, they have taken groups of Y9, Leigh's year group, for a morning in industry. We haven't got an obvious link between Leigh and him directly, but...'

Maarten sits up. 'What's the name?'

'Connor Whitehouse.'

23

Jenny is waiting for Sam on the corner, when her phone rings.

'Dad? What a surprise! Are you having a good time?'

'Jenny, pet, I've just read about the girl, about the drowning. Are you OK?'

'Yes, I'm fine. I know I was upset the other day but I'm—'

'Jenny, of course you are upset! God, love... I wanted to talk to you a few months ago...'

Again the static, the white noise. 'Dad? It's a rubbish line.'

'I know – we're in port at the moment. I thought it might be a bit easier than at sea, but...' Static.

'Look, Dad, you're back in a few days. I'll come and get you from the airport. I'm fine.'

'I could come home early?'

'Why do that?' Jenny shakes her head, even though he cannot see. 'Enjoy it. I'll see you soon.'

'OK... but call me if you feel upset. The drowning... Jenny...'

There is nothing else. The line dies.

She pockets the phone as Sam arrives, and Jenny throws off the question that is somewhere in her throat, caught, scratchy.

'We could go down to the lake?' Sam says.

'The lake?'

'I've been meaning to leave some flowers. I didn't get a chance yesterday, but the girls from baby-group have been down and I think Tessa would really appreciate it, you know, seeing that everyone has made a gesture, an effort to mark... to remember... Leigh.'

It makes sense. But it also feels like morbid curiosity. It's a graveyard now, and Jenny has never enjoyed wandering around graveyards. The thought of crowds, jostling, being eager...

They walk, and the snow holds off.

'It feels a bit... is it not too soon? Shouldn't we give it some space?' says Jenny.

'It's like nothing has ever happened there now – no police, no body; there's nothing to actually see.'

Sam is right. There won't be anything left there. Anything to see. And still, and yet... Jenny can feel her heartbeat speed, prepare for fight or flight.

Her feet follow Sam down the path; she pauses at the florist, stares at flowers.

'Here, do you want to write a message?' Sam passes Jenny the pen, and clutching it, fumbling, feeling sick, Jenny writes beneath Sam's round letters: 'So sorry, love Jenny and Finn Brennan.' The writing is uneven, and she wants to rip the card into pieces and toss them in the air.

'You OK, Jen?' Sam pauses as she tucks the envelope into the band of the flowers.

'It's just...'

Sam puts the flowers under the buggy seat and hugs her. Jenny can barely feel it: their coats and all their wrappings surround her like a moat.

'OK, love, if you really don't want to go, we won't.'

One sensible reason, one reason that when spoken aloud doesn't sound like badly written melodrama, but Jenny can think of nothing. So she nods, and says, 'Yes, it's fine. It's a good idea. And you're right. There won't be anything to see, I'm just being silly.'

They step into the cobbled alleyway that divides the cathedral from the city. The twisty, uneven stones muffle sounds from the street, the musty smell familiar. Natural light dims a little as the path becomes narrow, snaking the edge of the cathedral and the walled gardens, and they burst out into the light at the top of the park. Trees, white and dressed; children sledging and wobbly snowmen. The white world is bright. The sun bounces, dazzles on the ice. Tiny icicles hang in clusters from branches. The air is bracing. Jenny breathes in and holds it, expelling it slowly, beginning to believe her own words: she really is just being silly.

'How are things with Will?' Sam asks.

'Well, he's back to work now the trains are running again,' she says. Will. Back in the office, and she's relieved. The distance of his commute, some days apart, will ease the tone of the cottage. She has not wanted to pierce his good mood, glued together since their appointment at the hospital, but she can't sustain a cheery smile for much longer. It had been fine for the evening. But now her face aches, the corners held aloft in an uncomfortable upwards turn.

Neither Will nor her brain seem to be functioning as they used to. She is aware that she doesn't want to give in to frustration and tiredness when he is around. She doesn't want to cry, to seem incapable… He has never doubted her before; she doesn't understand these new rules.

'He's worried I'm going slowly mad. I had roughly two hours' sleep last night and Will slept the sleep of the dead. He rises and looks smart and capable, and leaves me grasping a mug of tea in one hand and a crying baby in the other.'

'What is it with our husbands? They have toilet breaks, lunch breaks, grown-up meetings. You know I didn't have a conversation with an adult the whole of yesterday? The snow was so bad, I just stayed in. Even my bloody mother had gone out when I called her.'

The edge of the lake comes into view. It's bright, like a sheet of mirror. Hard.

'Tessa will be touched,' Sam says, seeing her face.

Jenny steps forward, ducking under a low tree branch. The icicles are sharp, and one falls as she bumps against the branch, plunging to the ground and disappearing under the snow.

Looking down, as the path winds to the right, Sam gasps, and Jenny can see the edge of a crowd. There is no noise, just a quiet group. They flank the corner of the lake, near a crop of trees and the hut where children bird-watch during the summer. The ground is bare, and the snow has been walked away. The edge of the lake is lined with bunches of flowers, rows and rows of coloured petals, bright, wrapped in cellophane. Some in pots, some in vases. There are also single flowers: red, white roses with long stems, heads facing towards the lake, thorny stalks stark on the dirt. Petals have fallen and carpet the area. Cards and drawings colour the trees, flapping and clapping open and shut in the breeze.

Stilled, Jenny and Sam stand, heads tilted down silently. A prayer of sorts. A confrontation.

Jenny looks out, across the lake. It's not big; the other side is clearly visible, and if someone shouted from one end to the other you could probably still hear them. A city lake, a park lake. Not a graveyard. It's hard to imagine it in darkness, in all this sunlight with all these people. It's hard to imagine being alone, and being afraid. The sun catches the lake and it flashes, carbon sparks, diamonds. A figure moves on the far side. Darting backwards from the water, moving behind the trees. Indistinct. Disappearing beyond the threshold.

She is five again. '*Jenny! Jenny!*' Her head whips round – 'Mum?' she says, before she can swallow it.

'Jenny?' Sam looks at her, confused.

'Sorry.' Jenny's face burns hot with embarrassment. 'I feel…' Her eyes follow the movement into the trees. 'I feel as though something is waiting to happen,' she says. Or that she is waiting to remember what has happened – but she can't say this, and she can't shake the sensation. The cold cools her cheeks.

'What?' Sam asks.

Jenny shakes her head. 'Oh, nothing. But don't you feel as though we're waiting? For whoever did this to be caught and put away? It's like…' She stumbles for the words. 'It's like the trees have shadows that live; the noises at night in the house, I keep jumping…'

Sam puts her hand on Jenny's arm.

'Oh, it's nothing,' Jenny says, feeling ridiculous. 'Let's lay the flowers.'

They step forward and kneel.

As Jenny leans in, touching the earth with her gloved hand, she feels a jolt, a stab. She doesn't move. Her heart beats quickly. Her mouth dry, she daren't turn to look at Sam. She can't have anyone else look at her as Will does, as if she is mad. She needs an ally.

Her mother: she had been almost six when her mother had died. She doesn't remember much. And yet she's back there. There is a woman in a hospital bed – holding her hand. The image is so still, like a photo – she's not sure if it's a real memory, or a memory she's put together from the story her dad has told, over and over again. There are machines, with tubes – she doubts her dad would have embellished those. This memory, this fragment has been flashing up since Finn, since the birth, there are fresh details seeping in: a soft touch, the smell of milk, and the voice shouting – '*Jenny! Jenny!*' – she still can't place it. It's as though giving birth has opened a door. But she's not sure to where it leads.

In a moment, the tremor passes, and the earth returns to its solid, cold mass.

'God, there's Tessa,' Sam says. Her voice is quiet.

Looking up, Jenny sees the crowd part, and a murmur begins.

They stand quickly, stumbling on the slippery ground, and Jenny reaches for the buggy behind her, anxious and guilty. Her child is here, with her. She wants to hold him close, to ward off the grief she sees on Tessa's face. But she doesn't want to parade him. Taunting.

Tessa has two women with her. One looks very like her, and links her arm. Tessa leans against her, yet seems oblivious to her presence. She looks at the crowd as though she doesn't quite understand why they are there; doesn't acknowledge them. Her eyes are on the flowers, the rows of heads, colourful and bright. And on the lake. Her eyes stretch to the lake.

Kneeling, she begins reading the messages that are attached to the bouquets. She moves from one to the next. The paper in her fingers curls, as though her hands are wet. Jenny can see a tissue clutched in there.

It's uncomfortable to stand here, but they can't leave. No one can leave. Someone steps forward, and bends, saying quietly how sorry they are, what a waste, what a tragedy. Tessa nods, and places her hand on the woman's arm.

Rosie wakes and screams. Sam winces and lifts her out of the buggy, pulling her close and walking backwards to a bench. Like a baby's cry in a funeral, it's too loud, a bold shout of life against the hush of death. Tessa looks round.

Very briefly, in her sweep of gaze, she catches Jenny's eye. Jenny can feel that she has started to cry and, hating herself for it, for making this woman's sadness her own, for taking it away from her, she tries to smile.

The hollowness of Tessa's face, the loss – so evident, etched so deeply – takes Jenny's breath away. It echoes inside her: a child's cry, the first word, riding a fat dog across a garden, birthday cake, crying at a popped balloon, sandcastles, chicken pox, tiny kisses, a fallen tooth...

It's lost; out of reach. Pain so clear, so present. Loss. That whisper again. '*Save her.*'

'Leigh,' Jenny whispers. 'Oh, Leigh.'

Tessa's eyes have not left her face. Tilting forward, she reaches out towards Jenny.

Moving, just an inch or two, Jenny is still crying. Her arms reach forwards and Tessa, still holding her gaze, takes a step towards her, surprise writ on her face.

Tessa gasps, a small scream puffs out and disappears quickly, like breath. 'Leigh!' And then she falls, crumpling to the earth like discarded wrapping paper.

24

The heavy wheels of the car spin on the small, twisty lane.

'Shit, sorry,' says Imogen, as the car slides back a foot, moving down the slope and bumping into the stone wall. 'I should have let Seb drive us – he offered. My arm went on the handbrake.'

'It's fine. I'm not even allowed to drive on these pills. *Klere!* We're a wounded circus act this morning.' Maarten climbs out and stretches, slamming the door and setting off on foot. 'Leave it here.'

They walk up the hill towards the house. Maarten can feel himself spinning. He just needs to hold it together for another few hours.

Flinching as Imogen bangs on the door to the Whitehouse residence, he glances at next door. Through the window he can see Mrs Brennan. She doesn't see him, and there is something about her: the tilt of her head, the angle of her arm... he can see that she's crying.

The feeling again, of there being something she wasn't saying...

The phone had come back with a trace of Leigh – suspected, unconfirmed DNA trace – but no numbers. The phone was so waterlogged they had said it might take time to have a proper look. But the DNA, even faint, was enough.

There was a lot of work for their department to do to try to establish a link to the adult involved. But Mrs Brennan had found it. And they had not. That was interesting.

'No one in.' Imogen shivers.

The wind is cold, and his head spins again. He really must eat something. On the brink on knocking on Mrs Brennan's door, he changes his mind. What would he say? It would be better to wait until they had something concrete.

'Let's try again later.'

The drive back is worse, and he slams the dashboard. 'Stop!'

Retching at the side of the road, the straining exacerbates the pain behind his eyes. He kicks snow over the deposit, but he's barely eaten, so it doesn't take long. Dizzy, he reaches out for the fence post and leans against it, arching forward and staring out over the fields. Luckily, they have taken the ring road. Straight through the centre of town would have been embarrassing.

'Sir?' Imogen appears at his side with a bottle of water.

'Oh, fuck it.' He takes a drink. 'Thanks. Liv was right, I shouldn't have come in today; I should probably go home. But there's so much to do… we need to get a break from somewhere.'

'Do you think Whitehouse is a possible?'

'Yes, he might be. But other than the alibi, we've got nothing really… no corroborated link to Leigh. Proximity of the car, proximity of the class visit…'

The sky is dark and the wind cold.

'I'm going home,' he says.

The siren is deafening. Maarten had been at home all of two hours before Sunny had called.

He turns his face from it, reeling at the sound. Undeterred, he goes as close as he dare. The heat builds a barricade, a kilometre-high fence.

'What time was it found?' he shouts.

Sunny shrugs, turning his face from the heat and stepping back. 'Called in about half an hour ago, but looks as though it's been burning for some time.' His voice competes with the roar of the flames, as the gases expand and the chemicals sizzle.

'Get back!' A fireman appears, and puts a hand on Maarten's arm, pulling him hard. His voice is muffled through his mask. 'There'll be dangerous gases from the paint, and there's the danger of explosion, if there's any fuel left inside.'

Retreating further from the top of the hill where the car burns, Maarten shakes his head. 'If there is any DNA left in there, I'll be surprised. Shit. Are we sure it's the same one?'

'No, not sure. We've still had no confirmed plate. But what are the chances?'

Imogen walks up alongside. Maarten had sent her out that afternoon to follow up on a lead about the car. The wind on the downs is fierce and her hair whips over her face. 'The errant black BMW. I've checked four of them found abandoned in the last twenty-four hours. I'll bet my pension that this is the one we're after.'

'A sodden wallet, a jacket with a DNA we don't recognise,

and a phone we're still trying to make sense of – found by a member of the public. It's going to have to be enough.'

They stare at the bonfire, the DNA, evidence, leads, sizzling, curling in smoke.

25

Waking in the night is not unusual. Night feeds, nappies and all the other thousands of reasons that add up to wakeful babies have combined to disrupt Jenny's sleep for the past few months. It's different tonight. She is sure she heard something.

She can't wake Will. They have reached a truce of sorts. She will not mention the creeping unease, and he will make more of an effort to help out, to let her get some rest and not become so quickly irritated if she appears fragile. Nothing has been said, but the deal has been quietly done.

Her hand creeps out to Finn's crib, but he is warm, solid, and still sleeping. His gentle snores snuffle into the bedroom. Yet nothing feels quite as it should.

There it is again. That noise.

She sits up. Careful not to disturb either of the sleeping bodies in the room, she climbs out of bed.

The hall is quiet and the house is cold.

Again, the noise. Not quite a tapping, but repetitive and insistent.

A murmur of water, and a slow drip, drip, drip. Like drops from leaves.

She is in the garden. Her feet are wet and the damp is soaking up through the soft material of her pyjamas; they ride up, clinging to her ankles.

She puts her hands out before her. What is out there?

Soaking, soaked right through. How long has she stood here? There are trees behind her, again the willow, and the moon, a silver orb, hangs watchful above. Adrenalin surges, fuelling the feeling of urgency. Has she been running?

'Jenny! Jenny!'

She spins, the voice sounds urgent; it's more of a scream. Full of fright. But no one's there. She's not even sure if it came from nearby, or from within.

Teeth chattering, she shivers in spasms. The dark is closing in, despite the moon. A flicker ahead – is it a girl? There's movement behind the trees.

She steps forward, fingers – shivering – reaching. They unfurl stiffly; they ache.

There is a girl. The back of a head. It's too dark to make much out, but she has long, dark hair. She creeps.

'Jenny, Jenny!'

This time the shout is much closer to a scream and the shock electric.

Whirling, like a shying horse, Jenny flees back, bolts. Home must be up the hill. With scrabbling, trembling fingers, she finds herself inside, bolting the door. She can't remember where she has put the key; she can't remember opening the door.

Finding Will's keys on the table, she manages to turn the lock.

There are fresh clothes in the dryer. She changes into what is there. Will's gym kit, she thinks, but that will do.

Back in bed, she forces herself to think of sleep. It will be morning soon.

There it is again: rushing water, drip, rush...

Sleep. It is sleep she needs.

26

18 December

'Could you come down to the front desk? A couple, asking for you.'

Maarten can feel the weight of his tread heavy on the stairs. There had been something in the voice of the PC; it has turned him cold.

'Maarten!' There are tears spilling down the cheeks of the woman standing before him. He had met her very briefly at the vigil. It is Becky Dorrington's mother, the mother of Nic's best friend. He scrabbles in his brain and the name comes.

'Jess, what's wrong? What's happened?'

'It's Becky,' and there are more tears, as her husband leans forward to take over, but his voice cracks too.

'She's missing... she's...' His swallow is hard.

Maarten nods to the PC who buzzes them all through, and he opens a door to a side room. He can't remember the father's name. He curses himself.

'Mr Dorrington?'

'Kemmie, please.'

'Kemmie. I'm going to get a couple of my colleagues down to take some details while we talk. Can I get you tea, coffee?'

Stepping out of the room, to nod to the PC who waits outside, he asks for Adrika and for drinks to be brought.

He needs a minute. Nic has been so upset about Leigh. Devastated. And if Becky really is missing, if this is what he feels it might be, then this will be harder than it usually is. He doesn't want to waste time, so he doesn't give in to the pang that he feels, the pang for Liv. To call her, and to tell her, and to feel it between them – the pain that Nic will feel.

Adrika arrives with a notebook, and her expression tells him she has been briefed with the little they know.

He pushes open the door, introduces her, and they begin.

'She wasn't in her bed this morning.' Jess speaks, but Kemmie picks up the thread, and they pass the story between them.

'And she was wearing a red cardigan yesterday, which was gone this morning...'

'... and jeans.'

'And a backpack has gone...'

'... and her Velcro purse. It's plastic. It's got Rey on it, from *The Force Awakens*...'

'We've phoned round her friends already.'

At this Maarten feels a clutch: Nic will know. Liv will have had to ask her if she knows anywhere that Becky might have gone.

'So we came here. She's gone. I can feel it.' Jess finishes the story, and her voice is strong now. Unconsciously, she places a hand on her stomach, as she sits up tall. She's pregnant, Maarten thinks.

'I've heard you usually wait twenty-four hours. But not today. You can't wait today.'

Maarten nods. He leans forward, looks them both in the eye. 'You're right. We'll begin now. We'll find her.'

27

'How would you like to use today's session?'

Klaber sits across from Jenny. For all the delight she had felt at getting a last-minute appointment yesterday, talking is still difficult. Now that she sits here.

'Maybe you could start with what you're doing later? Have you anything planned, with Finn?'

Jenny smiles. 'I'm going to a class, at the local pool, then coffee at the café nearby. It's a baby swimming class, and Finn loves it, don't you?' She leans forward and waggles the rattle that he is sucking, as he lies on a playmat by her feet.

'Have you been going long?'

'A few weeks, I go with my friend Sam. She's got a little girl, the same age. I met her in hospital.'

Jenny can feel herself opening, finding talking easier.

'Thinking about the hospital, maybe we could talk a little about the birth? About how you found it?'

Jenny thinks back... the gasp as she'd heaved out of the birthing pool, to clutch the sides as the contractions gripped her. 'Surfacing,' she says. 'It felt like I was surfacing.' And it had. 'It felt I was breaking through something, that the water… that something was coming free, unsticking.' She'd felt exactly that. Even the eventual birth in the theatre hadn't dulled that sense that the pool had given her; that something had changed.

'And it's since then that I miss my mum. I miss her more than I've ever missed her. I miss her when I hold Finn – I miss her when I'm awake in the night, and he won't sleep. I want to ask her how she felt, what it was like for her. Breastfeeding was hard to start with, and there was such pressure… I had great friends but we were all going through it at the same time, all anxious. The midwives were all different. I wanted my mum. I wanted my mum to tell me it was OK. My dad was great, but how does he know what it feels like when it's two a.m. and I can't get a latch? And Finn is screaming…'

The room falls quiet as Klaber dips his head, making a few notes, giving her a moment. She had been going to cry, but it falls away.

'And this week? How have you felt since we last spoke? You mentioned the murdered girl?'

Jenny looks down, at her hands. She may as well tell him, otherwise why is she here? 'I don't know why but…' What to say? That she feels she's involved? That if she were to uncover the fears that plague her once the lights are out, that she might believe…

'Yes?' he says, encouraging.

'I don't understand what is happening to me.' And she cries. Her head tips forward, and she glances at Finn who plays with a teether, and she thinks of him, of the lake, of Leigh.

'Jenny,' he says. His voice is soft. Tissues are passed over, he waits.

'I can't explain it. I'm seeing ghosts. I'm sleepwalking. I'm sleepwalking in the *park*, bloody hell. What am I doing?'

'How often has this happened?' Klaber smiles. He hasn't laughed, he hasn't scoffed. He hasn't said the thing that scares her most. The thing that Will keeps almost saying, just holding himself back from outright accusation. That she might be going a bit... crazy? Mad?

'Oh, I don't know! Last night, and a few other nights before that. Sometimes I think it's just a dream. That I'm shivering because of a nightmare, because I'm panicking. That the cold is in my head. Surely I'd wake if I was leaving the house... but... well, I found the phone, the one I told you about.'

'Yes,' he says.

'And last night it was snowing, so I was wet. I changed when I got in, and again until I woke, I thought maybe it had been a dream...'

'What happened to the phone?'

'I gave it to the police. I thought maybe it was... evidence.'

'Evidence? What do you mean?'

'I found it in the park... and I felt that they might be...'

The police haven't got back to her yet, so is she making mountains? Out of molehills?

'What though? Evidence of what, Jenny?'

'That the phone... the phone belonged to...'

Klaber crosses his legs, leans forward slightly. 'Who? Jenny? Who?'

'To Leigh. To Leigh Hoarde.' Her voice is so low, Klaber has to lean forward to catch the name. To gather it up to consider it.

For a second there is a silence, and then he smiles gently. He hasn't said it. He hasn't said that she is going mad.

'Tell me more about the walking. Where do you go?'

'Well…' Jenny thinks. She hasn't really thought about the details. The fact of it happening has been the most terrifying part. She hasn't wanted to unpick it.

'I suppose I walk to the lake. And…'

'Yes?' He nods.

'Well, there's always the willow tree. The big weeping willow, where the river feeds the lake. I hadn't really thought about it before. That's odd, isn't it?'

'Let's not think about what's odd at the moment, let's just work with the facts. You say you've walked there a few times now, in the night. And it's the same place you're walking to?'

She nods. How come she hadn't thought of it before?

'Well, my next question would be why. Do you have any idea why you might walk there?'

'I don't think I'm deciding… Or…' Dare she? Dare she say it? In a whisper, she inches forward. 'The face in the window? You remember? I think *she* took me there.'

'Who, Jenny? Who took you there?'

She pauses, sighs. 'The girl. The girl with the dark hair.'

'So, is it holding? The peace with Will?' Sam asks, as they enter the changing rooms at the local pool for their WaterBabies class.

'Yes, though he's busy at work. I never see him, and when I do he's jumpy.'

Is jumpy the right word? Jenny thinks back to earlier that morning. Will had woken to find Jenny sleeping in his gym kit and she couldn't remember why.

'You must know,' he'd said, reasonably. Reasonably, but quite forcefully.

'I think Finn was sick, and I just changed into whatever was closest.'

'So you really can't remember? You are sure?' Will had pressed her to answer. Then he calmed down and said more gently, 'I suppose you're up in the night so much. You're just good at doing things half asleep.'

And that had been that.

It isn't exactly true that she can't remember, but more that, before she saw the clothes she was lying in, she thought she must have dreamt it all. It had been as much of a surprise to her, to wake and find she was wearing the shorts and T-shirt, as it had been to him. Klaber was helping her with her recall, but even now the memory is fading. She can't remember exactly what happened any more, but she has a vague recollection of getting wet.

'Your keys, Jenny! They were outside!' he'd said, coming back in after he'd left for work. He'd put them on the kitchen table and then left again, banging the door behind him. 'Look after your keys – we don't want any break-ins,' he'd called over his shoulder.

She jingles them now, popping them in her bag and putting them in the changing room locker.

It is the keys being outside that rattles her the most. She can remember, very clearly, hanging them up the previous evening. She feels invaded somehow, and the distaste of it is still fresh and unsavoury. That sensation she has felt recently, of there being someone peering over her shoulder, is stronger than ever.

If she is going to be honest, she is a tiny bit afraid.

'Morning, everyone!' The class begins.

Singing the welcome song, they lift the babies in and out of the water.

Finn loves the class. He splashes and kicks, giggling with delight. Jenny and Sam love it too. Jenny loves the feel of his slippery skin, plump and infant in the water. She feels weightless and carefree as she bounces and swims.

Laughing, they dress the babies after the class and make their way to the Watermill Café, ordering cake to replenish their energy. Snores breathe out from the buggies, everyone tired.

'Will's parents are coming up tomorrow for an impromptu visit,' Jenny says, reading her phone as the text alert beeps. 'They're visiting friends nearby so are popping in for Christmas cake.'

'Have you made a Christmas cake?' asks Sam.

'Not quite. But I think Waitrose might have done, so I'll have to nip in later and bash it about a bit. Any chance it will be remotely convincing as something home-made?'

'No.' Sam laughs. 'I wouldn't bother. Give it to them and dare them to say anything. Pray for Christmas spirit.'

Taking a sip of her drink, Jenny looks over at the buggies. 'I'm seeing a therapist now...' she begins, casually, unsure of what to follow it with.

'Yes? That's good, Jen. It can't hurt. Do you feel OK about it?'

Jenny nods. She's surprised that she does feel fine about it, good, even. The appointment that morning had gone well. After she'd told him about finding the phone, she had felt lighter – unburdened. He hadn't laughed, but then he must be used to hearing crazy things. Things that people conjure with tired, jumpy brains; vulnerable minds that work hard in the dark, when the world sleeps.

'Is he good?' Sam asks, a mouth full of cake.

'I bloody hope so,' Jenny says, and smiles. He'd asked her to describe the pain of the birth: it had been beyond her control. But when she thinks of it now, she feels calmer, and the jokes she had always thrown in when recounting the birth had already slipped away. She'd be able to just say it and smile next time.

When they'd spoken about her mum she hadn't been able to finish. She had tried to articulate the sense of nearness – a new thing. That she missed her when she rocked Finn at night. She didn't cry easily before, and now, tears lie beneath her skin as though she's been soaked in saltwater.

And more recently, since moving to St Albans – her sense of self had shifted further. A part of her was a little more out of reach, as though it was grappling with something to which Jenny wasn't privy.

Signalling to the waitress, Sam says, 'Another one?' as she points to the empty coffee mugs.

Jenny nods, and then looks out of the window, as Sam orders.

The pallid sky is empty.

'I think—' Sam begins.

'What's that?' Jenny interrupts.

'What?'

'That,' Jenny says. The fear, dormant at the pool, unwinds and rises. She stands, leaning forward, poised. Staring out of the window, she raises her hand, gesturing beyond the glass.

Opening her mouth to speak, the room spins, and she knows she must gather herself. This must not be ignored.

'There's something poking up. Something from underneath the waterwheel. There's something…'

Sam stands and looks.

'I can't see anything.'

The watermill windows are lead-lined and thick, looking out through the old, chalky walls. The wheel turns in the water, but only for decorative purposes. The current pushes its lazy circle when the river is full. Today it moves slowly, and from one of the rungs at the bottom, half trapped by bushes, there is a red object, waving and bobbing.

It is long and slender, and looks like it might be made of wool. As the water swells with each push of the rung, it lifts up, and offers a salutation. Grasping at land? Sinking? Disappearing in the icy current.

It is an arm.

Jenny tries to swallow the cake in her mouth. The room is a vacuum. Her eyes dim and her lids droop over the hazy view of the café. At the back of her mind, she can hear a drip, rush and drip again.

'Where are you going?' shouts Sam.

Jenny pounds the stairs. She's heading to the water. Finn is with Sam and fast asleep – not that she could stop the momentum if she tried. The pull towards the water, sweeping under the wheel, is magnetic.

'Jenny!' The shout carries loud and clear, but doesn't slow her.

She is outside. The cold hits, and running at full pelt, legs pounding and chest straining, she approaches the edge of the water.

She knows she will jump before she does it, and she closes her eyes; terrified of what she is doing, but unable to slow, to desist. Remembering to take a breath, just before she hits the water, she plunges.

As she flies, the air like ice against her face, her body soaring, time slows like a showreel winding down, there's another shout: '*Jenny! Jenny!*' It's not Sam, and she can feel it, coming from inside. It's there, bubbling up, ready to break through but not quite there… it makes her heart burn; she's heard it before. The split second before she enters the water, she catches sight of a figure in the water, splashing, flailing. Arms reaching upwards, and a head emerging and sinking. The figure is gone in a blink. *'Jenny! Jenny!'*

The force of the cold is overwhelming and she opens her mouth, choking, as she kicks her legs and moves towards the wheel. She is pulled forwards and manages to grab one of the old wooden spokes. She hangs on, a moving ballast, and reaches for the girl.

The wheel is powerful; the current throws her hard against the turning spokes. She is lifted out of the water, and as she rises, she catches sight of Sam at the window, caught in a scream.

A grind and screech, and the wheel slows. She can see a man lying over a lever nearby, thrown hard against it as though he's taken a flying leap. He wears the outfit of a waiter at the mill, and then she sees nothing as the slowing wheel plunges her once more beneath the surface.

The darkness is calming and she doesn't try to breathe. Opening her eyes, she looks clearly into green eyes in a pale face. Jenny's arms move out towards her and, abandoning the spoke she has been grasping, she stretches her arms wide for an embrace. The world goes dark.

28

Maarten's feet are cold, his hands are blue and he hasn't moved for a good fifteen minutes. He thinks of nothing, bar the expectation of a body, as he watches his team pull the clothes of a young girl from the river, upstream from the waterwheel. They have managed to shut down the power on the wheel completely; the steady flow of the water works against them, but there is no danger of being caught.

Imogen is down there, in waders, next to the diver, positioned under the heavy wheel. She is bent low, gesturing and calling out to the team. The CSI team have been at it for hours. Her arm is still wrapped in bandages but she had sworn the sprain had dulled.

'Another shoe,' comes the shout.

'Still no sign of a body!' Imogen calls.

A fucking shoe. Christ.

He moves forward to take a look. He has looked at all the items but it has been thirty minutes since they last found anything, and so far, no sign of the girl herself.

The hum of work is unbroken by chatter. There are people standing further back from the banks, watching silently. A second body will be big news. Just as the media was beginning to step away from the city.

Each time there is a shout to alert the crew that something else is coming up, Maarten steels himself. A body will be an utter failure on all accounts.

His head is throbbing. He's due more painkillers but in the rush he's left them at the station. '*Kak*,' he mutters, rubbing the side of his head.

The call had come from the café that two customers had spotted a red cardigan puffed up with water. One of the customers had jumped in, thinking she was saving a life. When she'd been pulled out, the garment was empty. She had been unconscious and an ambulance had been called. One blow of mouth-to-mouth had brought her round quickly. He looks at the spread of vomit and bile lying on the side of the bank, coughed up river water, clogging up airways. If only these girls were so lucky.

The woman, Mrs Brennan, is being checked now, and he glances at his phone to see if there is a message to confirm she is OK. They will need a statement from her soon. She seems to have a knack for entangling herself in this case. The phone she had brought in is still with his team. They are working to unlock the secrets that almost died with it, in its soggy grave.

Once the search had begun, the clothes found hinted at the very worst possible outcome to the report of another missing girl. He can hear the press in his head, the news bulletins.

The call from the mill had come close on the heels of the arrival of Becky's parents.

He still thinks of looking at Liv's face, as he'd looked at Jess.

He's floored, feels bottomless. This girl had been in his home only a few days ago, and he had promised Nic he would catch whoever... And now, Becky?

And then in had come the call. Rarely, in police work, do events conjoin so smoothly. A dull hush had settled in the station. Despite the rush of action to arrive at the scene, the tone was sombre. Jess and Kemmie, still present in the station, had been told. Not out of choice, but out of proximity.

Maarten would have preferred to have something concrete, some hard facts, to offer before he spoke to them, but now they are here, at the edge of the scene. Short of arresting them, he cannot keep them away. They are not permitted to enter the crime scene itself, as they are classifying the riverbank, but they will not be held back. Their audible, physical grief and hope, twinned in tears and their tangible longing, pin them to the very edge of the cordoned area.

Now there is just waiting to be done.

Soon he will have to begin gathering details of the girl's disappearance. He rubs his head, distracted by the dull ache. He will later allow anger to supersede the sadness of such a loss. Liv knows him well enough to allow him the space, but it isn't fair on his kids. None of this has been fair on his kids. He has missed two nativity plays in the last week. And now they will have to face this. How can he tell Liv?

He's due a sit-down talk with Liv. He's interviewing with Rotterdam in a few days and they haven't even nibbled at the edges of the offer, but now that will be impossible.

'Sir?'

He steps forward. 'Is there something else? Have they found anything?'

'No. I think that's it. We have the clothes, but as far as we can tell, there's no body. Not here anyway.'

He gazes up the river.

'Get the teams ready. We need to begin dredging further up and downstream.'

His phone buzzes in his pocket.

It's Liv. Oh, for Liv. He presses the green button.

'Maart? There's something on the news, about another girl?'

'*Ja*, I'm here now. It's slow and we've no idea what we're dealing with.'

'Nic's in a right state. There are rumours flying round, but if they're right, then it's Becky Dorrington. Maart...'

'Shit. I meant to call before the news came out. How is she?'

'I can't get much out of her but she's really distressed. You're going to need to speak to Nic today. She's sobbing – can you get back early?'

'Fuck, Liv, I've got no idea when I can get back. It's chaos here and we need to do the scene properly, I've got the press, the parents...'

'Look, it's hard, I know, but you make Nic a priority. Come home at some point today. Make it happen, Maart. She's her best friend.'

She is gone, and he watches his breath, cloudy in the cold, disperse in air, like smoke.

'Sir?' Imogen has come up behind him. 'Do you want me to speak to the parents? They're asking for news.'

His head throbs, the drab surrounds spin round him. He pushes his hand out towards her, and rests on her arm.

'Are you OK?' She peers at him.

Feeling steadier, he pulls away. 'Sorry, yes, I'm due some pills and I need a coffee.'

It is very tempting to let her deal with the parents. He is so tired, but it's too close. It needs to be him. 'No, I'll speak to them. But come with me, then I'll disappear off to get the next stage organised. You stay. They're needed to identify the clothes so I'll meet you back at the station. Let's go public with this as soon as possible. We have to assume she was taken by the same predator that took Leigh. If he's keeping her alive somewhere outside, she won't last long without her clothes. If she's not alive…' he pauses, and forces himself to go on, 'then we need to find the body quickly so that Forensics can nail this bastard. Let's get the press conference sorted and we'll need the usual: up-to-date photo, last known whereabouts. I'll leave that to you. We need to speak to Mrs Brennan, the woman who jumped in. I know she's recovering, but we need her statement quickly.'

Scanning the river, which leads down to the park, he makes a decision. 'Look, once we're done here, cordon off the area, but let's open the search up to the public. We don't have the manpower to cover the whole of the park fast enough. It's freezing. If she's alive. If. If she's alive, then we're on a countdown. We need to find her fast.'

The DCI shouts a few instructions out to the team and then turns towards the parents of the missing girl, his muddy boots marking out the slow, heavy footprints of a reluctant stride.

29

Jenny hears the front door open. Will had said he'd leave work as soon as he could. She hasn't checked the clock, but Finn has fed, is asleep, Sam has poured wine and she's had a shower.

The sound of shoes scuff the doormat and his footsteps tap tap in the hall. She glances at Finn in the buggy. She hadn't wanted him too far away from her. He lies beside the wooden table, on which stands the half-empty bottle of wine. His fist is raised high in a salute and his chubby face is soft and crumpled by sleep.

The steps slow. Will is pausing before walking through to the kitchen. She tenses against the possibility of anger, or gritted teeth.

'God, how terrible,' he says, moving towards Jenny as he enters the room.

She stands up, her chair screeching against the tiled floor. She wears a dressing gown and her hair is wet. There is no reproach in his face. She leans against him.

'It was... awful. It was just awful.' Her words muffle in his shoulder.

Sam takes a glug of the wine. 'Want a glass?' she asks.

'No, not yet. Tell me what happened.'

He sits down and they tell him. From the moment of arriving, to the point where Jenny thought she'd seen the body of a dead child, to finding out it was remnants of clothes from a missing child. A trip to the hospital, but only a quick check and then back home for a shower. No water in her lungs, up to date with her tetanus. 'A big gulp of water, but mainly the cold causing the problem. A bath, hot drinks, call if you feel unwell.'

'I had no idea what she was doing,' says Sam. 'I thought she'd gone mad. One minute we were chatting and the next she is jumping in the bloody river.'

Her hands fidget. 'I gave up smoking years ago, but I could go for one now. Christ.'

'Christ,' he repeats, slowly, sitting back. 'What the fuck is going on? Why haven't they caught whoever is doing this? Another girl missing? Are you OK, Jen? It was fucking brave of you, to jump in like that.'

'Yes, I'm fine. I passed out in the river, but they said I hadn't stopped breathing. The waitress tried to give me mouth-to-mouth and it made me throw up.' She can still taste the bile in her mouth. She reaches for the wine.

Will picks up the bottle and tops her up, pouring himself a glass after all. 'I'm sorry I'm late. I was in a meeting, and I just didn't get your call. It was bloody clever of you to call the firm, Sam. My secretary came to the meeting to get me out. Erin was in the meeting too – she's worried about you as well. When I heard hospital…'

'No problem. I've left you a stream of messages. God, I feel like shit now – I'm exhausted.' Sam stretches out again and then bends to pull her phone from her bag.

'I've left a message for your dad. Hopefully it will get to him – he will want to know.' Will pulls off his tie.

'The police are collecting us tomorrow to take us to the station. They want us to give full statements. They didn't want to go today; once we were out of the hospital and back, time disappeared. Can you work from home? Look after Finn?'

'Of course. How did you cope with the babies?'

'The Mill were great; the waitress changed nappies, and then came to the hospital with me to help out looking after Finn while Jen was being checked. I've had too much caffeine and booze. I need to get home,' Sam says. She rubs her head and pushes her dark hair up into a ponytail. Her phone beeps, vibrating on the wooden table.

'Is Ben coming for you or do you need a lift?'

'He's coming. He left work after I called. Christ...' She stretches her arms out again, and leans her head back.

They sit. Recounting the story, hearing it aloud, has loosened the atmosphere. The charge has gone, the crackle in the air. Now, it is just... sad. Jenny feels like weeping.

Will looks relieved.

'I'm just pleased you're OK,' he says to Jenny. 'I get that you thought you saw a child... It's bloody brave of you to jump in, but Jen, you could have been seriously hurt... think... calm down...'

It isn't as bad as she had been expecting.

'No,' she replies. 'I wasn't really thinking. I'm not really sure what I saw. It's a bit of a blur now.'

'Jenny saw it before all of us. I couldn't see anything out of the window. Until she came up again, clutching it, I had no idea what she was doing. You must have eyes like a hawk.'

Will looks tired. It has been pretty rubbish recently. His stores of reserve must be running fairly low. Jenny watches him. He leans forward to take her hand.

Jenny begins crying. She will be no use to Finn like this. She keeps thinking of the arm, of the red arm, moving up out of the water. And those green eyes. Staring like gems in the dark.

'They're searching the park now,' Sam says, glancing out of the window. 'I can see all the lights. Ben said he'd help once he's got us settled.'

'I should go,' Will says, looking out.

'Yes.' Jenny nods, shivering again. 'Help me get Finn ready first?'

The evening spins forward. The door bangs when Sam leaves. The bath runs for Finn and the heating comes on, warming her through, burning off the damp, clinging to her skin. Will cooks dinner, leaking the smell of garlic. He leaves to join the search for a few hours, then snakes back in bed.

They are lying in bed, side by side, touching from shoulder to heel. She realises she is talking, telling him again that there had been a red arm, then once in the water, eyes, and a mass of black hair.

And when she hears herself telling it afresh, she stutters and grinds to a halt.

30

The sound of the search helicopter is loud; Maarten feels the pressure burn at the top of his head, behind his eyes. The dogs roam the park, barking every now and again, from all directions.

The city is out, illuminating the ground of the St Albans' night. But they're going to have to call it soon. The park is littered with torches, dotted like a huge open-air concert; the beams reflect up from the snow, amplifying the light. The air is bright like gold.

'Jess, please. You've got to come home now.' Kemmie Dorrington is almost crying as he pleads with his wife.

'He's right, Jess,' Maarten says. This has been going on for a while now, but Jess Dorrington will not go back. Her back is rod straight.

'Not until she's home. How can I sleep?'

'I'm going to call it off now,' Maarten says. 'We'd agreed until midnight, but we can't ask anyone to stay out later. We will find her.' The last bit he says with a conviction driven by desire and determination.

'Please, Jess. Think of the baby,' Kemmie Dorrington says, his features fragile in the dark. He is tall, broad – the strain clear; it buckles him. His hand falls to hers, and he tugs gently.

'Oh...' Jess's hand moves to her stomach, and lies. 'Oh, but... how can I leave her, Kem? How can I leave Becky out here, in the snow? If she ever needed me, then it's now. She's only a baby herself.'

Maarten places his hand on her shoulder, as she begins to cry. 'I'm calling it off soon. It's late. It's time for us all to go home.'

'No, please... I need her back, if I can ever feel whole again.'

Kemmie Dorrington's hand slips, and Maarten watches them both begin to crumble.

'You have to trust that we will do everything we can. Everything in our power – in my power.'

He means it. Becky Dorrington is only nine years old. Nic had shown him that morning a comic they had made together: Becky had coloured in her figures bright and bold. She had jumped out of the page at him: her belief in the magic of stories, BB8 and the power of the stars. Her jokes had sounded from her characters, and her childish drawings, bold with life.

She will have that life. He will return it to her.

31

It is cold, out here in the snow. Her feet are freezing. Is Will still here? She reaches out to him, but no, nothing. Moving further she grasps a willow tree, naked, its leaves long abandoned, covered only with the dust of frost.

She is here again. She remembers. She must get back. It is too, too cold. Pulling her hands to wrap around herself, to warm her body, they rub across her nightshirt and she notices the blood. Long scratches of scarlet run in stripes. The trees have branded her.

There was blood before, the very first time. But on her legs. Its liquid red had been hot, and she'd been afraid. The voice from the water had shouted. People had come running. Her dad had been there, and she had been cold, shivering. She could remember the taste of her tears on her lips. No one had held her hand as her dad had dropped her and run.

Something lies on the ground. It glimmers. Picking it up, she clutches it to her chest.

Home. She will freeze to death if she stays out much longer. And she mustn't tell Will.

32

19 December

At the station, going over the notes, Maarten glances at the clock: half past nine. Time to start. Imogen should have the woman settled in the interview room now. She had been unconscious when they'd pulled her out of the water yesterday. Then hysterical when they'd tried to talk to her. Crying, and then she'd been quiet, unable to complete sentences. She had clutched her baby and spoken of what she'd seen, mistaking the cardigan, swollen with water, for a body. Her words had gone round in circles and he hadn't wanted to go to the hospital to speak to her, to hound her.

Hopefully this morning they will get somewhere. They had to make progress with this today. The press are circling. Eyes have swivelled.

He knocks and enters, preparing his smile.

'Mrs Brennan, Jenny,' he says, walking towards her with his hand extended. 'Thank you so much for coming in today. I realise you must still be upset after yesterday's ordeal. Is there coffee on its way, Imogen?'

'Yes, sir.'

Imogen moves up a chair at the table, so they each sit on different sides, preventing it feeling like an interrogation. Earlier, Imogen had rolled her eyes at the idea that Mrs Brennan had thought she'd seen a body. 'Bloody ridiculous!' she'd said, but she'd be on her best behaviour. She didn't put a foot wrong when it came to it – she knew how to handle people, how to get them to trust her.

Mrs Brennan sits up and nods, acknowledging him and sinking back into her chair. She has dark circles under her eyes, and her fingers play with a pencil on the table in front of her. She smiles, but only with her mouth, and her eyes are full of suspicion. He's not sure if he's imagining it but she seems to pull away from him, leaning towards Imogen. She's no pushover, he thinks. He will have to be careful with her. There is something delicate about her, and also some steel.

'Thank you.'

Jansen watches her smile at the officer who brings in the drinks, and she briefly opens up, her face genuine and her gratitude real. She is quite beautiful, with a strong face. She's intelligent; he adjusts his perceptions. He had written her off somewhat. She had been so washed out by the water yesterday.

The interview progresses and Imogen prompts. The paper before them fills up with notes. The tape is running too.

'I honestly thought I saw a body.' Jansen watches her hesitate. 'I don't want to sound mad, but I thought I saw her face in the water. Does that sound crazy?'

'No, of course not,' Imogen replies. 'If you were expecting to see a body, then your mind would expect to see a face. It's normal to remember something that you were anticipating seeing. Memory can be confusing.'

'Yes,' Jenny says. 'She had green eyes, her eyes were green. The face itself – I don't know – I couldn't see her features.'

She's faltering. Jansen smiles at her again, encouraging her. There isn't going to be much else. They just need to complete the statement. She's not going to be able to add anything. She looks as though she wants to leave; she looks irritated. He can think of no other expression to offer, so he smiles again.

She stares down at the table. He watches her hold the pencil in her fist, tight.

'I've brought something else in,' she says.

'Oh yes.' Jansen nods encouragingly, beginning to think out his statement to the press later, the right tone to take.

Jenny places a shiny plastic purse on the table. There's a picture of a droid on the front, and a girl, carrying a lightsaber.

'I've no idea if this is anything to do with the case, but I… I found it in the park last night. Well, this morning really. Anyway, it is either something to do with the case or someone has lost it, so either way…'

Jansen looks down at the purse. The edges are already curling from the damp. It doesn't look expensive. Becky's parents had reported a missing purse. Jess had stumbled over the description, breaking down.

'Where did you say you found it?' he asks. He keeps his voice casual, neutral.

'In the park, under a willow tree.'

'Can you tell us where exactly?' Imogen asks. She has leaned forward, and her tone has become more clinical. The softness has disappeared.

'No, not really.' Jenny falters again. 'It was quite dark.'

Jansen nods to Imogen, who takes out a plastic bag, and picks it up without touching it. Why was she in the park at night? After yesterday afternoon?

'Is there anything in particular that makes you think it belongs to the missing girl?' He holds his interest back. His nerves sit on stalks. The purse radiates on the table. His desire to grab it and run burns his fingers.

There is something about this woman; he can't put his finger quite on it, but she should not be dismissed. She sits quietly, holding a lit match, and she's entirely unaware. He feels Imogen stirring, next to him, itching to begin.

'Well no, nothing concrete. I suppose I just have a feeling.' Jenny sits back and finishes. She looks exhausted. She shifts her shoulders as Liv did when her milk was coming in. She looks as though she's been here longer than she wants.

Imogen stands up; Jansen watches her close the interview, saying the right things. He stands too, putting out his hand once more.

'We're so grateful for your assistance. We'll be in touch. Imogen here will show you out. If the purse does become important, we might need you to walk us through the section of park you were in, to check the ground. But we'll let you know.'

Once out, he makes a call, then races up to their floor.

'Imogen, Mr Dorrington's coming in to identify that purse. If it is the one they mentioned was missing, then we need to get out to the park pronto. We need to be ready to move. Get the team assembled.'

Later, as he nods to Kemmie Dorrington, who has come in to identify the purse, he's poised. The wallet does indeed belong to Becky. At least, she had an identical one. And they swept it quickly. Only one set of fingerprints, other than those they had taken from Becky's room. It had been Jenny Brennan who had handed it to them. So Becky and Jenny's prints. Only those.

Kemmie had leaned against the wall with one hand, holding himself up.

'Maarten…' he had said, faltering. 'Please… Becky.'

It's too coincidental. To find a phone and a purse, crucial to the case. And for her husband to have been one of the last people to see the car that they believe the girl was carried away in. It fits too perfectly. And murderers often can't keep away – she's been hovering round the case from the start.

He addresses the team before they leave for the park. 'Assume they're involved. We need to move carefully, but get digging: background checks, references – everything. Arrange for Mrs Brennan to meet us there, with her husband; we've got nothing more so they're just helping us right now, but be alert. Watch out for anything.'

'It doesn't feel right, sir. I'll get going, but I wouldn't have pinned it on her. She's a mother, and well, she just doesn't seem capable,' Adrika says. 'I'm not planning to have children myself – not something I've factored in. But I can't imagine being able to hurt them, once you've given birth.'

'Just because she's a mother doesn't mean that she can't be a monster. Who goes out walking in the middle of the night, in a park, and miraculously finds evidence? And she was the one to spot the clothes in that river…' Imogen says. 'It's got to be her. She's our one. Parents aren't infallible. They're not sainted beings.'

'Yes, there's something there, whatever it is… The husband maybe? There's something lurking in that house.' Maarten stands. His irritation with himself, with not knowing, rises and falls. He's exhausted.

'The evidence seems to be pointing to her,' Sunny says. 'We can't ignore it.'

The team clears out of the office and Maarten climbs into the car; Imogen takes the wheel. The snow is starting up again, which will cover the tracks they need to follow. She turns the keys in the car.

'Make it quick,' he says.

33

'Who was that?' Jenny looks at the expression on Will's face as he puts the phone down.

'It was the police.'

'Oh? What did they want? Have I forgotten to sign something?'

They're eating biscuits and drinking tea. It is almost lunchtime but Finn is having a nap and Jenny can't be bothered to waste the time making sandwiches. If Will was at work she'd just eat toast or cereal or something: apples, yoghurt, hummus from the pot with a spoon. The effort of doing any more is too much. They can always go out later, when Finn wakes. She'd only been at the police station for an hour in the end, so almost the whole day is left.

It hadn't been too bad. She hadn't liked Jansen any more than the first time, but it had been easy. She'd told her story and then they'd driven her home.

'Jenny, what did you give them?' His expression has changed. The rising tension, seeing his face, forces her ever so slightly upright.

'I gave them a purse I found, in case, you know, it was useful.'

'What? When? When did you find a purse?'

Jenny closes her eyes for a second. She knows it's coming and she's too tired. Her limbs still ache from the pull of the water yesterday.

'I found it last night, I think.'

'You think? What do you mean, you think? When last night?'

'Well… I went for… a walk.'

He stares at her. They're sitting round the wooden table in the kitchen. The tea is hot and she takes a sip. It's snowing, and the flakes fly at the window behind Will. She hopes Finn wakes up. She needs an excuse to leave the room. If she just walks out, it will be worse.

'When? When did you go for a walk? We didn't go to bed until almost midnight. When the fu— when on earth did you go for a walk?'

'It must have been after you'd gone to sleep…'

She should have said a run, she silently curses. She should have said she'd woken early and gone for a run. That would make sense to him. Impress him, even.

'You went for a walk, in the middle of the night, in the park, and you found a purse?'

'Babes, I don't really know. I was sleepwalking, I think. I kind of, woke up, outside. I don't really know any more than that. I was in the park; I was scared. I saw the purse and picked it up. I thought it was lost property… I didn't really think it was important.' That bit was a lie. She remembers seeing the purse, and it had shone, gleamed from the ground. As if it had been placed there just for her.

The big clock ticks loudly. Will looks at her, then past her. Then round to the side. He stands, walks over to the kettle and fills it, turning it on. He walks to the window as it begins to boil, heating water rattling against the limescale.

When he speaks, he does so staring outwards, watching the snow. His arms are resting on the granite work surface, palms down, leaning forward. Leaning away.

'Jen, is there anything you want to tell me? Before the police come?'

'What?' She feels confused. What is he talking about?

'Anything?' He turns round and looks at her, leaning back against the worktop, folding his arms.

He has picked up a peeler, gripped within his fist. His hands ball tightly either side of his body as he wraps his arms. His clench, tight; Jenny watches a slow drop of blood fall to the floor. She doesn't breathe, unable to pull her eyes away. Another – the peeler must be biting his skin – forms, clinging to his skin, hanging. Then it drops, round-bottomed, and splashes on the floor. She forces her eyes upwards.

'What do you mean? I've told you. I know it might sound a bit odd, but people often sleepwalk. I don't really know why... but there isn't anything to say about it.' She desperately thinks, thinks hard. Is there anything else to say, to make it sound plausible?

'Jenny.' He strides back to the table, wiping his empty palm on his trousers, pulling the chair out next to her. He swings it round, sitting so that the back of the chair is between them, legs astride the seat. 'Jen, you were outside in the middle of the night, finding evidence in a possible murder investigation, evidence the police haven't been able to find. Jenny, you saw the clothes for the girl, Christ, you can describe the girl! You bloody well gave them part of a description of her! You told me – green eyes… I checked the press details and she does have, guess what, green bloody eyes. What the fuck, Jen! You're going to be top of their bloody list! That's what the call was about. They're coming here. They want us to meet them and take them into the park, to go over your footsteps! Jen, do you understand?' His voice isn't actually shouting, almost but not quite. Still, the words slam against her. Battering.

'Will…' she says. It's all she can manage.

'No, don't say anything. We will say you couldn't sleep, you thought a walk would help… a bit of air. You were only out for five minutes and then you made yourself a drink, and came back to bed. That sounds more reasonable. Make sure you mention the drink; it's what people would normally do. In a normal situation.'

He sits more upright. His tone is calmer. He pushes the chair back and stands, pulling her chair out for her. Helping her up. 'OK, I'm not a criminal lawyer, but I know enough to tell you not to say anything. You've handed in the purse, so that's great, that's the right thing to do. They can't pin anything on you for handing across evidence that you've found, but nothing more. If you have any… visions…' Will stalls and stares away, fingers curling stiffly, arms held out at a slight angle. The hand holding the peeler finally releases it and it clatters to the floor. He looks back. 'Anything else, you say nothing. You show them where you walked, you show them where you found the purse, but anything else, you stay quiet.'

Jenny is shaking. She feels light-headed.

Will looks out of the window. 'I can see them, across the park. They've already started the search. They'll be here in a second. Jansen, and the other one, Deacon I think it is. We're going to help them, but say nothing else, and if we need to, I'll phone Azeem from work. He can come and advise you if they start questioning you. He's top of his game. You say nothing. You understand? I'm not going to call him now, because it would seem suspicious. Like we had something to hide.'

Jenny wants to steady herself, but there is nothing to lean against. She's in the middle of the kitchen, and she's afraid if she takes a step forward, towards the kitchen counter, she will fall.

Will is a hair's width out of reach. The distance of the thin edge of the blade of a knife.

34

'Get a team out to work up from the bottom. We'll go and walk with her, from the house. We'll trace her route. Watch her, Imogen, watch her. She's got something to hide. No question. And her next-door neighbour is Connor Whitehouse. Watch her like a hawk.'

The gate at the entrance of the cottage is rusted, and swings with a screech. Maarten goes first, pushing it open and walking to the front door. He knocks quickly, preparing his smile. He's got to be dressed for this. He does up the last few buttons on his coat. He's poised.

The door opens and it's the husband.

'Mr Brennan.' Maarten puts out his hand. 'Thanks for agreeing to help us.'

'Of course. We're happy to help. I can't believe the purse Jenny found has turned out to be important!'

'Yes, we were surprised too. We'd already made a detailed search of the park, yesterday. After the river, we searched the whole area. Of course, it's impossible to cover every inch.' He smiles. Genial. Both have moved a pawn.

Mr Brennan stands back, and he can see Jenny Brennan behind him. She's looping a scarf around her neck. Her coat gapes, and her husband gestures to the zip. 'Best do that up, Jen, keep the cold out.'

Her eyes dart to him, and her fingers fumble on the zip.

'I'll go and get Finn. He'll enjoy a walk out.' Mr Brennan goes up the stairs, and they wait for him in silence.

Maarten looks at Jenny Brennan, who is staring at the floor. She looks up and catches Imogen's eye, and smiles. It's a half smile. Watery at best.

'How are you?' Imogen says, stepping closer. 'You must still be exhausted after yesterday. It's so good of you to help us. You can't imagine how useful it could be.'

Nodding, this time the smile is warmer. 'It's fine. I want you to find her. I want to help.'

Mr Brennan comes down the stairs. Their baby is wrapped up in an outdoor bodysuit. He reaches for the baby carrier when he gets to the bottom, but his wife puts out her hands. 'No, I'll take him, Will.'

'Really? Don't you want to be free, to go ahead and help the police?'

'I'll take him.' She slips her arms in the carrier and seconds later the baby is secured, wrapped up against her. She circles his tiny frame with her arms.

Maarten watches the husband's face. The dynamic is not what he expected. The steel he had noticed earlier in her is gone. The energy comes from this husband. Chatty, joking, helpful: it's almost a convincing display. Just a shade too bright.

Colour returns to Jenny Brennan's face and she pushes past Maarten. He stands back quickly, letting her go ahead.

'Let's go,' she says.

35

Jenny walks out into the park. Her feet cold in her boots. Jansen is behind her. He towers above them. His proximity feels threatening.

'You walked this way?' It's the female police officer who speaks.

Jenny nods. 'Yes, I think so. It was dark, but I remember the cluster of the trees, by the water, further up from the willow. I must have come this way.'

'You don't know for sure?' Jansen says.

His voice carries an echo of Will's tone: how can she not know? She has no answer. She shakes her head, catching the exchange of looks between the officers.

Will walks by her side. He doesn't look at her. It snows, lightly.

Walking slightly down to the right, following the path that branches towards the lake, she moves apace.

'Down here,' she says.

'You're sure?' Jansen says.

Is he being facetious? His face is flat. No expression.

'Yes, I'm sure.'

They all trudge the path, arriving at the cluster. She shivers. The bare willow hangs low. The DI darts forward, sweeping the ground with her eyes. Jansen moves more slowly, walking across, around and around. He takes out his phone and speaks quietly.

'Careful about footsteps,' he calls to the DI.

Will puts his arm around her. It's stiff, and it doesn't sink down, following the curve of her shoulders. He still doesn't look at her. She can feel his body, like a rod.

'Sir,' says the DI. She's bent low.

Jansen walks over to where she stands. They talk, like a sports team in a huddle. Their voices quiet. The odd words drift over, but nothing she can make sense of. Will is straining to hear. His head is comically cocked.

Jansen takes out his phone. He speaks more loudly this time, but he listens, mainly. After issuing a few instructions, his tone alters a fraction. It's resolution, thinks Jenny.

'OK, thanks,' he says.

Finn squirms at her chest. He's hungry. He's been dozy since Will woke him from his nap, but she can feel him wriggling.

Enough of this. Enough.

'I need to feed Finn. He's getting restless. Can I walk back up now? Are we done?'

No one speaks. Jansen searches the park with his eyes. There is noise on the horizon, and she can hear teams approaching.

'We are done here; at least, we're finished with your help. However…' He takes a step towards her, to look her in the eye, and to include Will in the look. 'I'm afraid we're going to have to ask you to come down to the station with us. We'd appreciate it if you could come and help us with some more questions.'

Jenny can feel her arms close tightly on Finn.

'But I need to feed,' she says. 'I need to feed him?'

'Can you bring him to the station with you? Or your husband can take him home?' Jansen says.

'Sir,' the DI says, 'I'll stay with her – walk back to the house with Mrs Brennan, and wait for her to finish. Then I can drive her down to the station.'

Will's arm on her shoulder has become a grip. 'Are you scared of letting her out of your sight? Is that it?' His voice sounds hard, professional, tinged with scorn.

'Your assistance would be greatly appreciated,' Jansen says. His eyes still level. His face still blank.

The smile has vanished and in its place Jenny sees that his face has strong symmetry, giving it a sculpted look. And his eyes. His eyes stand out. Firm, clear. For the first time since looking at him, she feels fear. And she realises what is frightening Will. This man is fiercely bright, and determined. She will not be able to sidestep him, to cry and bow out. But what about Finn? She can't be caught up in this, in something as crazy as this, she has to look after Finn.

'Right, I'm calling a lawyer,' says Will.

'You're welcome to do that, Mr Brennan. However, I do want to reiterate that we are not charging your wife. We are just interested in speaking with her further.'

'What, because she came across a purse when out on a walk? And she handed it in? What about that makes her seem guilty, and in need of police detention?'

'It's not police detention, sir. We would simply like to speak with her further. And you ask why? DI Deacon?'

The DI steps forward. She carries something in a clear plastic bag, and she has put gloves on. Jenny has seen this before on television, and she knows it's about evidence. The

DI is carrying some evidence. She feels a thump to her chest, because as she looks towards the bag, as her eyes fall down to the level of the plastic, she can hear a sound in her ears. It's the whimper of a girl. '*Save her.*'

And she knows what she will see. She closes her eyes, afraid to look. The smell of sweat, and of fear, frantic fear, assaults her. She hears the whimper again, a blink of darkness and a voice, a male voice, from elsewhere, hisses in her ear: '*Be quiet!*'

She staggers backwards, Will's grip steadying her, holding her upright.

Her eyes open once more. Inside the plastic bag is a greyish, wet version of a pale blue rucksack, with a circle on the back showing a picture of a pop group. It's a rucksack of a young girl.

'Save her,' says Jenny, in a whisper, and she falls against Will, her arms clutching Finn.

36

Maarten steps out of the evidence room with Becky Dorrington's father. They're roughly the same age, but Maarten can see the scribbles of sleeplessness papering his skin.

'Maarten, I can't tell you how much I appreciate...' Kemmie Dorrington shakes his head.

There's nothing to say. Maarten places a hand on his shoulder. He sees his face; if this were Nic. Feels a stab of the pain as if it'd been Nic.

Time is passing quickly. He doesn't know if Jenny Brennan is guilty. She has led them to important evidence and she has helped the case. But police investigations are littered with seemingly helpful citizens who can't stay away from a crime they've had a hand in. Maybe she did find the purse by accident, and so in leading them to the same place, they found the bag. But from the start, there has been too much coincidence. With no real explanation.

There was a phone in the backpack. Becky's father hadn't recognised it. He had looked horrified when he had seen it. 'Do you think...? Does that mean...?' he had said.

It certainly pointed to an adult being involved, and the phone was very like the one that seemed to belong to Leigh. Maarten will not jump to conclusions, so tests will need to be carried out, but the similarities sting like a paper-cut: someone clever enough to have convinced her to take another phone. That is how these meetings must have been arranged. And, presumably, the same for Leigh. If both had phones, the same kind, he would bet he will find one and the same phone number in the call log, on both. They were still working on bringing Leigh's phone back to life. He was more hopeful with Becky's. It had been in the backpack and was not as drenched.

But how did someone have such easy contact with both of these girls, hidden in plain sight? There was no evidence to suggest that the girls even knew each other. One fourteen-year-old, one nine-year-old. Leigh from the other village and Becky at the city primary with Nic. Who could have had contact with both, and why could they not see it? The phone was being analysed: fingerprints, numbers, registrations. It's a long shot, that whoever gave out the phone has been stupid enough to leave a trail. But it's all they've got now.

And how does Jenny Brennan fit into all of this? How did she know where to find these things? There must be some route of involvement. This amount of coincidence...

Maarten checks the clock on the wall as he walks back to his office. Jenny Brennan will be here soon. The husband has slowed things up by calling in a lawyer. They could have let her go quickly, if nothing had turned up; now she might have to wait at the station if the lawyer is delayed. If the station is busy, then the usual route would be to place her in a holding cell, but that's a step further than he wants to take.

Walking through the office, his phone buzzes.

'Liv,' he says, answering.

'Maart, I've just had a call from Klaas to confirm your interview time for tomorrow, with Rotterdam. This is the main interview?'

'Yes, *kak*, sorry. I haven't had a chance to speak to you. They want to interview before Christmas, so they can finalise the offer. Liv, we need to talk about it...' He ducks into his office and closes the door.

'I've told you, Maart. Make your mind up and then we'll speak. I need to know what you want to do, not what you think you should do. We'll discuss then. My parents are coming over for Christmas lunch, but only staying the one night. We'll have enough time on our own. We're going out for lunch. I've booked it.'

'Great,' he says, thinking of Becky waiting to be found. Hopefully still breathing. Boxing Day lunch seems beyond reach. 'How's Nic?'

'She's devastated. They all are. The school have been great. They opened up this morning and brought them all in for a big assembly. They've been talking about Becky and said prayers for her. They've started putting together a big mural for her, based on *Star Wars*, made up of everyone's individual drawings. It's to give the kids an outlet, to be able to show Becky how much she was missed... when she comes back. And they've organised some counselling for groups who are upset. We all went in this morning. I took Sanne too. Luckily, she's too young to understand. It's a mess, Maart. Anything else turn up?'

'Yes. I'll fill you in later, when I'm home, but we've got another lead. I don't know where it's going just yet, but we'll see.'

The phone buzzes again.

The landline in the office rings. 'Brennan's downstairs.'

37

Jenny waits. It's the same room she sat in that morning. This time the clock ticks more loudly; the chairs scrape across the floor with an iron rasp. The table upon which she rests her hands wobbles, and the coffee she has been handed is both bitter and weak. It's a cheap brand of instant. She can't swallow it. There are footsteps in the corridor and, somewhere, a phone is ringing. The sound is shrill.

Beside her sits Azeem. She knows she's met him before at one of Will's work things, but she can't remember him. A bit bald, a bit podgy. It's not necessary; she's not being charged, as Jansen had kept saying, but Will's face had been ghostly as she'd been driven away. He's terrified. And Finn...

She can't think about that now. Azeem is speaking, saying things to her, and she's trying to concentrate. Her skin feels hot, as though she's just stepped out of a sauna; she fans herself with the pad on the table.

'... really nothing to worry about... you don't have to answer... to stop raise your hand, you're entitled to a break... great you handed in the purse... just a formality...'

Will's tone on the phone had been light-hearted. So light-hearted his face had almost cracked as he'd forced himself to smile into the receiver. 'Azeem! Hope it's not too much of an inconvenience…'

Will had helped him out with his divorce last year so is owed a favour.

Finn.

Finn.

Will had leaned in, just before Azeem had arrived. He had breathed into her ear, arms encircling her. She had thought he was about to whisper an endearment, and assurance: 'Is there anything else to tell me? Anything? You better do it now.'

After that, she had said nothing. Her lips had locked of their own accord, and all she could say, when the DI had come to get her, was his name, over and over. Finn.

Her head falls, and she cries. The sobs come in great gulps. Azeem, next to her, is still for a second, embarrassment she assumes; and then, surprisingly able. He produces tissues, and calls for biscuits: 'For the shock.' He doesn't plead with her to stop, and soon, it slows. Amongst her cries, her cries for Finn, to hold him, to be able to leave this place and walk to him, she hears another cry. The other cry.

She can still taste the fear, hear the scream.

The door opens and Jansen and the DI enter. Deacon's face is pale, and she comes in with the scent of tobacco smoke. It's odd, it's the first time Jenny has smelt it. But this moment matters. Noticing matters. Foolishly, she had discounted the police. She has let them be peripheral.

Jansen makes the initial overtures, 'For the sake of the recording…'

Then Azeem speaks: 'My client is here of her own free will. She has willingly given up the evidence she found…'

And now Jansen turns to her, and looks at her. The smile has not reappeared. Now it's the eyes, and the symmetry. Strangely, she likes him more. When he was trying to appear likeable he was fake, saccharine. Weak, ephemeral. Now he commands, seems insightful. Her opponent. He stands between her and Finn.

'Tell me about the walking. Why did you take a walk so late? Your husband said earlier that you had gone to bed late, and yet you got dressed in the middle of the night?'

'I didn't get dressed...' she begins, realising immediately that it's the wrong way to begin.

'You didn't get dressed? You went out in your nightclothes?' Jansen says.

'I wear pyjamas. I went out in my pyjamas.'

Jansen taps his pencil on the paper in front of him, glancing down.

'You went out, straight from your bed? You didn't get dressed?'

'No.'

'Was it urgent, your need to be outside?'

Looking at him carefully, Jenny thinks before speaking. She's not clever at this. She can't outwit this man. And looking at him, at the clarity in his expression, she suspects he's not trying to outwit her. Maybe it is easier to just be honest. Maybe Will's stonewalling is the weaker hand to play. Her skin prickles.

'I found myself outside. Something pulled me there.' She can't quite bring herself to say the word 'ghost'.

Azeem says something, but she doesn't listen. She can feel the trees on her arms. The snow underfoot.

'I found myself outside, again, under the trees. I knew I

needed to get home... I ran. I had found the purse. I ran, and then inside, I changed, and I went to bed.'

'Again?' Jansen tilts a fraction forward, towards her.

'Yes, I had been out earlier, the night before, and I woke in Will's gym kit. I thought it had been a dream... being outside in the dark, the cold. But when I woke... well, it must have been real. I put on what I could find in the tumble drier... I was so wet.'

'You were out before? The night Becky went missing?'

'Yes. I haven't told Will. I thought... well, I think, it does seem strange. That I wake in the park. I thought it was best not to say. People do sleepwalk. And I've found it hard to sleep sometimes. If Finn's up. I'm more tired than normal... Sometimes during the day, I don't even feel present, like I'm watching myself... Like I'm drifting between the world of sleep and day.' She feels it now. Like everything is fluid. She could reach out her hand and push between the barriers of the waking world and the sleeping. The living and the dead. Maybe the boundaries are not so clear... her head feels full of voices, muffled, somewhere under the surface.

Azeem's voice sounds loudly in her ear. 'My client needs to take a break. She's obviously very distressed, I would like a moment with my client!'

Jenny looks down. Her hands are shaking, and a bead of sweat falls from her face to the table. She's suddenly cold. Something's changed. Something's been said. How long has she been in here?

'What? What is it?' She's frightened. Her grasp on Finn feels as though it's slipping. 'What have I said? Have I said something?'

Jansen and Deacon exchange glances and Azeem says again, 'I demand that we take a break.'

Jenny feels his authority radiating. She had been wrong to take so little notice of him.

Jansen leans back, tilting his head to the side. He glances down at his pad, on which he has scribbled notes, and he looks up at her and then nods to Azeem. 'You're right. Let's take a break. No more for now. Just think about this, Mrs Brennan, please.

'You told us that Becky's eyes are green; you walked in the dark to her purse. You were out in the park the night Becky Dorrington was taken. You found her clothes on the waterwheel, you led us straight to her backpack. What do you expect us to think, Mrs Brennan? What are we supposed to think?'

38

'There's a call from Rotterdam, sir.' A PC stands in the corridor, just out from the main office.

'Hang on.' The noise buzzes around him.

'What shall I do with Mrs Brennan?' Sunny waits for an answer.

'Give her a room with her lawyer for half an hour…'

'Then the holding room, sir?' Imogen says.

Maarten hesitates. 'Yes, I suppose. We need to go over her statement before we can proceed. Find out where she was the first night – when Leigh was killed. See if it's just her husband who we've got down as her alibi. I don't trust it.'

'I'll take her,' Imogen says.

'Do you want the call transferred, sir? Shall I take a message?' The PC is still standing next to him.

'Transfer it upstairs. I'm going up now. I'll leave it with you, Imogen. Give her some food, drinks. Smile. We haven't charged her with anything yet. We don't want to go too hard, too soon. Meet upstairs in my office, but give me half an hour.'

39

'They're going to ask you where you were.' Azeem sits across from her in the room they've been given, right leg crossed over left, iPad on the desk, notebook out. He scribbles quickly on the pad in front of him, jotting down questions.

'What do you mean, where I was?'

'Jenny, you've just told them you were outside in the park the night Becky went missing. You've told them where to find evidence. You've no obvious motive, no obvious connection, there's no real evidence, but you have means. You could have been there. Now, can Will vouch for you?'

Would he? Would he lie for her? It was too late for that. She'd already told them he didn't know she'd been outside.

'But I don't know what to tell them. I was walking; I came back. I didn't kill the girls... of course I didn't!'

'Don't get upset, it won't help. You need to think carefully about the next steps. You could say nothing at all, but I think in this instance it would be better to be clear and get out of here.'

'I need to get to Finn. He'll be hungry soon.' The thought of his fists, tiny, waving in her air, sucking his hands.

'You will best help Finn by getting yourself out of here. You know on aeroplanes they say to put the child's mask on after you've put on your own? This is that. You don't help Finn without first getting yourself out. Now think. What did you do outside? Where did you go?'

Jenny lifts her hands to her face and covers her eyes. She imagines the cold underfoot. Her feet in the snow. Shivering.

'I don't know,' she whispers.

Sitting straighter, Azeem places a hand next to hers. He leans towards her. 'Think, Jenny. You said you were in the park.'

'Yes, I was in the park. I woke and I was near some trees. A willow.' She remembers their rustling, the whispering.

'And how long were you outside?'

'I don't know. When I realised where I was, I tried to come home. I was scratched.' She touches her arms. 'The branches scratched me. She pulls up her sleeves. 'They've nearly gone.'

They both look down. Her arms are covered, thin lines of scabs, snail trails of evidence.

'Anything else?'

'She was there.' The whisper is almost soundless.

'What? Who?'

'The face.' Closing her eyes, Jenny thinks of the black hair. In the lake, behind the willow tree. She had reached out, and the branches had taken their hold. She had reached through the trees. Reached for someone.

'Who, Jenny?'

'I see her, sometimes. I hear her voice. The night of the first murder. I saw her face…'

'When Leigh died? You saw her face?'

'I woke. I woke in bed, the sound, the cold. I woke and I reached for Finn, but he was asleep. I might have dreamt it, but it seemed real.' She looks up at Azeem, thinking of the night. She hadn't really thought of it before, remembered it, connected it; she had known and not known. Dreamt it. Saw it.

'I watched her die. In a dream, by the lake. I watched her drown. Black hair.' Had she? It had been, before all of this, just a dream.

'In your dreams, Jenny. You don't say you watched her. You had a dream. That's not relevant here. Your dreams aren't relevant. Focus on the facts.'

'Her hair, it lay across the lake. I felt the wetness.' Breath, sharp and sudden, fills her lungs, and Jenny grabs hold of Azeem's wrist. Rocked, she needs him to hold herself steady.

'What if… what if I didn't dream it? What if I really was there? What if…' Tears flow and she tightens her hold on his arm. His eyes are close to hers, and she looks into them, watching them fade from brown to green, to brown. 'What if I have been there? Who would know? Will doesn't wake… I could have been there, I could have let her drown. Maybe it was more than that… Jansen, he said so. If I know so much, maybe I…'

'Listen.' Azeem's face is close to hers. Not oppressively, but his voice travels to her quietly, fiercely. 'You had a dream. You say nothing. Not to me, not to Will, not to the police. You had a dream. Just a dream. And dreams are nobody's business but your own. Say it to me, say it now.'

'I…' She stumbles, the hair on the lake, the (she had felt it) wetness, the *death*…

'Say it.'

'I had a dream. Just a dream.'

40

'Sir?' Sunny puts his head round the door as Maarten finishes a list for the follow-up to the first interview.

'Yes?'

'First results back from the phone. All calls and texts have been deleted and phone records not through yet. But there is a saved number on there. Just one number.'

Maarten looks at Sunny. He can guess by the heightened colour, the fidgeting fingers, the wide eyes. He realises with a jolt it's not what he expected.

'It's Jenny Brennan's, sir. That's the only number on the phone.'

'Get everyone in here.' Maarten looks down at the list, and draws a line through it. It's time for a change of tack.

'Where is she now?' Maarten taps the desk.

'In the holding room. I'm sure it's her. How do you want to play this? I think she's hiding behind that child of hers.' Imogen stands by the desk. She had refused to sit down.

Maarten looks at her face, lit with certainty. Buzzing with conviction.

'Right. Let's give her an hour, and then we'll go over everything. This number changes everything. Now we have a link. I just…' What is it? His gut is still saying no. But it's always about following the evidence. There's no other way.

He looks at Imogen. Her back is stiff, her face impassive.

Adrika enters, followed by Sunny.

'OK?' he asks.

'We can't let her get away with that wish-washy bullshit. That other-worldly crap. There's a girl dead, and now another one missing. It's time to start calling it.'

Imogen sits; her face set like stone.

41

The lines are clean. The space is small, but uncluttered. Somewhere to sit, to lie. Somewhere to use the loo. Jenny can't sit, can't lie down. Glancing upwards, the ceiling feels low, and as though it's lowering further. The weight of the room, the building, presses down. She might suffocate.

How did she end up in here? A police station. What happened? If she had to decide where it all started, she still couldn't stick a pin in a timeline. Time has changed. Its softness, its malleability has pulled apart her ability to make sense of a day. In its fluency, it mocks the dead. It seems they can peer around the corners of the future, and fade back into the past. Her mother had never been more present to her than now – years after her death. The sense of her, the sound of her urgent voice, '*Jenny! Jenny!*'

And the other voice: the whisper. A face in the trees. Black hair, bloated garments aslant, floating on the lake. Everything disconnected. If Jenny were to reach out her hand, in the night, when the world sleeps and time bends itself through half-consciousness, through dreams, what would she touch…

Through a full mouth, brimming with pleas, with questions, bursting at the edges with desire, guilt, hope, fear, she will speak. She needs to get home. Her breasts burn with milk; her body aches.

Not for someone else's child. Her body weeps for only one baby. For Finn. Enough now. There's only one child who matters.

42

Maarten leans back in his chair.

'I imagine you're quite keen to get back home, Mrs Brennan. And we're keen to let you. How about we go over the events again, but this time, we will all be honest, lay our cards on the table. We'll go over the facts.'

He watches Mrs Brennan glance at her solicitor. His face is familiar, and Maarten's sure he's come across him in London before, when he was working for the Met. She will do well to listen to him. Hopefully it will make things smoother. He's quite a string to be able to pull, to pluck at when needed.

'Yes.' Her face is dust grey.

'On the night that Becky Dorrington went missing, and the following night, you have admitted that you were in the park, and that you were near where evidence has been abandoned. Would you like to go over the details?'

'As I have said, after jumping into the river, to pull out what I thought was a girl's body, I went home and slept. At one point, I woke in the park, beyond my back door. I must have sleepwalked there, and once I woke, I turned to go home. And I found the purse that I handed to you the next day.'

The expression has changed on her face. It had been creased in fear. A patina of steel has settled over the turbulence. She speaks with resolve. He wonders if she is lying, but nothing betrays her. Her hands are still; her eyes hold his.

'And the previous evening, when you found Leigh's phone?'

'I must have been sleepwalking on that occasion too. I woke in the park, and I returned home. I was wet. I put on my husband's gym clothes, was embarrassed. I didn't tell my husband, but I can't have been gone for long or he would have noticed. I'm still feeding Finn, my baby, at night. If I was gone for any serious length of time, he would wake and scream.' She lifts her chin and shakes her head a little. 'I couldn't…'

Silence falls like a curtain.

Maarten watches her, studies her. She had been about to say she couldn't kill anyone, but she can't say it. Despite the calmer attitude here, she couldn't say it. She couldn't say she didn't do it.

'Well, thanks to finding the girl's backpack this morning, we've a little more info on Becky Dorrington.'

Maarten can feel the stillness of the room. Imogen beside him barely breathes, and the solicitor can sense it. He sees composed impassivity setting in, to deflect whatever Maarten is about to say.

'We've plugged the phone in, and turned it on. We haven't had time for thorough tests, but there was one number on the phone.'

Still, nothing has crossed her face. She's watching him, but he can't shake the feeling that what he is about to say will come as a surprise to her. A shock.

'It was your number, Jenny. It was your number on her phone. And only your number. Nothing else.'

Watching, for even a flicker of guilt, there is a change, but what is it? Guilt? Confusion? Her face drops, and if Maarten were to bet, to lay his money all on red or black, he'd pick confusion. But beside him, he feels Imogen land the other way. Her exhale is one of satisfaction, of confirmation. Evidence, evidence, evidence. That's what it comes down to.

'But, I don't understand. I've never met her. I've never seen her before.'

Imogen leans forwards. 'But you told us you saw her face in the water. If you didn't know what she looked like, how did you know it was her?'

'Well, I saw a face. That's all I said; I saw a face in the water. I saw a body, struggling underwater, for a—'

'My client has no comment. We need some time to discuss.' The solicitor steps in.

'But honestly, I'm not lying about this. Why would I lie? I didn't know her, and I don't know how I—'

'No comment at this time. I need to speak to my client.'

'Your number, Jenny. Only your number.' Maarten keeps his tone clean, devoid of blame. 'You led us to the bag. Your number on the phone. You've admitted you were in the park the night she went missing. You—'

'I said *enough*.' His chair scrapes back, and the solicitor rises with authority.

Maarten nods. 'For the sake of the tape, this interview is suspended.'

43

'Mr Brennan has just arrived, sir.' Sunny appears round the door of the other interview room. Maarten sits with Imogen and Adrika, going over the details. The interview had lasted a while but produced nothing new. Nothing tangible.

'Come in, Sunny,' Maarten says.

They sit, the four of them, and Maarten outlines the content of Mrs Brennan's statement, so far.

Sunny says. 'A story and a half.'

'Yes,' Maarten says. 'What do we think?'

Sunny coughs onto the back of his hand, then frowns. 'She's guilty. It's all there: the timings, the link to evidence. But what's the motive? Where's the link to the victim? She'd met Leigh once, yes? But not Becky. We haven't come close to pinning it on her. I think she's guilty, but we need more, don't we?'

'Adrika?' Maarten turns to her.

'I think she's more confused and disorientated,' Adrika says. 'Yes, there's a link to the evidence but...' She dips her head, looking up again, reasoning, her face writing her thoughts. 'I can't...'

'Go on,' Maarten says.

'She's been sleepwalking, or maybe just escaping the house at night, not getting the rest she needs. As for her description of the victim, she possibly saw Becky's photo from the press conference afterwards, and added it to her story.'

Maarten thinks of the photo. She'd been all smiles, confidence, holding an ice cream, and wearing a pale blue T-shirt.

Adrika continues. 'We gave it to the media the afternoon she went missing. Mrs Brennan didn't come in until the following day to give us her statement. What's she actually done? What can we accuse her of?'

'The number?' Sunny says, shaking his head.

'The number on the phone is hers, but if she wants attention, if she's actually trying to claim attention, then we have to consider the possibility that she led us to a phone that she planted. If we'd found it, if it had turned up, that would be one thing. But she walked us to it, and gave it to us. All she had to do was hear about the first phone, get a similar one. If it *is* her, then why would she do that? Surely, surely she'd hide it, lose it... It's too... it's too easy.'

Sunny interrupts: 'Well—'

'But really...' Adrika continues, 'she saw something in the water, dived in. Then sleepwalking again that night, came across the purse. She takes us back to the same spot, where we find the bag. What else has she said? That she heard a whisper in the trees? That she saw a figure in the water? What does any of that mean anyway?'

'I agree, I think...' Maarten sits back, and rolls his head from right to left. He takes out a packet of pills and swallows two with the rest of his cold coffee; there's not enough to wash them all the way down and they catch in his throat. His headache is back. He's supposed to go in for a hospital check later, but he already knows he won't bother.

He says, 'No motive, and the evidence won't hold up until we get the phone records back – we need texts, calls. Until then it's circumstantial and fanciful imaginings. There's something here… but at times I feel sorry for her. She cowered earlier, when her husband was in full flow. And she gave us the evidence straight away, so she doesn't appear to be hiding anything. It doesn't add up. There's more to it – maybe she's covering for the husband? Or Connor Whitehouse – he's her neighbour, and we haven't ruled him out yet.'

'Yes, sir. No connection to the victim, or at least the second victim. It doesn't mean there isn't one…' Adrika sits back.

'Or we haven't found it yet?' Sunny says.

'Yes, you're right, but either way it's not enough to charge her. Walking in the park at night, on her own…' Maarten raises his eyebrows, about to ask what Imogen thinks, when she jumps in, with emphasis.

'I'm sorry, I just can't agree. How does she *know* what she knows? If we had someone with clear knowledge, a clear line of information to a crime, in any other circumstance, we would be on them in a flash. Surely her knowledge indicates that we just haven't discovered how she knows the girls – you can't argue with the facts. This flaky talk of sleepwalking and dreams. What kind of crap is that? Can you imagine that holding up in court?'

'So you would charge her?' Maarten looks at her, face shining with intent.

'Well, admittedly, not today. But give me a day or so. I'm sure I can find something. Let's get the phone records for both phones – they're nearly there with Leigh's – and if they don't prove her guilt, then it's Christmas drinks on me.'

'Fair enough. Let's let her go today.' He wonders if it's the right thing to do. He can't put his finger on it; she's at the heart of this case, somehow. But the murderer?

'Yes, sir. It won't do us any good in the press to be seen hounding her, when she dived into the river, in front of the whole café. She's given us a great lead. We look pretty hot to have recovered so much so soon after Becky's been reported missing. And we haven't enough to keep her today.'

Whilst less bothered about what the media say, Maarten silently acknowledges that the super will care a great deal. 'You're right, Sunny.

'Pickles – can we do a follow-up, to just check he was definitely in hospital at the time of Becky's disappearance? Is there a nurse or someone who could confirm? It's very unlikely, but we need to ensure we can rule him out completely.

'Imogen, fancy doing the press release now?'

Imogen nods, but her zeal, her lack of sympathy for Mrs Brennan will be obvious to the press. He tilts his head.

'Tell you what, Adrika, you speak to the press, and Imogen, you can start digging the back story for Jenny Brennan. Cover the husband too. Take Sunny with you. I'll speak to her now.'

He glances out of his office window. 'They're jammed outside. I'll go and tell Mrs Brennan she's free to leave. Adrika, say something public about what a hero she is for diving in to save what she thought was a child, blah, blah. Her husband has some important legal friends. The lawyer in the room with her is well-known in London; to mobilise him so quickly takes someone very well connected. We don't need the way ahead littered with complaints.' He stands. 'Good job, team. Everyone OK? We watch her – we let her go and we watch her. Pickles looks less likely now, unless they're two separate crimes. Two strong suspects: Connor Whitehouse, and now we have Jenny Brennan. I'll visit her. I'll go and see her at home – see if anything slips, when there's no one else there. We need to keep eyes on her.'

Time is pressing. They're all exhausted.

Knocking gently on the door to the interview room where Mrs Brennan sits, he enters softly.

'I'm sorry,' he says. 'We've kept you for longer than we planned. I know it's been difficult for you, but we'll leave it for today. Thank you for coming in.'

'My client is free to go?' the lawyer says.

'For the moment.'

'I can go home now?' she says.

'Yes, your husband's waiting in reception, and if you don't have a car, then my officers will drive you back. We will call if we have any more questions.'

Maarten stands and puts out his hand. 'Thank you for your help, Mrs Brennan.'

She looks at his hand, then looks at him, stands and takes a step backwards. Moving around the table, she walks out of the room, saying nothing. The lawyer steps forward, shakes his hand, and says, 'Go carefully, DCI Jansen.' He places some notes in his briefcase and, zipping it, he makes to leave the room. He looks once more at Maarten.

Walking behind them into reception, Maarten hears the end of Adrika's short address to the waiting press. As Mr and Mrs Brennan leave, their baby in her arms, a round of applause breaks out in the crowd, and a path parts to the waiting car.

'Gutsy thing to do!' someone shouts.

It's the perfect picture. Six days to Christmas and by then Becky Dorrington's chance of survival diminishes.

He thinks of her. He prays she is still alive. That this cold hasn't claimed her. That this beast hasn't disposed of her.

44

20 December

The kitchen is hot as she flicks the kettle switch downwards. The heating is on, and yet the front room is cold. It is as though the house straddles two continents, rather than about seventeen feet. It's only eight a.m. It will take a while for the warmth to penetrate. Finn had woken the whole house at five.

Will's parents, who had ended up staying to help out, are in there, waiting for hot drinks and making small talk about the missing girl.

Just making it small, Jenny thinks.

She can't think of the phone right now. She can't believe...

She stares out onto the park where the snow is starting up again, and she feels sick. Another girl lying cold, waiting to be found. With all the suspicion, the questions, it had become about her. What about Becky?

Why is there so much *stoic* disappointment or such titillation in the wake of yesterday? Why not hot rage? It isn't a soap opera. It isn't craic. They'd come rushing at her once she had got up this morning. Felicity admittedly not as fast as Henry. He'd wanted to know the story, what had happened.

The details of what she'd seen, why she'd jumped in, what the police had asked her.

Felicity, to be fair, was much more reserved. She'd said how sorry she was that Becky was missing, and how brave it had been of Jenny to try to save her. And still, Jenny had felt picked over, examined, assessed. Had it been sensible? Henry had asked. She'd just stared at him and suggested she make the coffee.

The kettle fizzes. Jenny bangs down the mugs and stirs them vigorously, rattling the spoon hard.

The phone. Her number. It doesn't make sense.

She'd not thought about the dream. She had deliberately not gone over the memory, the image, of the girl, lying... outstretched. She'd not pondered on the chill she'd felt, how *real* it had been. She isn't prepared to think about it. She's not sure she would even know how to begin.

Her number. Her number on Becky's phone. What is happening? Could...

'No news?' Henry is saying as she re-enters the room.

The local TV news is onscreen. A picture of the girl is staring out at them.

Jenny turns away and glances at Finn, in his bouncer, hitting the dangling toys that dance in an arc over the chair. Bending down, wiping his nose and the dribbles that leak onto his chin, which run almost constantly at the moment, she tries to breathe calmly. She can feel a surge of panic swelling. She taps one of Finn's swinging bears for him, and as his smell reaches her, and his hand grasps hers, her pulse quietens.

Behind her, Will passes round coffees and the conversation continues.

'So, tell me again. You thought you'd found the body, eh?' asks Henry.

Jenny stands up, more in control of herself, and sits near the bouncy chair as Will passes her a cup. To talk of anything else but this.

'Yes, but let's hope the police have better luck. There's still time left... it's so cold outside, but hopefully they'll find her...'

'You know, Felicity once got lost out in the snow, didn't you, Felicity?'

Felicity eyes Henry without reaction and smiles placidly, turning to Jenny. 'Yes, dear, I did. And I turned up in the end, so all hope isn't lost yet.'

'What do you mean, Mum, you got lost in the snow?'

'Well, much as it sounds. It was when you were very young.'

'Your mother found it hard, didn't you, Felicity, after William was born. Tricky for you to get the hang of nappies. One night, after putting you to bed, William, she went outside in the snow to post a letter, daft at that time of night, and couldn't find her way back. Bizarre. I had to wake the neighbours in the end. Get some manpower onto it. Found her in a field, lying down. She must have fallen and just couldn't get up. Bloody well nearly died out there in the cold. The doctor said she was very lucky, as hypothermia hadn't quite got a grip. Stupid thing to do.'

Henry takes a biscuit and passes them to Felicity. He has looked back at the TV.

Neither Will nor Jenny say anything. Jenny glances at Will, to see what his reaction is. She's never heard the story before.

'Mum...' Will leans forward. 'I didn't know... What happened?'

Felicity smiles again, glancing at Finn before speaking. Jenny notices that her hand holding the coffee cup tilts and wobbles, and she leans in to place it back on the table.

'Well, dear, not everyone swings straight into motherhood like Jenny here.'

'But were you…?' Will gazes at her, his question as clear and desperate as if he was three years old, and not thirty-three.

'No. No, dear, I wasn't. I was tired. And sometimes the easiest thing in the world is to take a walk away. For a while. There was never any doubt I was coming back. I just lost my way. That's all.'

The clock ticks ten long seconds and Will places his hand on his mother's. Jenny doesn't move.

'Mum's suggested they stay tonight as well,' Will says, helping her carry plates through to the kitchen. 'She wondered if you'd like it, an extra pair of hands. I thought maybe… given what's been going on… not until Christmas, but until you feel better? You could go back to bed… She's offered to take Finn out for a walk. Give you a break?'

Piling the plates by the sink, Jenny glances at him. His face doesn't give much away. She wonders how much was Felicity's suggestion, and how much Will's. Normally, she would baulk at the idea. But, well, something has given way a little. Felicity doesn't feel quite so… far away. Henry is Henry. Some things just need to be endured.

'Yes, OK,' she says. 'But only tonight. I need to get the spare room ready for Dad.' She relents. 'But ask them for Christmas. We can all squeeze in.'

'Oh good.' Will looks relieved. 'Look, I know you've been struggling, and I've been busy at work… But now it's behind you. Well…' He shakes his head, looks as if he's about to say something else. 'Let's just move on, shall we?'

He bends over the granite worktop, leaning on his hands, turning his head to look at her.

'I would have stood by you, you know.'

She looks at him, reaches out and touches his hand. She hasn't told him about the phone. She hasn't mentioned her number.

'It's over, isn't it?' he says. The words press down on her.

'Yes,' she says. It has to be.

Turning, he hugs her, and she can feel his arms tightening. She has forgotten how strong he is. 'Good,' he whispers, into her hair.

The tap, which she'd turned on to clean the dishes, is still running, and, locked in his embrace, she sees the bowl fill and spill over the side. Soapy suds cascade into the butler sink, frothing and swirling. She closes her eyes to it, to the tide, the swell, the water. Nothing will take her from Finn.

Her hands curl into fists and her nails dig deep into her palms. First there's a sting, and then there's pain. She uncurls them and glances at her palm over Will's shoulder. Small lines of blood track across the centre of the soft flesh. War paint.

45

Staring out of the window, at the iced cobbled streets and the outline of the cathedral which is just visible from the top floor of the police station, Maarten imagines the snow in Rotterdam: swept and dealt with; the streets broad, with tramlines running down the centre. Cycles bowling past. The city moving easily and quickly despite the snow. Its clean lines open, welcoming. Its skyline tall with bridges that soar.

The phone rings, and he answers.

'Hello?'

'So, you're moving back? About time. I thought you'd been turned.' Klaas's voice comes down the line, and Maarten smiles.

'Merry Christmas! Still filing paperwork while everyone else works?'

The loud belly laugh of Klaas Oomen sounds familiar as it crosses the wires from Rotterdam. 'Look, Maarten, the interview screen will be ready in a few minutes. I told them I'd make sure you were set up, but we've got five minutes.

Catch me up with this case of yours; it's even made the news over here in Holland.'

'Have they mentioned London over there, about me? The crash?' Maarten says, not hearing Klaas, thinking about how he will react if they mention the crash in the interview; how he could stall.

Klaas's tone is steady. 'They put that to bed, Maarten. It's behind you. It won't come up today.'

'Hmmm.' He thinks back to the Met, of the paperwork, endless streams of paper to sign, to be approved. Days at home. Knots tied in every direction. If they did mention it...

'Maarten – you'll be fine. You're the best at what you do. Your record is better than anyone's I know. Now, this Jenny Brennan – have you charged her yet, or decided to listen to her?'

'We're back to Jenny Brennan?' Maarten laughs. 'You believe in dreams and ghosts now, Klaas?'

'You know she might just be worth listening to. Perhaps she's trying to tell you something and she can't find the words. Why not humour the woman? Tell her you believe her, and see where it leads. Keep me updated.'

The interview is straightforward. A firm nod of agreement at the end. He hasn't said in so many words, but he knows he's intimated. He must speak to Liv. She's been waiting for him to make up his mind. It's not just his mind, though, he realises. He hasn't been deciding what he wants to do. He's been trying to decide what is best for them all: and it is that which has stalled him.

His grandparents had died before he turned twenty, and he had felt rootless. Here, there – Liv had given him footing, a grounding, and they'd moved closer to her parents after Nic had been born. But with this job offer, the yearn for Rotterdam, for his childhood city, to share it with the girls: Rotterdam. It's time to talk to Liv.

Maarten closes his eyes: he can smell the sea, knitted into the air. The lights of Rotterdam tall, round, stretch above themselves. The city breathes. He breathes.

46

Morning, and yet the darkness is still thick. The street lamps stay on. The cottage feels Dickensian, facing out onto the cobbled lane, which winds its way up into the mist.

Jenny is wrapped in a throw. She hasn't moved from the sofa since breakfast, and Finn is dozing. Henry and Felicity have driven home. Back for Christmas in a few days, Henry had started pacing in their tiny kitchen, and it had only taken a 'Jenny, dear...' from Felicity, for Jenny to nod in agreement, to conclude setting off first thing would make sense.

The knock repeats at the door. She had ignored it the first time. It will only be another parcel. The postman and the woman who delivers for Amazon had quickly realised she was the only member of the tiny lane who was at home during the day; she builds a small pile of their neighbours' Christmas shopping deliveries daily by the door.

It sounds again.

Heaving up, she straightens her jumper and shifts Finn onto her hip. The door is heavy as she pulls it back against the frame, its wooden shape swollen in the damp.

'Mrs Brennan, Jenny...' DCI Jansen stands outside. He rises higher than their front door, and she can't see the tip of his head.

She tightens her hold on Finn.

'I'm not here officially...' He starts again. 'Well, I am, but there's nothing new. It's a follow-up. Not an interview, just a chat.'

The mist from outside swirls into the house. Its clammy fingers lick her arm, and she shivers.

'Come in,' she says, jamming the door firmly closed as he ducks down and steps heavily into the narrow hall, wiping his boots on the mat.

Turning back to their lounge, she says nothing. She leaves him to infer an invitation to follow, and he enters the tiny room. She returns to the sofa; sinking in and curling her legs beneath her.

Sitting awkwardly in the leather chair, by the white built-in shelves which line the alcove by the fire, he looks down. Hands folded.

'So, you're not here to accuse me?' She breaks the silence first.

'No.' He half clears his throat, half coughs.

Staring out at the lane, the pools of light around the street lamps are like watercolours in the mist; she waits for him to explain. Nothing is finished yet.

'I've come to listen,' he says finally. 'Again.'

She nods, but she's not sure to what she's agreeing.

'So, if you want to tell me, then I'll listen.'

'I don't think there's anything to tell you that I haven't already said,' she says. The effort of speaking is exhausting.

His smile is soft, more in the eyes. 'Well, let's just say I might not have listened very well, the first time.'

Staring at the fireplace, she can see him from the corner of her gaze. The embers in the grate are grey, cold. Remnants of a fierce heat. Morphed to something else. She's not sure where she is. She's caught in this house, this street, this town. Now he's here. Can she trust him? Will talking release the hold that seems to have fixed her, pinned her here? Is it death? Is it death that whispers through the cracks of the house?

Talking is easier since she's been seeing Dr Klaber. The weight of it all, the strain of keeping it to herself has been lightened.

But she wants Becky to be found. Even through a simple choice of self-preservation, she wants it all to be over.

'You need to promise that whatever I tell you, it stays with you.'

He nods.

'I live here. You can't hold me up for ridicule.'

The room is still cold, and she pulls the throw around her and Finn again. His small body, sleepy and warm.

'Since that night... the night Leigh disappeared. I've felt... something.'

The light outside hasn't made its way through the mist. The world is grey and thick. Opaque.

'She's in my head. Or at least, something is in my head. I keep thinking about her.'

'And Becky? She's in your head too?'

'Neither of them are literally in my head; I'm not mad.'

He unbuttons his coat. It falls open, but he doesn't take it off, and she doesn't offer him a drink. She watches his face. It's blank, expressing nothing.

'And when you dived in, near the waterwheel?'

'I've told you. I saw her. Well, a face, I couldn't see features, just an outline, with black hair and those green eyes. For a second, I looked at her. I reached out for her but then I passed out. And then nothing.'

'It wasn't the water? You don't think you were losing consciousness, dreaming, hallucinating?'

Finn grabs her hair and he pulls. He's been starting to try to sit up. She lifts him so that he sits on her knee, facing Jansen.

'I don't know what to think. But if you want to know, if you want me to tell you, then you're really going to just have to listen. I don't have any answers.' She feels tears; the saltiness catches the edge of her lips, making its way to her tongue. She doesn't wipe it away, and he doesn't move.

The water drips. 'I wake, and I'm scared to open my eyes… in case I'm not at home. I feel something… the house, the streets, the lake… I feel it. And it's scaring the shit out of me.' *There's always a breath. A cold breath. Or is it the wind?*

Tipping slightly forward, Jansen remains silent. She looks at him, watching for some sort of flicker. There's nothing.

The room is quiet.

'I think if you can find him, whoever did this, then I think it will pass.'

'So, you've felt like this since the first murder?'

Looking him up and down, she still can't tell him about the first night. *A figure in the trees. The darkness. Was I there?* She can't trust him enough. She's not sure she trusts herself. *And why my number?*

'To be honest, I can't say when it started. I haven't been… well, I haven't been myself since I had Finn.' His fingers grip hers. She can't remember herself before Finn. Not right now. 'The birth threw me. We moved here. I'm doing fine, but I'm still finding my way. And then when I heard about Leigh, about her drowning…'

She looks across at Jansen. His frame remains still, his eyes clear.

'I can hear her. Her voice calls to me. It's a whisper, faint, but it's there. It sounds mad, and it's not all the time... but ... this weather: the cold, the damp, the wind... It won't burn away. Everywhere is fluid. And I'm so tired. But she says,' she is whispering now, her breath leaving her and she doesn't dare enunciate too clearly, 'she says, "save her".'

47

Ghosts, Maarten thinks, walking back. Jenny Brennan had spoken of ghosts. He can't take that to the station. He can't take that anywhere. He had texted Klaas: *Following your advice. If they lock me up hold yourself responsible.*

The team are out viewing CCTV and touring small second-hand phone shops.

Time presses like a falling brick. He still doesn't know what to believe about Jenny Brennan, but she is at the heart of this. Without further headway, Becky will be lost. He thinks of looking Nic in the face if that happened. He has promised her.

Brennan had stood like an island in the hallway, as he had nodded a goodbye. Despite the close walls of the cottage, she had been swamped by space. And the baby.

There is something she isn't saying. She had agreed to walk in the park with him. Covering her steps once more – she had found both phones. She is tied in.

Almost at the station, he catches sight of Imogen climbing out of a car, her phone at her ear, and waves. She waves back, and Seb drives off.

Imogen strides over to him, still talking on the phone. 'We're on our way in now.' She looks at him. 'They've got Leigh's phone working. They've found only one number on there.'

48

'So there are two different numbers on the phones?'

'Yes.' Maarten leans back. The team are assembled for a briefing and tiredness has blanched their faces.

'On Leigh Hoarde's phone, there is an unknown number logged in the contacts list. Just the one number. We don't have her call log back. On Becky's phone, we have only one number stored: Jenny Brennan's. However, her call log has come back. We're still awaiting texts, but the calls made are to the same number found on Leigh's phone – not to Jenny Brennan's.'

'It makes no sense,' Adrika says.

'What we know,' Imogen says, 'is that Jenny Brennan features in here somewhere. It could be that the other number belongs to her as well. Maybe she messed up somewhere along the way, and gave her real phone number out as well.'

'Or,' Maarten says, 'that there's someone else. Possibly working with Jenny Brennan? Possibly entangling her? Maybe her husband? Or even the neighbour – the proximity of

Connor Whitehouse, another suspect, is not to be overlooked. This city is small. Lines are crossed.'

Sunny shakes his head. 'But I still don't completely get it. Why have Jenny Brennan's number on there, if you're never going to use it? What can we accuse her of? I think she's guilty. But we still can't prove it.'

Shaking his head, Maarten glances at his watch. 'No, we need to wait for the full log from Leigh's phone, and we need to try to ascertain the identity behind the second number. Sunny, can you go over the husband's credit card et cetera? See if there is something on there we can link to somewhere that sells pay-as-you-go phones?'

Sunny nods, scribbling on paper.

'Adrika, can you go over the background for Connor Whitehouse, same thing? I know it's a tenuous link but I want it checked out.'

She nods, as Imogen finishes updating the whiteboard with the case details.

'Good luck. Let's hope we can unravel this today. I said I'd phone the Dorringtons with an update.' He glances again at his watch. He'd better do it now.

'Let me know how you get on. Right now, I'm going to go over the ground again with Jenny Brennan.'

'Do you want me to come, sir?'

Maarten thinks of Jenny Brennan, of how quickly she can close up.

'She likes me more than you, you know,' Imogen says, smiling.

Maarten laughs. 'That's true. But no. I think she will feel it less of a threat if I'm there on my own. We can't arrest her yet. I'll keep it informal. Just see if her story holds up, if she lets anything slip. I want to see how she behaves on her own in the park – without her husband to leap in at any minute. Let's keep this fairly quiet. The super will… well, there's no need to shout about it.'

Punching in the numbers from his desk phone, Maarten thinks of Nic. She'd not slept that night. Liv had been up with her. When she closed her eyes, she dreamt of Becky – sad and scary nightmares, she'd said they'd been filled with words she didn't understand, and when she'd asked him to explain them he realised they'd seeped in from news reports, from overheard conversations.

He wants desperately to save Becky, and also to wipe the slate for Nic. Sanne was picking up on it, and they clung to him each morning. Liv had to peel them off as he made his way out to work.

'Hello?'

Closing his eyes briefly, hearing the tremor in her voice, Maarten addresses Jess Dorrington. 'Just an update…'

He speaks as she begins to cry, and he tries to fill in some blanks, to create a feeling of movement, to sketch out a sense of hope. Each word so sharp, it cuts like glass. He imagines her sitting there, at the end of the phone, waiting for a daughter who may never return.

49

Waiting in the park is brighter than in the house. The slow burn of the sun has gathered pace, but hasn't managed to penetrate the walls of the cottage. Jansen is late. She lays Finn down in his snowsuit, gently, like a snow angel. He giggles and waves his arms and she takes a photo. She lies down next to him, staring up at the sky. It reaches up and out, far above them. The blue melts the clouds. When she had been small, her mother had told her heaven lay on top of the clouds, that angels jumped from one to the other, using their wings to break their fall.

Finn's fingers wave in the air, and she catches them, holding them in her palm.

'Jenny?'

Jansen's hand reaches down, and she takes it, pulling herself up.

'Are you ready?'

She nods, lifting Finn and fastening him onto the front of her chest.

They are almost at the huge weeping willow, winter-naked, before they speak. The silence is peaceful. The air is sharp, and she keeps her head ducked under her hood.

'Is this close to where you think you found the phone – you said you didn't remember picking it up?'

Jenny nods. Standing still, she braces herself against the turbulence, the scream. But there is nothing. The frost and ice, hanging from the leaning arms of the tree, brush her face as she leans to look beneath the branches.

'Why did you come here? Why here?' Jansen shifts his weight to the left, and lifts the curtains of the branches to peer with her. 'Do you… feel anything?'

Shaking her head, Jenny observes the silence of the ground. 'No. I was anxious last time; you were pushing me here. The first time I didn't choose it… I just came. It's always the willow, here by the lake. But I don't…'

As she takes a step away, onto the path that bends towards the water, she shivers. There is something. There's the sound again. The whisper. The noise. She stops.

'OK?' asks Jansen.

Closing her eyes, she wills it. She's been pushing it away, but this time she waits for it. But that's all it is. Just one slow blink, and it's gone.

'Yes, fine. I hear… I hear a whisper. And a rustle of breath. I can't quite make it out. I think maybe it's the wind… but I can feel it. I can feel something. And then it's gone, like now.' *Save her.*

Jansen nods. He looks lost, and he checks his watch.

'Come on, let's move round the lake.' He steps out to join her on the path, and they walk, him matching her stride.

She wants to tell him all her questions, uncertainties. She has spoken to Klaber, but it rolls out easily with him. He doesn't ask – he makes her feel as though he's been expecting everything she has to say. She has managed to tell him about the figure she sensed in the trees – and he had nodded. That the earth pulsed beneath her hands at the lake, and he nodded. That there was a voice – or more accurately – two voices. The half-scream in her head, *'Jenny! Jenny!'* and the whisper – *'Save her.'* Then the face that appeared at the window; like the one she saw at the watermill: black hair, green eyes.

Not however, that it was the death that had begun the unease. Klaber had tilted his head as she had pinpointed the birth, the surfacing. Since then, she has simply been treading water, trying to keep her head above everything: Finn's needs, Will's discomfort, the crevasse that had cracked between them, become cavernous. And arriving here, at St Albans, with its sense of home and its lake that pulled her, arresting, mesmerising.

Talking made things clearer, helped her sort through her thoughts, like she would a wardrobe: stacking a pile for throwing away, and a pile to be tried on later – some things just waiting until their time beckoned.

As they turn past the old pub, on the corner of the lake, Jenny halts. The lake lies out before her. Its stillness, its emptiness, quiet and stark. There are rows of flowers newly laid, up against the dying ones, black at the edges and wizened. The sun catches the cellophane and the burst of colour stands out, a rainbow heap against the muddy ice.

The whisper again, and she closes her eyes. There is a dark figure before her, turning away, and it vanishes, and there is no light except the moon. Jenny feels suddenly like a small girl, hunched, sobbing and frightened. The half scream again:

'*Jenny! Jenny!*' But it's not from that figure, dipping behind the trees: *Save her*.

She trembles, folds and bends to the left. Jansen grabs her arm, and without him, she would have sunk to the ground. Her heart beats. Panic suffocates.

No.

'I'm sorry.' She doesn't look at him. The flowers hold her eyes. 'I can't. I can't go any further. I'm not some...' She struggles with the words. They sound ridiculous out loud. This, this is ridiculous. Her pulse is still racing, her teeth chatter.

'If I think of anything, I will tell you.' But she doesn't know that she will. Not until there is something real to say. This scrabbling round in the dark... And tears prick her eyelids.

His bulk, more height than weight, hasn't moved. She can't look up; she doesn't want to turn to see his face. He might be able to persuade her, but she's sure that if she takes another step – she feels, deep within, with no sense of knowing how, that it might pull her in.

Sinking sand, collapsing clay: something will catch her, and she won't pull free.

50

22 December

'Where are we at with Mrs Brennan?'

Maarten looks up. The super has appeared in his doorway. His smaller frame has slipped in quietly.

'Sir?'

'Mrs Brennan. I hear you've been to visit her?'

'I was just following up on procedure – going over the route she took when she found the evidence.'

'You? Why you? Surely that's a job for your team. Is there something more to this?'

Maarten pushes his chair back, half-rising and gesturing to the chair at the other side of his desk, but he makes no move to sit.

'I thought it might seem more courteous if I made the visit, sir. Considering. Keep the tone even.'

The super looks at him hard. 'Well, we've had a letter from her solicitor; if she did it then go after her, but you need to be a hundred per cent certain before you make a move. Don't do it too soon. There's a lot pointing that way, but the press we would get if we called it wrong...'

Nodding, Maarten says nothing.

'Any further leads? Surely with the evidence she found we've made some headway?'

'Some. The first phone is working again, but the numbers are different. Jenny Brennan's number on Becky's phone, but an entirely different one on Leigh's. One of the reasons I wanted to go over the route with her was to see if she let anything slip, if she tripped up.'

'And did she?'

'She seems as confused as we do.'

'Anything else?'

'We're ruling out both fathers now. There's no link between the two girls – this isn't a crime that comes from the home. Based on limited CCTV and eyewitnesses we know where the girls were last seen, so we're interviewing again. We're assuming the perpetrator knew the girls well enough to give each of them a phone. Likelihood is that he was someone they trusted, perhaps someone they looked up to. We're pretty sure Leigh got into that car willingly. She was meeting someone she liked – we know that from the hearts and question marks in her notebook. I doubt she suspected how that night would end. If we're right that her murder was a first offence, our theory is that she rejected his advances, he tried to rape her, she fought back and he killed her. Then he has to abduct Becky to keep her quiet. Did she witness something perhaps? Did she know Leigh? Or is it just that she was the only other girl he gave a phone to? We can only pray he hasn't killed her, and won't while the area is swarming with police. But what we still can't figure out is the link between the girls. Different schools, different ages. Why did he choose them? And why is Jenny Brennan's number on one of the phones? It just doesn't fit. We need the phone records to come back before we can move again. I've been thinking we could pull together a re-enactment?'

'Hmm… sounds good. Check the Hoarde father's estate again. I've heard on the grapevine that the BMW had been seen near where the Hoardes live. Whoever took it, and presumably for this purpose, is someone who knows where stolen cars are easy to get hold of. Keep me informed. What's the plan for Brennan?'

'DI Deacon is fact-checking, but she will do it quietly. She's pulled up Jenny Brennan's history. Her mother died in Tonbridge, in Pembury Hospital as it was called then, when she was five, and we're looking into the rest of her background.'

'No PR nightmare, Maarten, not this close to Christmas.'

'No, sir.'

'And the car is from Sunderland? Where does that leave us?'

Gesturing, moving his hands apart and his palms half turning upwards, Maarten says, 'To be honest, not much further forward. We managed to trace the car, but it seems it was stolen and then sold on down here. To be able to trace the sale, we'd need someone to come forward to admit their part in dealing with stolen goods.'

'Can we announce an amnesty?'

'In my experience, that may work with the minor criminals, but not the professionals. It's more than their livelihood's worth.'

'Well, let me know where you get to.'

'Will do, sir.'

As the super leaves, Maarten watches the empty space in which he stood; the whiff of aftershave slowly dispersing.

51

The phone sits on the coffee table, and it screams of Klaber. Jenny feels it. Outside is drenched white, and still it comes. Finn feeds as some terrible Christmas film plays out quietly on the TV: a missing Santa, elves in plain clothes.

She hasn't contacted Jansen, and she doesn't think she will. It's too much to cope with. But Klaber, he helps her cope. She glances again at the phone.

The doorbell sounds and she jumps. Tucking Finn under her arm, she pulls open the cottage door to Connor, standing on her doorstep. He doesn't speak, and she grips the lock, cold under her fingers.

The waiting pause is long. She watches his face. It's blank, and his eyes, bloodshot, swivel down the lane and back. *All the better to see you with.*

'Everything OK, Connor?' she asks. The silence is heavy.

'I know you've been talking to Erin… ' He breaks off immediately, looking uncertain. 'Do you know… Have you told her…'

A loud, metallic rattle sounds from the kitchen, as the

washing machine finishes a cycle. She jumps, and Finn stares up at her in surprise.

Connor takes a step towards her and, unthinkingly, she slams the door. It doesn't catch him, but he's only an inch away, and he punches the door, slamming hard on the old wood. With the ricochet a picture falls from the wall, and glass shatters on the floor; shards fly. Stepping backwards, she leans to put the chain on and holds Finn, and her breath.

Jenny sits back on the sofa to finish Finn's feed. Picture and glass swept away. She looks out of the window and sees Connor walk past, on his way home from town.

Whatever he had wanted to say will keep. His body is stiff, jerky as he disappears out of view. She will need to apologise for slamming the door. She's not quite sure why she did.

Still looking out the window, she spills hot coffee; it bites into her hand.

Picking up the phone, she dials.

'Hello, Dr Klaber's office. How can I help you?'

'Hello, this is Jenny Brennan. I'm calling to make a follow-up appointment. He said to call… I'm not sure how long I need to phone in advance?'

'Mrs Brennan? He said to put you straight through.'

'Mrs Brennan, Jenny. How are you?'

Gesturing to a chair, he makes small talk about the weather. His chair swivels; he smiles.

After a burst of nervous chatter, apologies for the last-minute appointment… it doesn't take more than a moment to feel as though the fizz has been released, a Coke can settling after having been shaken. The anticipation, tension, seeps away.

'And how are you?' he says.

Klaber glances out of the window, allowing her to respond, and watches the snow for a second.

She stalls.

'No let-up from the weather, is there? How's your week been?' he says.

Looking down, the list of things she had been planning to say locks within her.

'Has your sleep been any better? Any more night-walking?'

Playing with Finn and his teether gives her somewhere to look, to focus her hands.

'Let's start with something easy again. Tell me what you're giving Will for Christmas. My wife's getting me a new wallet; I'm buying her a silver bracelet, with charms. What about Will: a watch? Socks? What will he want?'

Jenny thinks. 'With everything going on I haven't got him anything. Maybe...' She really doesn't know.

'What about you? What do you want?'

What does she want? 'I want this thing, whatever it is, to be over,' she says, looking up, meaning it. 'Do you think there's any chance it will?'

He smiles. 'You feel involved? Like it depends on you?'

The words come. Pulling. Like cleaning chewing gum, glued into the carpet. They're embedded. They're released with something sharp, pinging inside her:

'When I had Finn, when I gave birth, I was in the water for quite a while. The labour was longish – no longer than normal for a first birth, I suppose, but I began to feel... I felt as though the wetness was part of me.' She shakes her head. 'I'm not making sense... I felt, I felt as though the wetness *reminded* me of a part of me. That I was more myself – but a me I didn't recognise. I felt something shift.'

Klaber nods.

She looks up. 'I can't shake it. Some ghost from my past – like I've been not confronting... something. And I've no idea what. When I heard about the girl in the lake, for a second, I thought of my mother. It's a jumble in my head. And I'm just so *tired*...'

Klaber pours more water. 'You mentioned the murdered girl last time. Has that been something you've been thinking about?'

There is a flash, like a shot of blue, before her eyes. She can see the hair, black on the lake, she feels the cold. The clutch of the water pulls at her waist – the waterwheel...

'Jenny, are you OK? You've gone white.' He stands and leans forward, placing his hand on her arm.

The shivering in her limbs takes hold. She bends, almost convulsing. Her teeth chatter.

'Jenny! Jenny, can you hear me?' He's standing over her now.

She tips forward. She's going to fall out of the chair. Her arms are like ice. The sound of water rushes over her. She opens her mouth to scream, but nothing comes out.

Then suddenly she's lifted. His arms are round her, pulling her over to the sofa near the coffee table. He lifts her, lays her down, pulling a rug over her. Her hand is gripped, and her brow covered, his palm warm.

'Jenny, listen to me. You're having a panic attack. You need to breathe; you're not breathing.' His voice gathers volume as he speaks. He lifts a paper bag, and pushes it into her hands.

The air is lit by tiny pricks of light. Dots flash before her eyes. Her head spins.

'Breathe, Jenny. Deep breath in. It feels much worse than it is.'

Sucking, pulling, as though through a thin straw, she inhales.

'Again.' His hand is firm on hers.

Slowly, the blackness lifts, the lights disappear. Her body calms.

She opens her eyes to Klaber, sitting next to her. His hand still on hers, his face smiling, and as she looks at him, still trembling, still in part submerged, he answers his question.

'I will take that as a yes. How about we start with that again.'

A minute passes. She finds her voice. 'I feel… not watched, but not entirely alone. There's a… breath over my shoulder.'

He nods.

'The police – they've asked me to help. Well, the detective. He asked me to walk him to the places I've been… think I've been. And he said he wants to hear me, to listen to me.'

'That's good, isn't it.' It was a statement, not really a question.

'I suppose – I'm too scared, I think. Will, he's scared. I think he's scared for me. Having me involved isn't part of our plan. It's not really what people like us "do". Get involved in murders.'

Klaber smiles.

'And I've just lost touch with him. Our neighbour, Erin, seems to see more of him than me.'

'Is that something that bothers you? You think he might be spending too much time with her?'

The words land heavily. Jenny jolts, thinks for a second. What, would Will stray?

'You said he's been home late… is this something that's making you doubt him?' Klaber continues.

An affair? How would she feel? Erin? Would it be the end of them? 'He wouldn't do that to me…' Would he? Has she become so blinded she can't see something in front of her? She glances out of the window. 'No. I honestly don't think that's a possibility. My head is so full. It doesn't really feel like *my* head, not any more. But Will… beneath all this, he's still Will.' Would he?

The clock ticks and soon they are standing.

'Come again,' he says.

'I'm sorry,' she says.

'It's my job.' He reaches for a handshake. It's gentle and he covers her hand briefly with both of his.

His touch is soft.

52

Got a bit of update about your copper. Hollyhocks OK? Half an hour? Or can email you.

The text arrives just as Jenny reaches the top of her road. After Finn's nap, she had headed into town for a bit of Christmas shopping. A bag of gifts and a few groceries hang off the buggy. It's a five-minute walk, no biggy, she tells herself. Her stride is quick and easy as she tackles the hill back up to town, her steps light.

'Here you go,' Matt says, sitting down across from her. 'We've almost finished. Press release this morning so we're fucking off back down to London tomorrow. I had a fish around in the notes last night for you.'

She takes a sip of her coffee. He wears a T-shirt with a French slogan scrawled across, and there's a tiny tattoo on his wrist.

'Thanks,' she says.

'Right, so this Jansen bloke, started out in Rotterdam, then the Met. Something fucked up there and he was suspended for a while. Reinstated, but then moved north. Like I said, no details, no black mark on his file apparently. But you never know. And there was a kid involved...'

'What do you mean, a kid?'

'No idea. I've only got half the story, but I heard he was suspended over something that happened with a kid. There might be some shady covering up of something shitty.'

Jenny thinks of Jansen: first there was slickness, now a plea for help. She can't imagine him under crossfire and yet his presence makes her tense, strained. Is he not what he seems?

'What do you think?' she says.

Matt whistles through his teeth and waves his hand in a twist. 'I'm tainted; I always go dark. I reported on Yewtree and the cover-ups there would blow your fucking mind. All that mess doesn't help the next generation. There was some statistic bandied about: thirty per cent of abusers have been abused themselves.'

He drinks coffee, still chewing. 'It's all about transparency now, but I take that with a pinch of salt.'

'So, he's new down here?'

'He's been here about eight months. He came out of his last case up in Sunderland with a commendation. There's some whisper of him moving away again. Could be suspicious? Having to move on? Or maybe he's just got itchy feet...'

Jenny watches him take a gulp of coffee, and bite into a caramel square. Crumbs scatter on his chin. His eyes glint.

'However, in the past hour, we've heard that the car that was found, the BMW your husband saw... was from fucking Sunderland.'

Holding her cup too long, distracted, Finn swipes at it and it spills hot on her leg. She yelps, putting it down, out of his reach, checking it hasn't landed on him.

'What does that mean?'

Matt shrugs. 'Too soon to be thinking anything really. It throws out all sorts of questions – the father, he's from the north. Or it could just have been nicked and sold on down here – it doesn't mean anything in particular.' His eyes flash a grin at her. 'But it's fucking interesting.'

Nodding, Jenny thinks of Jansen. Of her initial dislike of him, of whether he might be capable…

'How are you feeling about it? Jumping at the shadows?'

'No,' Jenny says, automatically, too quickly.

'It's a great town,' Matt says. 'I'll miss it. Makes a change from trying to avoid the dog shit around Wood Green.'

She smiles. 'Thanks for looking into it.'

'No problem. We'll be down for a follow-up in a few weeks. That teacher I told you about has bitten his fucking bullet. Sweaty perv. Took a beating and resigned when he woke up. No loss to the school there.'

'There are no new suspects?'

'One. I've heard the name, but if I tell you, you can't say. Seriously, it would cost me my job.'

'You can't tell me then!'

'Yes, yes I can,' he says. He eyes her appraisingly, holding her gaze.

Jenny can feel herself hot under his look.

'You've got an interest in this girl… there's something you know.'

'What do you mean?' Flustered, embarrassed, on the spot; she rubs furiously at her spill on her leg with a tissue.

'Well, I've got a fucking good nose for this shit, and if I tell you something, then I think you might be able to tell me something. Not now, but at some point?'

She thinks. Would she tell him? He's far enough removed. 'Yes,' she says. 'If I knew something, I would say.'

'Connor Whitehouse. That's the name. I got it on the quiet though, so seriously, tell no one.'

The name carries a sting, sharp. Shocked, she leans forward.

'Connor? Connor Whitehouse? You're sure?'

Matt nods, eyebrows raised. 'I had an inkling you'd know him... Tell you what. I'll ask you nothing now, but I'm heading down to the cathedral later. I'm doing some shots for the story. How about you come with me and give me a few local quotes? I'll buy you a beer afterwards for your help, for the insight.'

The mention of Connor has thrown her in a spin – does that have anything to do with his visit the other day? – and going to the cathedral and park later, in the dark, leaves her cold. But a beer, just for half an hour. To be someone else...

'Let me know. I've got a couple of interviews to do this afternoon so I better get going.'

Jenny watches as Finn stuffs handfuls of tissue paper into his mouth, and then she leans forward and pulls them out again, making him cry. She's not sure what to say.

'I'll be in touch. Shit, is that the time?' He glances at his flashing lime watch, and jumps up. 'I've got to do another visit to the station too – best be fucking off. Take care, yeah? Might see you later.' He taps Finn on the head. 'See ya, dude.'

53

Knocking hard on the door, Maarten's hungry. He wishes he'd thought about lunch before heading out to follow up with the questioning. It is almost three thirty, and he's eaten nothing since breakfast.

'Mr Whitehouse? Are you inside?' There's no movement. 'Go round the back, Imogen. Let's just check before we head home.'

Waiting for Imogen to return, he sees Jenny, walking up the lanes, pushing the buggy. He stops himself calling out to her. He's still watching her when the door opens before him. Could it be the two of them? Deceit laced between the stone walls of the cottages?

'Hello,' says the man he recognises from their first meeting. 'Is it about a delivery?

'Police, sir,' Jansen says, showing his badge. 'Can we come in?'

Connor Whitehouse is unshaven and wearing a dressing

gown over a pair of boxer shorts. He yawns unapologetically, and bangs the kettle down.

'You caught me on the hop. I've only just got up from a nap. Can I get you tea? Coffee?' He bangs cups, sloshes water.

Maarten sees Imogen give the man a glance. He's attractive, young, must be almost thirty. He has dark hair and can get away with being caught in his boxer shorts and not feel at a disadvantage.

'Mr Whitehouse, we're here about your alibi for the time of the murder,' Maarten says. 'Playing golf, I think you said?'

Still banging cups, Whitehouse turns towards them, stirring his coffee. His face is expressionless. 'Yeah?'

'Sir, the information you gave us wasn't corroborated.' Imogen's voice is firm.

'Wasn't it? Can't remember really. What day are we talking about?'

Maarten's head is aching. There is a pulse, a pull, just above his right eyebrow. It lifts, or feels as though it's lifting, every few seconds.

'Your alibi, Mr Whitehouse. You've lied to a police officer.'

'Oh, I didn't mean to lie. I'm sure I just got the day wrong. I can't remember even talking to you… fucking hell.' The last bit is muttered into his coffee, and he drops his spoon on the table with a clatter.

'You know it's an offence to supply incorrect information?' Imogen says.

Maarten can hear that her voice has gone up in pitch. She's becoming angry, and usually he would step in and calm the situation down, but he can feel his own blood begin to heat, his teeth to clench.

'Sir, we're asking you a question. I'm not sure you understand, but we're here, asking you to clarify where you were.'

Connor Whitehouse pulls a wry face. He doesn't look sheepish. He puts down his mug and leans back, appraising Maarten. A packet of biscuits lies half eaten on the table, and he pushes them forward. 'Here, help yourself. Yes, I'm sorry about that. I thought that might catch up with me...' It peters out, then he starts again. 'You kind of caught me at a bad time. I was with my wife, you see, when you asked where I'd been, and so I had to stick with the story I'd told her. I've been a bit... well, a bit... you know, naughty, recently.'

'You're not in school, Mr Whitehouse. If you want to lie to your wife, that's your business, but it's not ours.' These grown men, dressing up their behaviour as charming, their betrayals, their self-indulgences. Maarten can't hold it back. He feels his fists clench, his voice become louder. He bangs the table hard with the flat of his hand. One of the mugs falls on the floor, smashing. Imogen sits like stone next to him. He takes a breath, holds it, and releases it. Ignoring the mug, pleased he hadn't stood up, Maarten fights for his game face and loses.

'Where were you?'

'I was here, at home, with another woman.' Whitehouse looks frightened now. He doesn't look at the mug on the floor. 'I can give you her details. Look, I realise I've been stupid, I'm sorry. I realise that you don't owe me anything, but if you could please not mention it to my wife... We're having a tough time at the moment, and I'd just let off a bit of steam... I'd be lost without her. She's struggling... I've never done anything like that before.'

Jenny Brennan crosses Maarten's mind. Could he have been with Jenny Brennan? If so, then this might fall into place. He catches Imogen's eye.

'And I believe that Leigh Hoarde visited your place of work? Can you tell us about your relationship with her?'

Connor Whitehouse's face before him blanches, whitewashed. 'No... no relationship; she's never been to my office?' He bleats now, like a sheep. Like a lamb.

'She has, Mr Whitehouse,' Imogen says. 'She visited Same But Different, your creative agency, over six months ago, with a school group. They had a tour of the office, and took part in some workshops there.'

'Hang on.' He collapses into the chair, tapping his fingers on the table, eyebrows moving as he shakes his head. 'Yes, I remember, the co-owner of the company has a kid here in St Albans and she arranged a day – gave a speech. I had nothing to do with that day – nothing. I'm no good with kids! You have to believe me... I lied because I was with someone else, but the girl... I had nothing to do—'

'Can we have the details of the woman you were with?' Imogen takes out a notebook and writes down the name while Maarten stares out of the window. The park lies stretched out behind the house, and behind Jenny Brennan's house. It would make perfect sense, if you lived here, to lure the girls to a meeting in the park. In winter, the lane is dark from four o'clock. And the park is so easily accessible from here. You could slip out at night, and enter it, and maybe no one need know.

'And you were here all night? With this other woman?' Maarten rises and walks to the window. There are people sledging on the hill, down the slope that leads to the lake. 'You think she will corroborate your version?'

'Why wouldn't she?' His voice is a whisper.

'Well, if you lied to protect your wife, will your girlfriend not do the same, if she has a partner?'

'But, it's the truth! You have to believe me.' Whitehouse is shaking now. His grip on the table, white-knuckled, steadied so he doesn't fall from the chair, dizzy…

'We don't, sir. We have to do no such thing. You've lied once to us. You better pray that whoever you were with is going to agree. And we'll speak to your work. If you have so much as exhaled near those children…' Imogen stands.

Maarten rises too. 'Now do I have to ask you to wait at the station, or are you staying here this afternoon?'

'Here, I'll be here. There's a woman next door… I'm sure she knows about the other woman… I know she's been talking to my wife, and I was going to try to speak to her again… I went earlier, but she slammed the door in my face.'

Maarten looks him up and down, seeking any clue that this isn't true. That maybe he's trying to throw them off the scent.

'Please, please don't say anything to Erin. It's over now. I really regret it. It would tear her apart!' The man's lazy appearance now looks desperate, his boxer shorts and stubble now pathetic.

The slick kitchen has two huge black and white prints in frames at the side, showing the married couple on their wedding day. He thinks of Liv, of her standing next to him. How she trusts him.

54

23 December

Pulling into Tim Pickles' estate, his head still hurts, more so now that he's so close to where he took the blow.

'You OK, sir?' Imogen says.

He is and he isn't. They need to do this. Once Becky had gone missing, and he had been in hospital, Pickles had fallen off the suspect list. But something had come up.

'You think it could be him?' she asks.

Sunny had double-checked with the hospital, and Pickles had discharged himself late the night that Becky had been taken. He'd gone back in at eight thirty a.m., to A&E, worried about a bleed, and had been observed for the day.

'Not really. The CCTV Adrika has found looks like Becky walked into the park at eight forty a.m. She wasn't seen again. Pickles was in triage at eight thirty, then in all morning. But it's a funny coincidence.' This whole case was filled with holes.

Maarten looks out at the sky. Grey. Dark.

Imogen turns the car into the street, and swears. 'Fucking hell.'

Maarten shakes his head. He's seen worse, but this is pretty bad.

Pickles is outside his house, locked up in a duffel coat, hat and scarf, and with bucket in hand is scrubbing spray paint from the front of his house: *...urderer, ...king ...unt, Peedo.*

'You think they could have at least checked the spelling,' Pickles says, as he sees them walk up the path. He drops his bucket and throws the sponge on the snow, all signs of the scuffle covered with fresh fall. 'Want a drink?'

The kitchen is cold as Pickles turns the kettle on. He doesn't take his coat off.

'Takes ages for this bloody house to heat up, and I only turned the heating on this morning. Too knackered last night.'

'I thought you had a housemate?' Imogen says. 'Has he gone away for Christmas?'

'Gone away full stop. We're fine. I've known him for years; he knows I didn't do it. But they've been coming and coming. Non-stop. Broken a window, someone put shit through the front door. That was when he left. Cleaned it up first, which was good of him. He didn't need to. It's not his fight.'

Plonking coffee down, it splashes out on the wooden top but Pickles makes no move to wipe it up.

'Not my fight either. Not any more,' he says.

'What do you mean?' Maarten asks.

'I'm clearing off. Enough is enough. The school don't want me back, but I haven't ever actually been charged with anything...' 'Charged' is emphasised, hangs long, sits above the steaming coffees.

'I called my old school, where I boarded, and they're recruiting. They said to lie low for a while, until whoever did this is caught. Should have done that in the first place, really. Much easier. I can be friendly at my old school. I can be myself.'

Maarten sips the coffee, wondering how long it would take Tim Pickles to be himself again. Suspicion lingers. He'd seen suspects, tainted with unproven, unfounded guilt, change a tiny bit for ever. Shame and suspicion can lie thick. Fester.

'Good,' Maarten says. 'But no travel just yet. You discharged yourself? Were you well enough?'

'I have epilepsy. I'm exhausted for a few hours after a fit, but after that I'm fine. The attacks seemed to exacerbate it, and I feel dizzy, the bruises ache. But I couldn't stay in there another minute. They had me in a private room, but still, people peered in. Nothing like a suspect to drum up some business.'

Maarten listens to his bitter tone. 'You're free to press charges against the men who attacked you. Come on in, and we'll get the ball rolling.'

Pickles begins to unbutton his coat, pulling his hat off. His face is still bruised, and Maarten can see his stitches. There'll be worse under his clothes, under the dressings. And worse still in his head.

'No. I'm not going to press charges. I just want rid of the whole thing. I'll never stop being sorry that Leigh died. She didn't deserve that. But I didn't deserve this, and all I want is to leave here, and not look back.'

'Is there anyone who can corroborate your presence here? At home, when Becky was taken?'

Pickles sighs, sagging like a defeated man. 'Yes, Alex was here. He dropped me at A&E the next morning and then left. But he was in the house.'

Maarten listens as Imogen takes down the phone number, and leaves to make the call.

'So where will you go?' he asks. 'When you leave?'

'I called my old girlfriend. The one who went travelling? She's spending Christmas in Santiago, in Chile. I'm planning to fly out tomorrow to join her. We didn't end badly, so a month or so backpacking over there sounds about right.'

Maarten takes a sip of the coffee. 'You need to keep an eye on those friendships.'

Pickles' eyes are sharp: narrowed, like a rat. 'What do you mean?'

'Well, to you those friendships come easily, go easily. Young girls in your care, young boys. They look up to you. The young feel their friendships deeply. Those poor girls put their trust in someone who betrayed them horribly. There are rules in place about teachers not fraternising with pupils for a reason.'

'Are you saying I've been grooming? After everything I've been through? That I'm as bad as the twisted bastard that killed Leigh and took Becky?' The anger spits.

'No, nothing like that. I'm saying be careful. Not for you, but for them. The young deserve to be treasured, to be helped, to be liked… but don't stand in their way. Know when it's time to step aside.'

Imogen steps back into the kitchen and nods.

'That's big of him, not pressing charges,' Imogen says, sliding the car into reverse, and they turn in the street, Pickles standing on the lawn watching them go, bucket in hand.

'Yes, it's the right decision. He'd get a pay-out, but unless he needs it, there's no point in leaving this unfinished. They'll get what they deserve anyway, for attacking an officer. They'll see their day in court.'

'How is your head? If you need me to drop you home, and have a rest, I can?'

His head is aching, thick, like he's been wearing a swimming hat pulled too tight all morning. The throb starts at his eyebrows and comes in waves up and over. And his vision has its odd blurry moment. The moment this case is finished, he needs a few days off. Fresh air, hydration, rest.

'Fine,' he says. 'I'll be fine.'

55

Jenny opens the door, and sees a retreating figure. 'Erin?'

Turning, as though caught out, Erin glances around and stills. For a second, Jenny wonders if she's here to shout at her because she wouldn't speak to Connor.

But Erin, instead, starts to cry.

'Oh, Erin!' Jenny moves out to the step, and stands in her socks, putting her arms around her.

'No… your feet will get wet. Can I come in?' Erin's mascara is running, but this time she makes no move to wipe it away.

'Well…' Jenny begins, thinking of the walls, the shrinking room, the mess she hasn't cleared away.

'Oh, I'm sorry; it's a bad time. I shouldn't have come…' Erin starts to walk backwards, shaking her head.

'No, it's not that. I've got a bit of a clean going on for the in-laws. We might be better off at yours?'

Jenny glances at the half-empty bottle of wine on the table. 'You started with something stronger than coffee, then,' she says. Finn plays happily in his bouncing chair, easy to lift round from next door.

Erin fills two glasses, pushing one to Jenny, and also puts a mug under the coffee machine, putting a capsule in and pressing the button.

'You can choose,' she says. 'But I need a drink. Shit, Jenny… oh God, I've lost it all.' Fresh tears spill.

Reaching out, Jenny puts her hand on Erin's. 'Tell me,' she says.

'Well, I had an appointment the other day, for… for a scan.'

'Wow…' Jenny begins.

'… and they're not sure I can… I can conceive. I need more tests, but there's a problem with some cysts… You know I thought I was pregnant, because I had been late… five days.' Fresh tears.

Picking up the bottle, Jenny tops her up.

'Have you told Connor?' she says.

'Connor? *Connor?*' Erin says, shaking her head. 'Connor has fucked off. You know I hung around the police station for him for hours, while they unpicked the bundle of lies he'd been fabricating. He hadn't been with his mates, hadn't been to the work conference the other month… he's been seeing some girl who he met at work.'

Jenny sits back. Erin's sobs grow louder.

'I never thought he'd do that. Of all the things… we always swore, no affairs. I just don't know why I ever believed him. I feel such an idiot! Such a fucking loser…'

'Where's he gone?'

'He's gone to his parents, for Christmas. He said he can't deal with me at the moment. He said the baby thing is too much for him. The stupid thing is that I know he wants to be a dad, but I think he wants it to arrive gift wrapped, with a manual.' She takes a swig of wine, and despite the fact that it's not yet noon, Jenny takes one too.

'I've got to have an operation. They're fairly hopeful – if I can have the cysts taken out, then they can give me a fertility boost with some injections, and then I should be able... but he said he's sick of all the stress of it.'

'Do you think he'll come back?' Jenny asks. 'Do you want him to come back?'

'He said he's coming back. He said he just needs Christmas to unwind, kick back. He said it's all been too much. And the girl meant nothing to him... I believe him. I think.' She runs her hands through her hair. 'I think that if I wasn't so far on with this, then I would walk away. But I can't.'

'You could, Erin, if you wanted to?' Jenny thinks of the bruise. 'Does he... has he hurt you?'

Erin glances up, surprised, then touches her cheek. 'Oh that. No, he didn't hit me... he didn't actually do it but... Well, we had a row. He stormed out the room. I followed him and he was slamming the door behind him. I don't think he meant for it to... But we're fractured at the moment. There's no other way to describe it. We've splintered, and I feel if I let him go, then it's all gone.

'We can start trying properly in a few months, and if I leave him, well... It could take years for me to meet someone. What I want, more than anything, is a baby. I want the baby more than I want him.'

Jenny wonders briefly about Will. Does she feel the same about Will? They have drifted so far. But she does. Even despite all the tension. She would still choose him. She just has to trust that some peace will arrive, once all this is behind them.

Erin pours another glass, and offers Jenny a top-up. She pulls out a box of chocolates from a drawer of their breakfast bar. The clean lines on the expensive shaker-style wood units are polished, something Jenny's kitchen hasn't been for a while. Jenny lifts the wine glass, heavy and etched.

'Here, lunch.' Erin rips off the wrapping. 'I was going to give these to Connor's mum in a hamper for Christmas. I can think of a better use for them right now.'

Biting into a truffle, soft and rich, Jenny wonders what to say. She's never really known Erin like this. She's always been so… in control.

'You know it's not really true,' says Erin.

'What?' asks Jenny.

'You know, that I want the baby more than I want him. I want them both. I love Connor – he's the perfect antidote for me. I used to laugh when he'd show me another number he'd got from a girl on a lads' night out. His mates all thought I was really cool, the cool girlfriend, who didn't tie herself up in knots if they went to a strip club. But honestly, I didn't care. He loved me, loves me.'

Jenny chews, watching Erin.

'It's a bit like, I allow him… no, not that, I'm not going to start excusing his behaviour. But because I've always been so driven, at work. I always sort the bills, the insurance… I struggle to let go. I just think that I'll do a better job… and then we started trying for a baby, I couldn't control it. Nothing happened. I've done everything right – wheatgrass shots, coconut water…'

She drinks the rest of her glass, swallowing quickly. 'He's the relaxed one who makes me calm down. But not at the moment. At the moment I'm a mess, and I think it's the first time he's had to face up to being the grown-up.'

Jenny lifts the bottle but it's empty, and Erin gestures to the fridge. Pulling open the door to the Smeg, she stares in amazement at the rows of wine, fruit, Charlie Bingham meals. Her fridge is full of leftovers, stored milk.

'Which bottle do you want?' she asks.

'Anything – anything white. Oh God, what am I going to do?' She cries afresh.

There is a knock at the door. Jenny walks to open it, glancing through the spyhole first.

'Erm, Erin,' she says.

'What?' Erin turns.

Jenny pulls a face. 'It's Connor. It's Connor outside.'

56

'Hello?' Maarten answers the phone.

'Sir, we've got some press on the phone, asking for a quote. They're running a series of human interest stories on Becky Dorrington. They're doing it with the support of the parents, to try to make Becky seem real, more vulnerable to her captor.'

'Put them through,' he says. He checks his watch.

'Hello? DCI Jansen here.'

'Hi, my name is Matt Peters, calling from the *Guardian*. We ran a story today about Becky and we are going to run another tomorrow. We're touching on some vulnerable stuff – the fact that she's so young, that she was anxious and not eating at school. Could we quote you?'

'No, I'm sorry. I believe the latest press release went out this morning, so that's the only official source you can use.'

'And what about Mrs Jenny Brennan? Do you have a quote about her? We're mentioning her jumping in to save what she thought was Becky. Any quote there?'

Mrs Brennan. Again. It was harder than he thought to keep her out of profile on the case. 'You can say that the

Hertfordshire Police thank her for all of her help, and that anybody with any information should step forward. We are always grateful for the help of the public.'

Maarten taps the phone with his fingers once the call is finished. Anxious at school – he'd just said Becky had been anxious. Her parents hadn't mentioned that. There could be something… He calls Adrika. 'Can you and Sunny pop round to the Dorringtons' and ask them about Becky's anxiety? Get some info?' He needed to ask Nic too.

'Of course, sir.'

'Oh, and the counsellor in Hong Kong – Dr Bhatti wasn't it, can we chase him up?'

Whoever did this is watching. Running the story is not a bad idea. They're watching, and if a sociopath can be reached out to at any time of year, then maybe it is Christmas.

57

'Dr Klaber, it's Jenny, Jenny Brennan.'

'Hello, Jenny. How are you?'

'I'm actually feeling a lot better. Will said you'd left a message.'

'Yes, I just wanted to check in. No more clue finding?'

She laughs. 'Not yet.'

'I hope you have a good holiday, Jenny. Make sure you get some rest.'

'Thank you. Really, thanks. I really do feel… well, I think it's helping.'

'You know where I am if you need me,' he says.

Should she tell him? She hasn't told Will. It's more than she wants to share with anyone, and she has managed to push it back, into the pockets in her mind. 'They found my number on Becky's phone.'

'What?' He sounds confused.

'I found another phone. Another one – this one belonged to Becky, and they found my number on it.'

There's a brief pause.

'And what do you think it means?'

Surely, Jenny thinks, surely it means that... But she can't put words in his mouth. If there is any way that it could mean anything *else*, then she's desperate to hear it.

'What do you think? Do you think it might mean that maybe I was there? That somehow, without knowing, without even having the first clue how... do you think that...'

'What, that you murdered Becky Dorrington? Is that what you're trying to say, Jenny?'

She hasn't said it aloud. She hasn't finished the thought in her head.

'Is that what you're worried about?' he asks.

The figure in the trees, the lake behind, white in the moonlight. She had dreamt it. She holds it tight in her head.

'Do you want to come in? Talk about it?'

'No, I can't today.'

'Look, it's not about what I think. And the police haven't charged you. If what you say is true...'

She hears him talking, but the last bit catches. *If what you say is true.* Is it true? She doubts so much at the moment. Should she doubt the facts she thinks of as concrete and real?

He's still talking, offering time. She hasn't got any today. But she can feel her heart beating a little faster.

She hears herself say goodbye, that she has to go, and they make another appointment. She stares ahead, out of the window. The world is white, and all her usual markers are gone. She doesn't recognise this landscape any more, buried under the snow. Herself.

And she misses her mum.

Holding the phone in her hand, Jenny feels like she is holding a panic button. She can press it if she starts losing control. She knows it's his job, but it's like he knows her, he sees her. As Will drifts further away, Klaber is there for her. She thinks of his hand, warm on her skin. The phone on the line is dead, but she presses it against her ear.

58

'Maarten?' It's the super. Maarten can detect a conciliatory note in there.

'Sir, come in.' Maarten stands.

'I've had a letter from Rotterdam, to address your possible finish dates. It's decided? You're thinking of leaving us soon?' He doesn't sit down, but stands at the other side of the desk. Maarten can't sit either.

'Yes. I need to give an answer the day after Boxing Day. I do need to think about it.'

'Well, good luck. Not that you'll need it. I know how keen Rotterdam are to get you back. Seems a couple of your old colleagues have climbed the ranks. It's always good to be wanted. I just wanted to say again, how pleased we are to have you here, but I won't stand in your way.'

'Thank you, sir.'

'One last thing. With it being Christmas Eve tomorrow, we were thinking that one last press conference, one last appeal...'

'Yes, sir. Good idea. We're all set with clothes, timings, et cetera, to run the re-enactment of Becky's last movements; to jog someone's memory.'

'Well done. I didn't think you'd get it arranged in time. It was a big job. Fingers crossed.'

'Yes.' Maarten nods, glancing at the clock, thinking of the things he still has to do. He thinks of Leigh's headmaster and his desire to promote the school, his help had been invaluable. They can't use Becky's primary. Too young and so unsettled. And it's Nic's primary too. Some things need to be kept an arm's reach away.

'Good stuff. Did that wallet turn anything up?'

'No, sir. It could have been dropped at any time. We can't find any link to the case.'

The super nods his head, looking tired. 'And Maarten, I know you've been speaking to the Brennan woman, the one who seemed to think there were ghosts involved. Keep the force out of that, will you? I know you've been humouring her, but Rotterdam won't want to hear about any of that. Not before the job has been signed.'

There's not a flicker on his face. Maarten admires his impassivity. Being able to deliver such a threat without blanching even a shade takes some stoniness.

'Yes, sir.'

'Christmas Eve drinks in the office are kicking off at four o'clock tomorrow. I'm not in, so if you wouldn't mind leading them?'

'Of course.'

'Happy Christmas, Maarten. Let's hope it's a happy Christmas for the Dorringtons as well. There's still time. Statistically, not looking good, but all is not lost just yet.'

59

Christmas Eve

Heathrow is packed. They are struggling to get the holiday passengers through immigration. Queues of people, piles of luggage and litter are scattered higgledy-piggledy all over the terminal. Even the cold, conditioned air seems thicker than usual: hotter, almost humid, plastic. Christmas has sent the travel world into overdrive.

Jenny had left before seven a.m. to collect him and is early for the flight; she thinks about trying to find a seat in a coffee shop with a book for an hour while Finn naps, but there is barely anywhere to sit down.

Picking up a paper, she finds a spare red plastic seat near the screen. A bottle of water sits in the buggy cup holder. It's warm and the bubbles that had fizzed down her sleeve when she had opened it earlier have dissipated, leaving a mineral saltiness. It will have to do. She sips at it, for something to occupy her hands. She can't settle.

Reading a discarded newspaper, a distraction, she is exhausted, and the print swims before her. She had spoken with Matt and another reporter late yesterday. Will had thought it a great idea; he is now a force to be reckoned with: full steam ahead on the Jenny PR train. She understands his success at work. His tenacity. He's building a wall of goodwill around her in the city: the woman who jumped. His hackles have not gone down. He prowls.

The headlines are about the disappearance of the other girl, but there is nothing new about the case. The story describes Becky's family life: she has an older sister and a dog; she loves ice skating, Harry Potter, *Star Wars*; it's her birthday next month… Her mother's voice, fragile even on the page, said she hoped that wherever she was, she was being strong now: frightened. Alone. The article repeatedly names her, appealing to her captor: Becky, Becky, Becky.

It is the same sad news, and she is away from St Albans. She doesn't want to think of it today.

Will had called when she'd got here, asking about Erin and Connor.

'Thank God we're not them,' he'd said. 'What a way to carry on.'

In some ways, Jenny agrees with him. Had Will had an affair, she wouldn't have known what to do. But babies are hard. They're hard when you have them, but getting them can be just as hard. She glances at Finn. They are lucky. It is something she has to remember, even if she's been stuck in the house all day, if she's exhausted, if she feels as though Will has it easy and she's fraying. She would never be without him, and neither would Will.

The tannoy announces movement and she checks the Arrivals board. It is almost eight thirty. She flicks the brake up on the buggy and pushes Finn towards the long line of people, who wait, some carrying boards with names written on, some carrying flowers.

Jenny squeezes in, searching for him. They pour out like Lego figures spilling from a jar, tumbling in a crush, all faces looking the same. The last twelve days have felt like the longest of times.

There he is. She runs the three steps.

'Oh, Dad!' Jenny falls against her father.

The noise fades.

'Dad, oh...'

'He looks like your mum, you know. Just like you do.' He glances at her, throwing his arm around her shoulders.

The car park is huge, and because she was in such a rush to make the flight, Jenny can't quite remember the number of the floor level where she'd parked.

'I've missed you both, Jen love. How's it been? I'm sorry I haven't been on the phone much, there was limited reception on the ship.'

'Well, there's been a bit going on.' Where to start? 'You heard about the murder, in St Albans?'

'Yes. And another girl's gone missing?'

Jenny spots the car, and pushes the buggy towards it. There is so much to say, starting is hard. But there's no rush. Not now he's back.

'And Will? Busy at work, I bet.'

'As usual.' She nods. 'But things are starting to even out a bit.'

'Oh, Jen. You know your mum and I rowed all the time when we had you. I wasn't even allowed in the room when you were born. She felt from the start she'd been expected to do it alone.' He smiles, lifting his bag to load into the boot. 'Has it hit him yet? That he can't write a contract with Finn, forcing him to sleep through the night?'

She laughs, feeling better herself. 'I'm pleased you're staying for Christmas, Dad. Be good to have someone on my side, once the Brennans are all here.'

Clicking Finn into his seat, she climbs in the car.

'Don't you worry about them, love. I'll have Henry eating out of my hand; I tell him how clever he is, ask his advice. I don't take it, but it keeps him busy. And Felicity needs a sherry, and to have someone else to entertain Henry.'

'I've missed you, Dad,' she says.

'Missed you too, pet.' He leans over, clicking his belt in, and kisses her on her brow. 'I love you. I always wish your mum was with us at this time of year, and she'd be so proud of you. Of the mother you are.'

He places his hand on hers, just as she begins to release the handbrake.

'I know you've had a rough time recently: that the lake has been bothering you…'

Jenny opens her mouth to speak, but he shakes his head.

'Let me speak, I've been too nervous… I've wanted to say, but I know you've had a lot to deal with since the birth, and I've not wanted to add to that. When your mum died, I wasn't in a great place.'

'None of us were, Dad.'

'No, well I missed out part of… about her death.'

'She died from pneumonia, didn't she?' Jenny shakes her head, confused.

'Yes, yes she did. But I've never really told you about how she developed it. I was trying to protect you… you were so young.'

The car feels as though it's suffocating. The car park – its concrete roof lowers. She wants to scream, to run.

'She drowned, Jen. We were fishing from the riverbank, near a waterwheel, staying with some friends for the weekend. You held a rod, and tipped in, and she plunged in after you.

'You were only five, and you were both splashing, thrashing, floating down. Your mum managed to pass you to me, and I pulled you out, but she disappeared under, and she surfaced downstream in the lake. She was calling your name, desperate to hear you were alive. You stood on the side, and you hid behind a willow tree. You screamed. I can still hear you, even now. Your legs all scratched, bleeding.' He shakes his head.

She is a young girl again. She is underwater, terrified, looking into her mother's face. She is by the willow tree, wet, her mother calling over and over: '*Jenny! Jenny!*'

He continues. 'I managed to run down the bank, and she grabbed my fishing net. She got out, alive, but in a bit of a state. We thanked our stars and thought that was the end of it. But the next morning, after we'd driven home to Tonbridge, she was sick... shivering, high temperature, and when we visited the hospital, they found water on her lungs.'

'But I remember her in the hospital, I remember visiting her... I don't remember the river,' Jenny says, things blurring.

'It's called secondary drowning. She developed pneumonia. You didn't remember at the time. One of the doctors said you had probably blacked it out. The screaming and the splashing.'

'Oh, Dad!'

'We were both with her when she died, so it's not like it was hidden from you. There just never seemed to be any need to tell you the whole, horrible story. It was horrible enough. But now, this girl dying, drowning, nearby...'

With shaking hands, Jenny releases the handbrake and starts the car. She doesn't look at him, but she can feel his eyes on her. She knows he's waiting. But she's not ready. Not yet. Nothing has really changed: her mother is still dead. She had died as she remembered her dying. Only now there was sinking, flailing.

'And there's another thing. And I've wrestled with telling you this over the last four months.' His face twists, eyes close then open.

Jenny's breath is hot in her mouth, and she holds it in. Full of air, inflated. Light-headed. She knows.

'Well, you might have guessed from the description, I don't know... but our friends we were staying with, they lived in St Albans. You both fell in the river, by the waterwheel. Your mum was in the same lake when I pulled her out. And with the girl dying in that lake... you've been in that river before. You and your mum. Your mum drowned in that lake.'

He leans forwards, places his arms around her.

'You started to flow downstream, away from me. The very worst moment of my life... the start of the hardest part of my life.

'Jenny, love. I don't even know if telling you is the right thing, but I can't just tell you half.'

Dizzy, heady, Jenny's vision swirls. She has been wrestling with a dream or a ghost. Or a memory. Black hair – but whose? Her mum had black hair... Giving in. The damp: familiar, singing to her, calling her, leading her. Had she been there the night Leigh died? She had been there years ago.

Seeing a face, in the water. Green eyes. That her mother's eyes were green had never even occurred to her. Jenny struggles to remember what she thinks she had seen: it had been so dark underwater. The eyes had shone. Fetid water had clouded everything else. And that mass of black hair. Had it ever been Becky, in the water's gloom?

If places hold memories, if they soak up even a fraction of a footprint, of our most vivid moments; if we spread ourselves around the earth, and blend – dust to dust – then surely part of her mother remains here. And in returning to St Albans, in coming back, had she found the part of herself she had abandoned... buried deep? If time bends, is her history echoing now, even now, with Leigh Hoarde?

Ghosts – not white, flying creatures – but traces, echoes, imprints. Ourselves, déjà vu: already seen; always seen.

60

Loss snakes amongst the crowd, weaving, parting; grief and shock vibrate afresh. Maarten's fingers are cold, even in his gloves, and his mouth is dry as he prepares to speak: arid. He can feel Jenny near him, her body swamped with wintry layers: more for the cover, he suspects, than simply the cold.

She had looked frightened, an hour ago, when he had picked her up from the house.

'Look after her,' her husband had said, his face set hard as his gaze locked on Maarten. She had squeezed past him to get to the door; his fingers catching her sleeve and tugging her back.

'I need to go, Will,' she'd said.

'I could still come?'

'No, I don't want Finn there. Stay here. You and Dad look after him. I'll be fine. Sam's meeting me there.'

'Have you told her?'

'Not everything; I said I wanted to go, and she's got Ben's mum to look after Rosie.'

Brennan's fingers had still been holding her sleeve when she slipped out of his grasp, kissing him goodbye and then joining Maarten on the path, ducking into the car.

'Will's angry. He thinks we should stay out of it.'

Maarten had nodded. It wasn't his business. But it was easy to dress yourself in the safety of distance. This community, made up of its invisible lines, provides the comfort of zoning. In the right zone, you could feel quite impregnable. But then Becky had vanished too, and the centre of town, with its 'outstanding' and 'good' primaries, had rippled with terror. A ricochet.

He wonders if there would have been more opposition in closing down one of the main streets for the afternoon had it been only for a girl from Abbey-Ville. But he is being unfair. Surely communities pulled together when it mattered. Despite this new-world order of protectionism: door closing.

'Are you OK?' Maarten asks Jenny.

The smallest of nods. She is white-faced, blending with the snow, washed into the background. It won't hurt, he thinks. She shouldn't really be here in any other capacity than another observer in the crowd. No penalty.

It is Wednesday, Christmas Eve, and the market is in full swing. Busyness thronging outside the blank street, lined with police tape, behind which the crowds breathe and rustle.

The streets paving the way to the lake have been cleared. The media is here, and the police. The two families stand in huddles; packed together, hostile, vulnerable.

'Sir?' Adrika is at his right.

'Yes,' he says. It's time. He had instructed them to scan the crowds. He can feel it in his bones that the killer will be here. Somewhere.

'Good afternoon.' His voice is metallic through the loud hailer. 'Thank you for coming along. As you all know, we're tracing the last known movements of Becky Dorrington. We have managed to piece together a few sightings, and some locations based on evidence retrieved, and they lead us from here, down through the park, where some of her belongings were found. I ask you to stand well behind the barriers at all times. There is a leaflet circulating with a number to call, should something occur to you.

'As you all know, another girl was also taken and killed. We believe the two crimes are connected. Assistance may help us locate Becky and may also lead to solving the murder of Leigh Hoarde.'

The rustle, the murmur, takes hold, like the buzz of a hive, and the press – clicking all around him throughout – begin to move; swarming in clusters, and stepping forward as the young girl, chosen for the part for her long brown hair, and the following police car begin inching their way forward.

It's slow, macabre walking.

They have prepared a signal. If Jenny sees or senses anything in the crowds, she will text the word PACKAGE.

It is ridiculous, really: he is placing such faith not in the sightings of the public, but such fantastical imaginings. He is hoping for some sort of sign; some sort of supernatural stirring?

61

'Shit, this is weird,' Sam says, muttering quietly. 'Are you sure you don't just want to leave? We've not got the kids. We could just go and get pissed instead.' Her head leans to Jenny, moving instinctively away from the throng of the crowd following the girl.

Long brown hair falls down her back, as the girl, aged about twelve, Jenny guesses, walks slowly over the cobbles, moving into the park. She leads the town, walking metres ahead of everyone else. She's older than Becky, but Jansen had said someone of Becky's age was too young to do this.

Shaking her head, Jenny grimaces. 'Can we do that after? I think I'll need a drink. Let's do this bit though, just in case.'

The park is grey as they enter. A huge crowd has turned out for the re-enactment. The media moves at the right and left of the public. Jenny can see Jansen up near the front. Matt is over to the right, and he waves as she catches his eye.

'Who's that?' Sam asks. 'He's fit.'

'He's covering the case,' Jenny says, trying to sound casual, but she can feel her face heat up.

'How do you know him?'

'I bumped into him…' Jenny starts, and although that was exactly what had happened, she knows it's now something more and it's tied up in this feeling, this connection (*haunting?*); she can't talk about Becky. Not to Sam.

'Did you indeed? Well, I bet that wasn't unpleasant.'

The snow underfoot has begun freezing. They pass the cathedral and the crust of frost breaks as they plunge off the path down the bank towards the Watermill Café. The narrow path that leads through the park, past the willow tree, skirts the edges of the lake. They won't need to go there, and Jenny is pleased. She had visited it countless times, felt a pull there. But now, after what her dad had said… well. The bells chime the hour behind them: ding-dong dell.

'Fuck, there's Tessa.' Sam nudges Jenny.

The crowd have spread out a little. Tessa and John Hoarde are up, almost at the front, just behind the police and the Dorringtons; space rings their unit: respect and fear. John walks with his arm through Tessa's. She leans on him, and her other hand is held by her sister. Tessa stumbles every now and again, but cuts such a slight figure, barely perceptible.

Jess and Kemmie Dorrington are up at the very front. They hold their heads up, searching forward; desperation and hope stream like banners above them. Their child's fate still unclear. Still hanging.

Pulling her eyes away, Jenny forces herself to move with the crowds. The wind is fierce as they tip over the hill, and she pulls her hood even further over her head.

'Jenny!'

Looking up, she sees Dr Klaber. He looks as surprised to see her as she feels to see him.

'No Finn today?'

'No, Will's got him. Hi... I didn't know you'd be here?'

'I told you I do Parkrun here sometimes. A few of us thought we'd come down, you know, to support it. You never know what you've seen, do you?' He waves over at some people on the left. Looking, Jenny can see a few more of the police up at the front, ahead of them. DI Deacon and the other woman – Jansen had called her Adrika – are up, with phones out.

'I better get over there,' Klaber says. 'I'm giving some a lift back afterwards. I'll see you after Christmas?'

She nods and he smiles.

'Merry Christmas,' he says, disappearing into the crowds.

'And who was that?' Sam digs her elbow into Jenny's side, and despite herself, Jenny laughs.

'That's my therapist!' she whispers, aware of eyes turning at the noise of the laugh, pulling her hood back up.

'Jenny Brennan. You're a dark horse. You never mentioned he was so attractive.'

'Is he?' Jenny catches a glimpse of Klaber's back. 'I suppose he is. Will came with me the first time, but not since. It's made a real difference... at least I think it has. I feel... I feel more able to *say* how I feel.'

'That's a start... and once this murder is behind us, I think we'll all feel better.' Sam shivers, wrapping her arms around her coat, stepping even closer to Jenny. 'I know you and Will live much closer to the lake, but I don't mind telling you, I don't like it when Ben's home late now. If he's not due back until after I'm supposed to go to sleep, I double-, triple-check the door... I slept on the sofa the other night until he got back. I was sure I heard something.'

The crowd surges together as they turn the corner past the clump of willow trees. Jenny sees Matt pause and take a photo. Jenny thinks of Sam's reaction, and with a glimmer of *schadenfreude*, feels less extreme about her own.

'Not long now,' she says.

Sam smiles a reply, tucks her arm into Jenny's, and then grimaces as the snow begins to fall in fat, white flakes, that fly towards them, obscuring the view.

Cold bites as the slow tread of the crowd moves towards the waterwheel. Jenny rewraps her scarf, but it's wet, and it clings damply to her face.

Jansen has stopped up ahead, and is explaining that this is where Becky's clothes were found; that the police suspect that whoever took Becky was disposing of the evidence of his crime. He reminds the crowd that there is a glimmer of hope that Becky is still alive. The profile the police psychologist had created was one of a man who wanted power and control over a younger girl, but may not have planned to kill her. A man with the capability to kill again, but perhaps not the desire.

Jenny shakes her head. The dampness is spreading upwards, inching in and under her hood. She reaches up and rubs, finding a drop of water on her cheek.

And another.

Stepping back, she bumps into someone behind her, and stands on someone's foot.

'So sorry,' she mutters, feeling another drop.

Sam raises her eyebrows, seeing her movement.

'Will's on the phone, back in a minute,' Jenny mouths, lying, and pushes her way through the throng. Faces blur as she ducks her head down; she can feel drops down her back, trickle, run, drip...

Breaking out at the edge of the thick push of the crowd, she pulls open her coat and rubs at the back of her neck. The sensation of cold water is overwhelming, her throat begins to close, but… nothing. There is no wetness on her fingers, but still she can feel a trickle: its cold, damp path burns.

Breathe, breathe, breathe… she thinks. Sweat, perspiration, a glow… it won't be water. Memory, now, takes hold like a physical state.

And then the whisper. Out beyond the willow tree.

Her head whips quickly. But nothing, it's nothing.

Eyes catch hers. Connor and Erin are up front, a good ten people away from her, but Erin lifts her hand and waves. Connor stares, stonily: looking, but not acknowledging.

'Sorry, love,' says a voice, as she feels something bump her at the back.

Her hands tremble; she turns, feeling pushed in, and the crowd begins to surge forward, following Jansen, as the walk begins again.

A whisper. The whisper, the rustle sounds again, breathing out: '*Save her.*'

'Who's there?' she says, blindly looking, but she can't hear her own voice. Her throat is thick, filled now with a thick warm air, clogging, cloying.

The faces come towards her as she pushes out to the edge. She ducks her head to avoid making eye contact with the swarming crowd, and arms brush hers as she squeezes out.

Something raises its head, appears as a picture, a card held aloft carrying a photo, before disappearing. What is it?

The rustle is louder. The noise of the crowd dims, and she begins to feel dizzy; spinning and winding, her feet are heavy, pulling away from the crowd as she fights to surface, to breathe. The main mass of people move ahead of her. She's alone. Except for… something.

It's not just a whisper. There's a noise. The rustle isn't breath. The wind, the sound of the trees…

The park fades. The cold air becomes icy; it stings. She reaches out to steady herself – there's the willow tree. Its branches wave like arms, covering her, hiding her.

The bells are ringing. The cathedral bells. Ding. Dong. Ding-dong dell.

'*Save her.*' The whisper is against her cheek. She's here again. And the voice, which sounds like milk, calls her. But there's something else, between her and the lake.

Her face is brushed by the willow, its twigs scratching and coarse. Someone is here. Someone is frightened.

She needs to pull away, to get out of here. Banging her hands to the sides, her fists move aside the waving branches, but she feels caught. Her pulse races. Her mouth makes no sound as she opens it to scream – like a dream, but the panic is real.

And there is the cry again, soft like a footfall, up ahead, beyond the branches, beyond the willow tree, closer to the clump of trees that stand towards the exit to the park: '*Save her.*'

Only it's not. Of course it's not. That's why he had sounded familiar. That's why there has been a pull.

The musk is sweet and pungent, moist. Dead leaves, rushing water… the chill like a sharpened blade.

The dark is physical. It moves, shakes. It lives. The weight is oppressive. Hot, cold.

Jenny peers forward, one step at a time. Is she alone? She can hear a breath, a whimper, a shout.

Now she remembers. In the depths of the night, she'd come for her mother, to hear her call her name: '*Jenny, Jenny!*' And before she had reached the lake, she had run into the willow tree, and heard it. Heard her. Heard him. Beyond the willow. In the black of night, she had heard the rush of water.

'Hello?' she calls.

The opaque air, the darkness. This time, in answer, there is the voice. The whisper. Guiding her forwards. Encouraging her to lean even closer to the ground, to reach out.

And then she'd been scared, because he'd shouted. And she'd run. She'd run so fast she had felt as though she was choking. The wind against her, like cold breath.

She'd searched for one voice, and found another.

Not 'Save her'; the cadence was wrong. The girl behind the trees had been calling a name. The cold wind had delivered it, and the rustle, the rush, of the water. And Jenny hears it echoing round in her head, with the smell of the willow, the sound of the water, and the lake, lying ahead, like an invitation.

The world darkens.

Jenny pulls out her phone, head dizzy and thick, and types a text: *PACKAGE*.

62

The jolt of the words, bold, leaping out from the phone, sends Maarten spinning out from his role at the front of the crowd. He had prepared Imogen and Adrika: were anything to arise, he would need to step out and one of them could take over. Sunny is at the back.

PACKAGE. It buzzes again, its repeat spurring him forwards. He tips his head at Adrika, who is closest, and he slips round the edge of the crowd, moving back up the hill.

The trees that line the curve of the path heave with snow, bent to accommodate the weight; their branches bulging with expectancy, of load; the sharpness of the icicles, the sparkle of the frost; the night-time shadows and light from the moon mix to cast a melancholy shade: bright and subdued, sparkle and fade.

Leaning against a tree, up ahead, Jenny is alone. Bent, following the curve of the branches. The weight upon her clear to see, but when she turns to face him, her face full, she passes it to him, and she drains before him.

'I'm not sure what happened to me... I don't know... The whisper... there was running water. It's the sound... and the bells. There were bells – I know that whatever I saw, I heard bells, so it must be near here. The sound of water and cathedral bells. And him. He's here too. I can feel it... he's here.'

He sees her eyes scan the crowd, a mass moving downwards, below them, away from the cathedral.

She stands, lifted, lighter.

'Are you OK?' he asks, although he can see something has changed.

'I panicked – I was certain I knew something, but now, I'm not so sure. I think I saw something, when I was sleepwalking. I think I saw something that I didn't really understand. But it was near here. You'll look again?'

'Round here?' He sweeps the park in his gaze.

'Yes... I... I think... I think I saw Leigh on that first night, with him. And I know something, I'm just to wait for it to bubble up. I think...'

He watches her stumble; it's still locked her up, whatever she's reaching for.

'I have been so afraid of it being me, just me who knows. I spoke to my dad today... Well, it doesn't matter, but I thought maybe I'm haunted... But maybe I'm just obsessed – obsessed by something I didn't realise... I heard running water and drips. You *must* be able to find her. She can't be far... He comes here. He came here with Leigh. The rustle I've heard, been hearing – the rush of water. But I can't hear it now. Maybe I dreamt it? And there was something else: "Save her" – I keep hearing it. But somehow it's wrong. Those weren't the exact words. And I'm sure I knew what it meant, but I passed out... my head is aching... it's all confused...'

He nods.

'I'm going now.' Her voice is tired.

Looking hopefully, expectantly, trustingly at him, he nods again. What else can he do? He can't make her stay. Her hand is bleeding. She must have fallen.

'OK, I'll get on it. Anything else?'

'No,' she says.

Maarten nods. He is already pulling out his phone, making the call.

'Can I go, now? Did it help?'

He tilts his head forward. 'Thank you,' he says.

The dial tone sounds as he watches her move up the hill. Her friend joins her as they turn up the path towards the cathedral, and they link arms. Moving up towards the moon.

63

'Thank fuck that's over!' Sam takes a gulp and checks her watch. 'And we've got about half an hour. I told Ben I wouldn't be back until four thirty, so got time for another at least. Happy Christmas Eve, my lovely!' She winks, and clinks Jenny's glass.

Jenny's arms lift almost of their own accord; she feels as though she's shed two stone. She's given Jansen everything she can, and she's free. She'd seen Connor again on the way out of the park. He'd waved. Conciliatory. There was a way forward, out of this. It is over. She can go back to Will, and they can start again. Buy a house. Would they stay? Now she knew her mother had drowned here? She hadn't died here – she had died at home, in Tonbridge. She was buried there. But is she closer to her mother here? Is that why she had felt so out of kilter, positioned on the tip of a pin, since moving?

'Let's leave the lake until the New Year,' she says. 'Once they've caught him, no shadows.'

The pub is warm and bright, Christmas songs play through the speakers and groups of drunk office workers sit nearby, wearing paper hats and talking too loudly, clearly been here for some time already.

'Are your in-laws here yet?'

Jenny checks her watch. 'They will be. They were arriving at about three. Luckily my dad's there. He's great at smoothing things over.'

She glances at her phone as it buzzes on the table. Will has texted: *Mum's offered to look after Finn so I can come and join you for a drink. I've sorted a bottle for him. See you in 10?*

'Will's on his way here,' she says, surprised.

'Great!' Sam says. 'Let me call Ben. His mother's over from Trinidad so we're taking full advantage while she's here; I bet he'll come out too. About time we let our hair down.'

64

'Anything?' Maarten shouts over to the other side of the room, where Sunny and Imogen are marking and crossing on the pinned drainage maps: every conceivable place where you could hear rushing water, near the lake and the river running from the waterwheel, close enough to hear the cathedral bells too. The search has been ongoing since Becky had gone missing, but they'd moved further outwards, the lake area had been covered.

'We've a team phoning round and one team has left already to start searching,' Imogen calls.

Nothing else had come from the re-enactment. Whilst Maarten believes in his bones the killer had been there, they don't have anything to search for.

But if they can find Becky. If they can complete the search and find her, then finding him will be easier. Maps, pinned on the walls, span the room, and pens are already crossing off various points further up the river, leading out from the lake. He can see Imogen at the far side of the room, going over the photos on the board. She picks up a packet of cigarettes, a lighter, and heads out of the room.

Announcing another search had been hard. He'd had to say he'd had an anonymous tip.

The super's face had been grimed with anger: the lack of advancement, the re-enactment. He had hissed at Maarten in his office, promising a call to Rotterdam, to take him off the case. The usual calm, the structure had vanished: 'Do you know the pressure I'm under? This has been going on for almost two weeks and still we're no closer! An attack, men in jail and no closer to the killer. Sort it out, Maarten. It's a waste of funding right now. We need real police investigation. If we're going backwards in the search it had better be for a bloody good reason... or Rotterdam will receive an up-fucking-dated reference.'

The faith, which he has placed entirely of his own accord, in Jenny Brennan is being tested.

'Sir!' Adrika's shout is loud, and she runs through the room, knocking a chair which spins to the side. 'Sir!'

'Yes?'

'I've got him on the phone – Dr Bhatti, you asked me to chase. He couldn't remember treating Leigh, so he had to locate his old files, and he found them... But he didn't. He didn't treat her.'

'What you mean? We've got the data here – three sessions, with a Dr Bhatti, on the school premises. CRB checked, and it's all here.'

'Yes, but it wasn't him. The CRB checks happened ahead of the appointment and then his move to Hong Kong was speeded up. He asked a colleague to take over; someone he trained with.'

Maarten sits like stone. 'But the signature is his name?'

'I know... which means this colleague must have lied. This other counsellor must have lied. Maybe he thought he could get away with it, as Bhatti was moving abroad. And it's not photo ID on the door. They take a driver's licence photocopy, but when it comes to actually signing in on the day, there's no photo check. He has lied, and lied deliberately. And there's more.'

'What is it?'

'When I asked the Dorringtons about Becky's anxiety, they said she had been tense since her SATs last year, and it was making her stressed in school. She wasn't really eating properly, so they have had a few recent counselling sessions. The name of the counsellor who Bhatti passed the case to is the same name as the counsellor that the Dorringtons went to privately with Becky. It fits, sir. We've found it. It's the link.'

65

'We'll be fine,' Felicity says, smiling.

'Come on, Jen. It's just a drink and Midnight Mass. We'll only be a couple of hours and he's already had enough milk to last him until at least three. It's only ten o'clock, and we'll be back by one at the latest. Snowball? Advocaat? Lambrusco? Hmm,' Will strokes his chin, raising an eyebrow, 'do you feel like a Babycham?'

She laughs. Will's a bit pissed already. So is she, come to think of it.

'Yeah, let's go. If you're sure, Felicity?'

'Yes, dear. You two go. Henry's snoring in front of the TV and I've got your dad for company. It will be quite relaxing really.' She smiles. 'I'll go to bed in a bit, but I promise to take the monitor with me and William can collect it once you're back.'

Woolly hats, thick scarves, lipstick and she's ready. They walk up The Lanes towards town, holding hands. Jenny can feel Will's grasp, like a paw in his gloves, curl round her fingers carefully, gently. The sky is clear and full of stars and the coldness makes her lean towards him. Walking out of the house together, Finn fast asleep and cared for, she feels released.

'So, what you got me? A Maserati?' Will says.

She laughs. 'I considered it. Gone for a country retreat instead, complete with labrador. You know I'm expecting loads of diamonds?'

'Got you a tiara and a yacht.'

'Chocolates then?'

'Might have done…'

He grabs her round the waist, and lifts her over a frozen puddle. She shrieks with the suddenness, the brief flight. His arm remains tight, close.

The Kings Arms is bustling and Will brings a large red for her and a pint for him. And crisps. They share a stool by the bar as the tables are all taken; the noise is thick and lively. Holly is woven on the wooden beams. His fingers brush her hand as he reaches for his drink; she thinks of their first meeting. He had laughed at her jokes: out loud, belly-laughed. Her fingers had itched to reach out for him.

Words bump and roll in the air above them, rising with the heat. She hears snatches from all around as they float: 'white wine for me…'; '… can't stand the stuff but I know she's gone and bought it again'; 'bet I've just got socks'; 'your mum's at it again…'; 'book about therapy – as if he…'; 'God, look at the time, got to get the presents out for the kids…'

Something stirs. She tilts her head, leaning into the conversations. What was it?

'So, go on, what have you got me, babe?' Will bends and kisses her. His lips land south of the top of her head, and she feels her ear turn slightly damp.

'Let's see, Finn's been doing some arts and crafts. I've been a bit more predictable. You'll have to wait and see. It might be slippers...'

'Socks? Gardening gloves?'

She laughs. 'You'd be lucky.'

What was it? What had been said?

'You OK? You've got that look again.' He peers, eyes narrowing. His features loom in, and she rocks back slightly as the beery breath hits her.

'I'm fine. The parents have got on well, haven't they? I was a bit worried about, you know, the mingling and small talk.'

'Yes. Even my bloody dad. Your dad started to tell me about your mum earlier. He said you'd fill me in...'

The bell rings for last orders. Jenny checks her watch.

'Shit, it's nearly time for Mass, come on.'

The streets are busy. People shout out to them, 'Merry Christmas!'

Jenny sees Sam and waves. 'Have a good one!'

'You too, my lovely. Lots of love!'

'Watch out!' Ben catches Sam as she slips in her heels in the snow.

Jenny watches Sam laugh, hanging onto Ben's arm, and Will throws his arm around her shoulders. From the weight of it, Jenny assumes it's part affection and part for support.

'Looks like you're on early morning duty tomorrow, Ben!' Will waves at them, and wobbles next to Jenny with the effort.

They head down to the cathedral. The snow has stopped. The moon is full and the air is crisp, clean. There is a crowd beginning to cluster around the huge wooden doors, overlooking the park.

'Quick,' Jenny says. 'We don't want to be right at the back.'

They cut through the graveyard lying to the right, to enter by the side door. It would be creepy but for the streams of people doing the same. Gravestones loom in the dark. Just as they duck to enter the side door, built a century ago for people shorter than they are, Jenny halts.

'The therapy book, Will. Someone in the pub mentioned a therapy book, and it's been ticking over in my mind. I didn't know why, but I'm sure...'

'What? Come on, the music's starting.'

Through the heavy doors, the stone floor stretches smooth before them. The thick of hush is velvet. Three cathedral volunteers lean in, offering paper programmes. A tall, young, bearded man reaches out to Jenny. His face is familiar: cafés, the market, the odd service they've attended. People she can nod to now; the community knitting to a pattern of house improvements, good schools, moaning about the commuter trains. An older lady stands next to him, her smile painted in pale lipstick, sitting on a lemon scarf.

Moving without jostling, people nod as they squeeze into a pew. They're more than halfway back, and TV screens have been erected behind the thick stone pillars, wider than the span of Jenny's arms. The smell of ancient stone becalming.

Will leans to Jenny. 'Have you got a tenner? I'm out of cash.'

He fills the gift aid section of the donation envelope, and Jenny flicks through the programme: 'Away In A Manger', 'In the Bleak Midwinter'. The melodies from the well-worn carols roll in her mouth like toffee, gooey and sweet.

A teenager lolls forward in the pew before Jenny, elbowed by his mother.

'I'm going to be sick,' he says. His cracking voice pitches high and low.

'Oh, for goodness' sake, you'll be fine for an hour. I told you to lay off the beer.' Her voice is crisp and her whisper brisk. 'Hold it together.'

He lolls forward again. Jenny grins.

The organ begins, rich and heavy, and the thousand-plus people, flooding the cathedral, collectively stand.

Soft lighting illuminates the tall, arched ceiling, not quite reaching the edges of the shadows. The chorister boys sing at the front, wearing high-necked white frill collared shirts, under long, dark red robes.

Jenny thinks of the therapy book comment. Why? It is stuck in her head, hanging, dangling, glistening. A hand knocks on the door – and warmth, a giving way. What is it? Its presence pulls, niggles.

'*Sanctus, Sanctus, Sanctus…*'

The choristers' voices lift high. Jenny feels the pull, the tugging cord in her brain release. She can lift herself free. This need not be her fight.

'*Pleni sunt caeli et terra gloria tua.*'

The service is gentle, a balm. Hymns familiar and the voice of the bishop soft, soporific. Will looks sleepy; he stands for the third hymn a fraction of a second after everyone else, giving himself a shake. He winks at her, turning the hymnal to the right page and joining in loudly and off-key, after everyone else has begun singing. It is warm and Jenny takes off her jacket, hanging it over the back of the wooden seat.

Are they OK, then? Maybe they are. It is stunning in here. There is a real feeling of belonging. She is not a newbie any more. This is where she lives. Where she loves living. The past few months have been hard, the past few weeks harder, but time is suspended in here. The town no longer seems daunting. People nodded to her as they entered. She jumped into the river to try to save a girl, and she has woven herself into the fortunes of the city.

'*In the bleak midwinter, frosty wind made moan...*'

The voice of the soloist rings into the cathedral, slicing like a blade of lace.

'*Earth stood hard as iron, water like a stone...*'

A stone. Water like a stone.

The music lifts with the crescendo, gathering pace. The forte signals for the congregation to join, and Jenny stands, adding her voice, lost in the swell.

'*Our God, heaven cannot hold him...*'

Why...

'*But his mother only...*'

The gust over her shoulder is gentle, '*Jenny.*' Now she knows this is her mother's voice, she treasures the word. Her palms moisten, her tongue dries.

In a blink, and flash, there she stands to her left. Her face is the same one that has peeped out at her through the waterlogged streets of the town, through the windows of the house. Through her dreams.

It is the same face: but softer, her mouth still an O, a plea. She is drenched. Water droplets run down her arms and off her fingers, pooling on the floor. The flames from the candles are reflected in the beads of water, sparking, flashing. The image from years ago, dancing before her eyes.

The ages of the cathedral fall away. Time disappears. What was yesterday is today. What should be today is years ago. The pit of forgotten things is not a place of stillness, but writhes with vitality, yearning for remembrance.

Her eyes meet Jenny's.

How did she ever think she could be free of this? These memories now lie like two halves, a yin and yang.

In the blink, in the flash, she appears and then she is gone.

Jenny remembers. She remembers that she has known all along. She knew at the very beginning. The sound of his name. It had leapt out at her, from the clean, white page.

She had been there. She had walked to the lake. Compelled there again and again, to hide behind the willow, as she had done on the day her mother had died. It's not a haunting, it's the rising reclamation of her darkest memories. It's not a ghost, it's a distorted face that haunts her dreams. Her mother, wet, ghost-white, calling for her. Desperation rewriting her beauty. Panic hollowing her eyes.

And she must have stumbled nearby. She had heard the whisper, the cry – like a yelp, gasping for air: not 'save her', but falling cry of his name: 'Klaber'. She had heard the whimper on the rise of the wind, and it had hidden itself in her mind, Swiss-cheese with lack of sleep.

Her heart clenches and the heat of the cathedral hits her like a spear. She rocks back. Her feet slip and she falls back into her seat, hitting Will on his side.

He grins down at her. 'The wine?'

Looking up at him, her mouth dries. She can't tell him. Not now. She will be undone. She will undo them.

'No, Jen, no. Please no.' His face pales as he stares down at her.

Moving is hard. Her limbs are heavy, weighted and cumbersome. Even sitting upright is hard. She fights for the vertical. Flailing. She needs to be outside, in the cold. This heat will burn her. She claws at her neck, pulling her top.

Will links his arm through hers, about to pull her out. The service is almost over.

'Peace be with you...'

Faces turn, hands outstretched. She is reached, grasped. Her hand lifts and falls, her hands boil, burning from the grip of others.

Faces look her way... She searches just for one.

Will heaves the huge doors at the back, and he leads her out. The moon is bright. The park opens up before them: a velvet map. The lake lies hidden. Jenny feels its wetness, its coldness.

66

'And what's his name?' The room is silent. No one even breathes.

'It's a Dr S. Klaber.'

Maarten exhales. The blood pounds in his ears.

'Sir, are you OK?'

His body is sweating, and his fingers type quickly, pressing the letters incorrectly, fumbling: *Liv, where are you?* He knows eyes are watching him.

The zing of the reply is fast: *In town. Meeting Mum and Dad, then heading to carol service. Seb meeting us there. Probably leaving around 11.30pm – late one for girls. We're hoping you and Imo will make it too?*

Fingers damp and sticky, he replies: *Don't go to carols. Come to station.*

The faces. Expectant.

'We need to bring him in. Now.'

'Yes, but I need to get his address, sir, and there's no one at the clinic today. I've tried. I suppose I can try the medical council.'

Closing his eyes, Maarten feels the room swirl further

around him, and says, 'It's OK. Dr S. Klaber – I know what the S stands for. It's Sebastian Klaber. It's Seb – it's Imogen Deacon's husband.'

'Fuck! Shit... But...'

Maarten scans for Imogen, but she's not back from her fag break. He looks at the ashen faces before him. Of course they'd never even considered it; not Seb. And yet he's been hovering. His mind flashes to the night Seb had put his back to the cameras of the press, to shield him and Imogen; only he hadn't been shielding them, he'd been scared of having his face in the press. Of being recognised. And he's been around, all the time, asking about the case...

Christ, the stuff they've told him... He'd known when they'd finished with the search in the local area. He would have known where it was safe to put her.

The room is motionless, like a collection of statues. He needs to break this moment. But his daughter, planning her party with Becky...

'Move. Sunny, take one car and Adrika organise the other but you need to check CCTV. We need to act now.' And like a broken spell, the roar of the sound of movement in the room is deafening.

He thinks about Nic again – his girls – the whole of his calm tips on its head.

The vanished sun, bright with hope that afternoon, is long gone. The shade of night hangs heavy, and pushes them into Christmas Eve with force. The eleventh day, and the proverbial eleventh hour. They must find him.

'Where's DI Deacon?' Maarten grabs his coat as he prepares to run down to the car. He needs to get Liv and the girls here. Until he knows they're all safe – until he can see it, he can't relax.

'No idea, sir. Does she know?' Adrika says.

'No – we need to put her in a room. She's got to get out of the way. Have Sunny find her – I don't care what you tell her, but she goes in a room. Out of the way.'

'She headed out for a fag and I haven't heard from her since. I've got a team ready. We're looking at outhouses up from the waterwheel that we think might fit a child in, and there are some sheds, the Roman ruins... We're going now, to see if any are likely,' Adrika says. 'We've also sent Forensics to DI Deacon's address, and a team to Klaber's clinic.'

'Right, good. Pull his bank statements too. See if you can find a link to the girls, or the phones he gave them. Shit...' Too many thoughts in his head. Liv's not answering her phone – she must have gone to the carol concert anyway and turned her phone off. Is Seb there, sitting next to Liv, unaware of their search? He feels sick.

Sunny was due to call in five minutes to confirm they had Klaber – that they had Seb.

It is still too much to reconcile. How can Seb be involved in this? How can it be him?

'Oh, and... sir?' There's a hesitancy to her tone.

'Yes?'

'It's Tim Pickles.'

Pickles? It feels weeks since they had thought about him.

'What is it?'

'Well, the hospital's called the station. What it will mean for John Hoarde, for that poor family...' She is tired.

The lights are bright and Maarten can see shades of pewter in her skin.

'He's in trouble. He had a heart attack. It looks bad.'

67

Christmas Day

'I just can't do it anymore! It's more than I asked for and it's more than I can handle!'

Will stands in a pool of light on the dark cobbles surrounding the cathedral. Mass is exiting; the crowds a backdrop, a retreating huddle adding texture to the tableau. His figure is dark against the light. A tall frame, with hidden eyes: the silhouette of his figure paints in the colours of his shape with an inky grey, a midnight blue, a granite black. A moment passes, and then no shade remains. His cardboard cut-out outline darkens as it stands, an arm's reach away.

'You know, babe, I know I'm so bad at telling you this, but I love you so much. When I thought the police might keep you in, charge you... Fuck, Jen, I just shut down. I don't know what I'd do if that happened. But now that we've got through that – well, I feel so hopeful for us again. I just can't stand for you to disappear again. Don't do it!'

Jenny wants to know if he's crying; if his words cut him. They cut her. The intangible line that has frayed over the past weeks, tied between them in promises, kisses, hopes, childbirth, holds by only a single strand. It strains under the weight of the cut, and with one breath more, it will sever. Her solitude will take root.

'Say something, Jen,' he says. 'Say something.'

She wants to speak. But the marbles have grown in her mouth. The words that rise, carry resonance, weigh her down. She can't spit them out. They are lodged, pressing her tongue flat to the floor against her bottom gums. Her teeth are wedged between them. One must be chipped because at the back of her throat, a sharp sliver of glass is stuck. If she tries to pull it out, the blood will flow.

'Please, Jen. Jenny, babe... say something. Where have you gone? When did you go?' He is crying now and the silhouette dips. The droop of his shoulders bends down into Thinking Man.

'How can you just stand there, staring? Don't you want to save us? Don't you want to try?'

Her heart breaks. She wants to tell him, but she can feel the panic rising, the need to run. To run to the lake. She can't form the sentences in her head. It's a jumble now, and there's no time. The lake is pulling her. She feels in her bones that Becky is out there; where she's sure she saw Klaber with Leigh. If he is going to kill Becky, she is sure he will choose the lake.

Will turns and walks away. The curtain is falling.

The bells sound out one o'clock. 'Ding-dong dell,' she whispers. Her feet, already petrifying beneath her, refuse to allow her to follow him. She wills them, but they do not move. The pull behind her is intense and when she does manage to lift a foot, to wrench it up and to step after him to say, 'YES', it will not go forward, only backward. Her feet turn her away from the city and out towards the park. Her coat is still inside; it sits on the wooden pew where she sang carols and leant towards him less than an hour ago.

There. The noise again. The drip of water from the trees, the rush of water coming from somewhere nearby. And the voice. There is clarity now.

Aware of Will, walking home, crying in the snow, to Finn, the drip still pulls her like a metronome. Her feet move with each drop. Andantino.

The darkness of the park a shroud. The whisper louder. The voice stronger. She needs to save Becky, when she couldn't save Leigh.

68

Arriving en masse, Maarten shakes with relief: Sanne won't let Liv go – in-laws trailing, hand-wringing, in their wake. Sanne is crying: she had been woken from a sleep in the car, wound round and embedded herself, buried deep under Liv's chin. 'Is it Christmas? Will Santa know where I am? How will he know?' And Nic. They are all there. Whole.

'Papa, have you found her? Have you found Becky?' Nic sobs, falls against him. He would hand over anything to be able to say yes, but instead he holds her, and silently promises her that Becky will be found. Nothing will stand in his way.

His whole team are out. St Albans is ablaze with them.

'Oh, Maart. Where is that little girl?' Liv holds each of their girls tight.

And he puts his arms around them all, and for the first time, he has no words to offer up. He is dry.

69

The dark ahead, the blackness, is like ink. She dips her hand in, pushing forwards, watching it be swallowed, then watches it come out again. Her withdrawing arm emerges pale. The ink has an alluring wetness. She can finally give in to it. Its embrace is a long-held promise.

The snow beneath her feet is soft. Her shoes offer no protection; they are wet too.

Finn? Will is with him. She will not be long. This is not for ever. She will save this girl. She will be back before light.

Drip. Splash. Drip. Drip.

Jenny carries on, deeper into the dark park.

70

'He's not there, sir. I've checked everywhere I can think.' A PC stands before him, pale like snow.

'CCTV, now,' Maarten says, and Liv whimpers behind him.

Adrika runs to Maarten as he rages in the office – ordering, shouting – trying to impose discipline in chaos.

'There are loads of outbuildings here, farms, stables… Sir, I don't know how to limit this. We can't have long.'

'Think.' Maarten sits. 'She'd been so certain, about the lake, the willow tree. And yet there had been no sign of them there this afternoon, when they'd checked. She said she had been walking to the same spot each time. But why?'

'Who, sir?'

'Jenny Brennan. It's not going to be ghosts – but what if it's something else? Do a scan of news stories about incidents in the lake. Is there something else going on here? Do it now, Adrika. We know her mother died in Tonbridge, so I don't see how it can be that – but search. Look for something.'

'Maart – where is he? You need to find that man. Becky…' Liv's face, pale, like ivory – cut like stone.

Maarten's phone buzzes and it's Sunny.

'I've got DI Deacon and she's off the scene. I've put someone outside the door – in case we need to interview her. Do you want me out, sir?'

'CCTV, Sunny. Can you go over the local film we have available for tonight?'

'Maart?' Liv grabs his hand, cold, firm. 'It's OK – I'll stay with the girls. Nothing will happen to them. You go and do what you need to do. I promise I won't let anything happen to them. We'll stay here.'

'OK.' He leans and kisses her. Hugs them both. Struggles to let go. Liv's arms: they bend round him, firm, tight. He leans his head on her shoulder and he feels stronger, his limbs more stable, head steadier. He's home: Rotterdam, Holland, Hertfordshire, England... home is here. Home is Liv and the girls. Beyond that, it means nothing. He doesn't need to take the job. He needs to hold them close.

Adrika shouts across the room. 'Mr Brennan called too: his wife's missing. They had a row and he thought she'd follow him home, but that was ages ago. He called to ask for help.'

'Now? Tonight?' Does that mean she knows something? They have no manpower. But Becky is waiting to be found. Can he afford to ignore it? Her truth has illuminated the case. If he could ask anyone for help right now, it would be Jenny Brennan.

71

Too tired for walking. Just a little sleep before going home. Just here... just lie down. The snow will be soft, a cushion. Bullied by the cold.

So sleepy. Only five minutes.

72

The lights of the cars outside are bright, flashing against the snow, lighting up the outside of the station like midday. It's not yet two a.m.

Adrika's voice shouts as he leaves the building. 'Will Brennan's coming in, sir. I told him he could. He's desperate. I will get someone to take a statement from him.'

'Fine, whatever.' Maarten goes to speak to Kemmie Dorrington, who has just arrived. And he thinks of Jenny, of how she'd directed them. Urged them to look again. And he shouts over his shoulder, 'Take him seriously, Adrika. Update me when I'm back.'

73

Jenny opens her eyes a second too quickly for her mind to catch up. A fuzziness of view. Something has thrown her awake. It must be the pain that she feels stab through her right thigh. God, it hurts. Her head aches and she longs to close her eyes again and sleep.

Through squinting eyes, the light black and green, she sees daytime hasn't quite begun. The air is thick and translucent. If it weren't for the burning in her leg, real and throbbing, she would assume she is still asleep.

It must be almost morning. Reaching out for the clock that lies on her bedside table, it isn't here. Instead, she grabs a handful of cold, wet leaves. Her fingers curl tightly around them and fasten. Soft, slimy, thick with morning dew and frost, turning black: withering.

The damp seeps upwards, moving quickly, and within moments she shivers from head to toe. The only warmth is the fire in her thigh, a hot hole into flesh. She's lying on something sharp, something metal. Like a drain grid. She sits up. That rush of water. She can hear it.

There's no bed. There's no Will or Finn. Her thigh is red. The blue cotton of her jeans shows blood: a small pinhead soaking through to a palm-size stain.

The shivering is intense now. Her teeth are chatting and her fingers are numb, moving in the air as though playing rapid, uneven scales on an unseen piano.

That she finds herself outside is no longer a shock, but it is still terrifying. Embarrassment sets in – what will she do if someone spots her here? She can't explain it away. She glances around, left, right, left again.

This time, however, is worse than before. This is the first time that it is near morning – it must be. She had left the cathedral just after one o'clock – she had, what, walked into the park? She couldn't have been asleep long as she would have frozen to death. It must still be only about two or three a.m. Christ. She's got to get back. She's got to get back before Will wakes to find her gone.

And she's got to get back to Finn. His first Christmas.

Her memory kicks in and Jenny thinks of the fight. She had run through the park: no phone, no purse, no coat.

The lake is frozen and swathes of moonlight cascade from the cloudless night sky. There are a few remaining patches where leaves circle round in pools of water. Stranded. Standing slowly, her leg hurts, but not enough to stop her getting back home. So, despite the shivering, ice cold, she takes a step forward and moves behind a bare tree. Once back on the path, it won't take more than five minutes to run up the hill. Finn will be awake and need feeding, but Will is there. There is no reason to panic. She just needs to stay calm.

The scratching branch of the tree pokes her as she squeezes past. The branch holds her fast. Pulling free her T-shirt, snagged on twigs, she catches sight of something else caught higher up in the branches. A soggy jumper, half frozen.

Jenny opens it out, to see if she can wear it home, to cover up a little more, but it is too small. It is pink with flowers decorating the front panel. It isn't an adult's jumper at all.

Looking out at the lake, at the other side, near the swings and the small café that serves toasties and hot chocolate, she sees a body on the lake, not far from the edge. And also a figure.

It is the adult that holds her attention first. Dressed in dark clothes and running away, looking both exactly right and horribly wrong. Like many runners out on an early frosty morning: a hat, gloves, jogging suit bottoms, sweatshirt. But it's not day – it's the middle of the night. There can be no doubt they have placed the body on the ice. The run is fast, the woollen hat pulled tightly on the head, obscures the face.

Jenny chokes on her breath, falling against the tree. The sharp twigs push her back out again, refusing to let her rest.

The body lies flat on the ice. The position is awkward, one leg bent back and outwards in a way that legs shouldn't bend. One foot dangles into a watery hole, and it won't be long, maybe even now, that the cracks will appear, and the body – it must be Becky – will disappear for ever into the waters. They might pull the shell of her out, but the girl will have vanished.

She runs. She needs to get round the lake. The figure is moving away and the body lies helpless. It isn't far enough away to mistake for anything else. She can see arms outstretched on the ice, immobile and sprawled; a head, long hair, spread out in a chaotic tumble, and Jenny runs faster.

Looking once more at the runner, terrified to see it, but more terrified that if it changes course, and returns to the girl, it might throw her off her stride; she is relieved to catch sight only of a diminishing form. A small black spot now running into the trees that leads to the road. There is only her now. It is up to her.

The bluey hue of the darkness ignites a flash of a memory of earlier Christmas mornings and packed stockings at dawn. The childish delight of Christmas. There is so much to save.

Running faster still, she skids over a mirrored puddle and falls, heading down towards the lake, almost at the point where Becky hangs on the ice. Jenny skids, falling onto the edge of the lake, and she hears the cracks of pressure as she lands hard.

Her arm plunges into the freezing water and she withdraws it quickly. She is so cold now, she isn't sure she will make it out to the girl in time.

Slowly, so as not to crack the ice further, she begins to pull herself flat, gently reaching and sliding, inch by inch.

She can feel splashes of tears on her face and she thinks of Finn, of how he won't know her if she moves too quickly and falls in; all the mass of love she has felt, and been swallowed up by, might vanish into the water and be lost. He will think of only Will as he grows.

Reaching the long brown hair first, knotted and damp, it frames a white, ghostly face.

'Please be alive,' Jenny whispers. 'Please.'

As though carrying a newborn, she places her shaking, shivering hand under the head of the girl, to protect it, and then with the other hand she grasps her shoulder, before beginning to pull her backwards: slowly, very slowly. She is heavier than Jenny had thought, and in pulling, she hears the small splinters of ice giving way all around. It is taking an age: seconds, minutes, hours. There is only each tug of the girl and each movement towards shore.

Becky stirs beneath her fingers: 'Help me.' The voice is faint.

Jenny can see the edge of the shore coming closer out of the corner of her eye.

'Come on!' she shouts, to no one, but as she does so, she feels a surge of warmth in her feet. She pauses, and pulls her legs underneath her, kneeling, and then squatting. Her legs ache as she raises one leg, and she stamps, hard. She will be waist deep now; they will not sink.

The ice cracks with the sound of shattering glass and she pulls the body into her arms and wades backwards, in the frozen waters. Each step demands more, and she grunts loudly with the effort; her voice releases the strain of each thrust into the shallow shoreline. She breathes rhythmically, puffing out the exhaustion.

She bursts out of the lake with the body carried aloft; head first they reach the shore and she feels the earth beneath her bare and freezing feet. She gasps for air and screams, piercing and loud.

The warmth in her legs holds her upright for only a moment, and she falls over the body of the girl, and shivers, too cold for thought. Becky's eyes open briefly, and Jenny whispers, 'I've got you.'

Before Becky passes out, she can feel her hand grip her thumb, before fading.

A voice whispers at her ear. 'Got you, you bitch.'

74

'Here, sir! There's something here.'

Adrika is leaning over a list she's printed off. 'The bank statements! There's something here, a direct debit that leaves his bank account to a local farm. Sir, they will have outbuildings there. What if that's where she is? Where he's kept her?'

'Get a team there now.'

75

The shock of his voice is like a fist, even before he hits her.

Jenny isn't sure her heart is still beating as her chest tightens so quickly. Too quickly, and she pants out air, her muscles flooding with the roar of adrenalin. She is rising upwards, to push away from him, when the punch lands.

Her cheek crunches beneath his knuckles. The sound – rice crispies exploding in her mouth; a dog biting down on a bone – worse than the pain, numb at first.

Rolling, falling, she lands on the edge of the ice, which splinters and, sharp like shards of glass, cuts her cheek, her face, her lip. Her eyes close as her head dives into the inch of water beneath, and she flings her arms out, palms down; instinctively, saving her head from the full force of the fall.

'You fucking bitch!'

And then he kicks her, and the only direction in which to curl is further into the water. And she bends, foetal-like, turning on her side. Water soaks along her back, her shivering increases. Or is it the shock? Shock makes you shiver too, she thinks. She is amazed she can think, her mind has slowed it all down. Or has he stopped?

Jenny opens her eyes, and he stands over her. Klaber. His tall frame, once so graceful. His hands, once so warm, so calming. It all now looms. Looming, imperious. Vengeful. Vengeance.

'Why? If you had gone home. Just gone the fuck home. Why is that so hard?' And he kicks her again.

This time she manages to roll, and the blow misses her body, just glancing her shoulder. He seems to neither see, nor care.

'What is it with you? Why will you not just stay away? She was in there, I was finished – and now I have to do it all again, and you too. Do you think I like this? Enjoy this? The things I'm driven to do, by you fucking bitches! You give me no alternative. Force my hand. For fuck's sake!'

He looks around him, and she sees his fear, his jumpiness. He is tightly wound, like an electrified coil. He zings; he stings.

'I won't say anything,' she whispers. Her teeth chatter, and worried he didn't hear, she tries again, as loud as she can manage. 'You could just leave. I won't tell them I saw you.'

Teeth baring, his lips curling up, she realises he is laughing, and he leans close.

'You're lying to me, Jenny Brennan. All you've done since the start is talk. Talk, talk, talk. And how you know the shit you know, I have no idea. But I sat across from you, and you've spilled stuff that means I'll never let you go.

'I tried to stop you. I put your number in that phone for them to find. After the sob story about you walking in the park – I knew you'd go back there. And you gave them the first phone! Fuck – it threw me, then I thought, let's play you at your own game.'

He gestures around, and again jumps. Shadows on the lake making him uneasy.

'And you played right into my hands. Leading the police to that backpack. Finding Becky's clothes by the watermill. You told me you'd be at the café that afternoon – why the fuck you jumped in I don't know! But it did what I wanted it to. It slowed them, redirected them. Gave me a chance to get Becky settled in the stable whilst the police searched the river. So if I can make it look like you did this... maybe...'

He pulls her up.

'If it hadn't been for you... They had *no idea* before you!'

The shout is fierce, intense, rather than loud, and Jenny flinches back, expecting another blow, and his arm rises; but dropping it, he shakes his head.

'Doesn't matter anyway now. I've got no choice. I'm running, once I'm done with the two of you.'

Glancing at the girl still sprawled on the dirt at the side of the lake, Jenny sees she's unconscious. If he manages to kill her, Becky has no chance.

Finn... can she run away, back to Finn? What will Finn do without her? She can't leave Finn, like her mother left her.

Klaber grips her wrist and his fingers cut deep, the blood spilling away beneath them. Pins and needles shoot up her arm.

Strangely calm, her mind thinks clearly, steadily; in contrast to her body which is shaking, almost convulsing, her mind runs thoughts out in full. There's no getting away from this. But surely somebody will come. He's jumpy because he knows they're looking. She thinks of Maarten Jansen, of his promise to search outwards from the lake. If she is to be saved, it will be Jansen.

She can't give up. She needs to fight. She needs to be clever. He had played her, talked her into self-doubt. To doubting Will. He had set her up. She can outwit this man. He might be stronger, but she has more to live for. And Becky has everything to come.

Klaber pulls her up, heaves her over his shoulder, but she is heavy, waterlogged, and she slips to the side.

Swearing under his breath, he grabs her waist and she tries to wrench free. Her fingers fumble at his, and he is wearing gloves which slip off. Diving forward, she manages half a step. A plunge, the start of her run, is blocked as he scoops her round her waist and hauls her back into the water, calf deep.

'Come on.' He yanks her backwards, jerking her from her middle, and she starts to cry, pain and frustration.

It is Finn she can see. It's all she can see. She can't leave Finn.

'Come on!' His voice is louder this time. 'I wish I knew how you found the phone. I hid it near the willow tree. That wasn't for anyone to find.'

She is almost thigh deep as he drags her backwards, and she tries again. She throws her weight forward, leaning hard on his arm, spinning her head round and trying to bite his shoulder. She kicks her foot back, and it lands on his shin but it's difficult to swing it in the water, and she knows she hasn't hurt him. Even the bite… it's his sweatshirt she can taste.

'For fuck's sake! Do you ever stop!'

'Please don't kill me,' she says. Her tears flow. How can she win here? To plead, to cajole? 'I don't know why you killed Leigh, but I won't tell anyone, I can't say anything…'

'Not here. I'm not doing it here. We're going.'

'Where?' Jerking in shock, she panics. The only hope they have of being saved is being out in the open.

The water soaks almost to the top of Jenny's legs, and he swings her round, facing him. His hand locks round her throat. He leans in.

'We're going into the water.' He smells like death. 'Under the ice.'

76

Maarten sits to speak to Will Brennan. There is barely any time left. Seb will move quickly – he has no choice.

A buzz has begun in his ears and his eyes flinch as he catches the beam from the ceiling light.

'I should never have left her! I was so angry – this bloody stupid ghost crap; I just want my wife back. Maarten – can I call you Maarten? Can you help me?'

His face crumples, and his head shakes; shoulders sagging. Will Brennan is as lost as he is.

'We think we might have a word on where Becky is. Maybe when we find her, we find Jenny.'

'Oh God... I've phoned her friend but she's not there. It's my fault. Since we had Finn, she's up all the time at night, she's tired when I come back from work. And I want to talk to her about all the things we used to talk about, but it's like I can't any more. Restaurants, client trips – she just looks at me... blankly. And I've hidden from it. I've stayed at work, where I know what I'm doing. Where I'm the one in control... So it's my fault?'

Will looks at Maarten, and there's nothing to say. Maarten remembers the first six months after Nic. It's a rite of passage.

'Let's focus on finding her. Both of them.'

77

Her heels scuff the dirt and he drags her. She has to half run to keep up with him, her arm wrenching in its socket. But she keeps falling, and the pull when she does is immense; she digs down with her feet to heave herself back up, to prevent her arm breaking. She has lost a shoe. The cold, the overwhelming cold, presses so hard she's afraid she will black out.

'Here.' His voice is short, a bark, and he ducks under the willow tree.

So close to passing out, Jenny wonders if she is dreaming as she hears the voice again, 'Save her.' But she realises that it's her own voice she can hear, and she's not saying, 'Save her,' but his name, over and over again: Klaber, Klaber, Klaber.

The first night; the fug of sleep, the image creeping round the corner of consciousness. Sleepwalking. There had been the voice, and the figure of a girl behind the willow tree. And it had been him. She hadn't done more than glance that way, as the lake had been pulling her. But as Leigh Hoarde had gasped, 'Klaber,' Jenny had been locked in. She hadn't even known what she'd seen – it had been a dream to her. It was here she had found the phone. And here, each time she returned, the haze of memory had sounded an echo of a cry, the sound of distress – a last fight.

It can't end here, not for her, not for Becky.

They are moving under the far side of the willow tree, up towards the clump of trees. Close to where Jenny woke up. Klaber drops her on the frozen ground. Becky is lying over his shoulder, and he tips her nearby. Jenny reaches out, holds her hand, whispering, reassuring: 'Don't worry, don't worry.'

There's a flicker from Becky. Her eyes open briefly, and look into Jenny's. The deep green flickers, sparks, and then the lids close again. But she's alive. Jenny grips her hand, warming her, reassuring her. She will not let go.

Klaber leans heavily on a long metal bar, and the grating noise is loud.

'Fuck,' he mutters, and whatever he is lifting falls, and he begins again. He leans out and picks up a brick, and balances the edge of the grille on it, leaving half of it raised. Wide enough to lift in a child. An adult.

'Please, no,' Jenny says. 'No, don't… I won't tell, I won't say.'

'Oh shut up,' he says, and he reaches out and lifts Becky to the edge, lowering her in, feet first.

Jenny feels Becky's fingers slip from hers. She's not finished.

Jenny wants to run, but there is nothing left. And how can she leave this girl? The first time she didn't even know what she'd seen. But still, if she'd woken, could she have saved Leigh?

'I only killed Leigh because she made me do it. I gave everything to that girl. She was so broken when she came to me and I built her back up. The love and attention I gave her! I had nothing like that when I was a teenager, no one to look out for me. No one gave to me what I gave to her – I grew up alone. But she wouldn't do what I told her. We were in a relationship, for Christ's sake! When she turned on me, rejected me – well, I didn't have a choice.'

He grabs Jenny and pulls her towards him.

'When Bhatti gave me that file... I knew it was my chance to make a difference. But after weeks of saying she loved me, she turned out to be just another prick-tease. Right here, under the willow, was supposed to be our first time together. But she said no, said it wasn't what she wanted. So I put her in the storm drain to think it over. When I came back, she said she was ready. But she was a lying bitch. When I touched her, she fought me. She hit me! When I hit her back, she just went down. What could I do?'

He swivels Jenny, preparing to lower her in after Becky. 'It was the job that gave her to me. It's pathetic that there are all these rules about relationships with clients. But this way I was safe. To pretend to be Bhatti, to get to know her without prying eyes. I was safe – even when she was dead, I was safe. And Becky didn't even need to get involved! I didn't want her to die. I just wanted to help her. She was beginning to trust me. It was only because you gave them Leigh's phone that I had to take Becky too. She was the only other person I'd given that phone number; I haven't seen more than a couple of children since. So when Becky dies, it will be *your fault*. But how did you know? I tracked the case from home... from...' He shakes his head, like he can't say her name. 'You told me details about the case even the police didn't know. How?'

His face is now pressing up close to hers. His nose almost touches her nose. He tilts her up from the throat, and pinpricks of light pop up all around.

'You said "she" led you to Leigh's phone. Who is this "she"? Who were you talking about?' He growls, and she can smell his breath. His arm is raised, and it's coming. It's coming soon. There's almost no time left.

'Who, Jenny? Who?'

And from behind him, she sees a lift and fall of the willow branch. And she thinks of the dark hair, of the whisper, of the shout.

And now she knows there's no ghost, that it's the lack of oxygen, lack of sleep, her darkest nightmares rising up in this state of semi-wakefulness. But he doesn't know. And she understands now how the fear of the dead can cut to the quick.

She opens her mouth, and rasping, with rationed breath, she says, 'Leigh. It was Leigh.'

78

'Sir, we've found some clothes! There are a few bags here. Looks like he was prepared for her – all seems like charity shop stuff but she's been looked after. Blankets too, food and water. There's a stable. No horses, just a stable in a field off the estate just outside St Albans. No Becky, but I'm getting Forensics down here now, going over the evidence of someone having been held here.'

Sunny's voice is buzzing down the line. They have evidence, but they don't have Becky. Where the hell is Becky?

'I've just got off the phone with Jenny's father!' The excitement in Adrika's voice is contagious.

'Yes?'

'Well, one of the articles that had come up was about a mother and a daughter who fell in years ago, and the mother later died. I've spoken to Jenny's father: he told me that Jenny fell in, then watched her mother struggle in the lake. She died later.'

'Where?'

'She fell in by the waterwheel, but her mother was swept

downstream to the lake – by the weeping willow. That's why it was the same spot – it must be!'

That's it. 'Adrika, you are a star. If she was out there the night Leigh went missing, then she probably has no idea what she knows, or how she knows it, but I bet she has seen something. Do we know where she is now, any update?'

Adrika shakes her head. 'No, and her husband is frantic. He's still here – I told him to wait.'

'Well, I'll try the lake. If she's been going back there, chances are she has returned. She talked about rushing water near the willow, but we couldn't hear any. But maybe it was nearby – somewhere you can see from the willow, and still hear the bells. You stay to focus on the search for Becky. I'll get Will Brennan. We'll head back to where it all started.'

79

Klaber's eyes widen. He shakes his head. 'What do you mean?'

The water soaks. The cold. The pain of it. Jenny feels so much pain. Her cheek burns. Lights pop all around, and she is fading.

Sound becomes faint to her, remote, like a distant line, a bad connection. The cold, so cold.

'What do you mean?' Is that fear in his eyes?

'I…' But she can't speak.

The world darkens; again Jenny tries to reach out, to fight. Becky and Finn. Becky and Finn. She manages to grasp at the arm holding her throat, but her hand slips. She tries to grab the other, but loses her footing. She feels herself lowering into the depths. The river lies above them, the frozen ground.

'*Jenny, Jenny!*' The memory of her mother, calling out, and with it comes a burst, a final clutch at life.

She grabs his arm, hard and fast. She is already lowering into the storm drain, already almost at the final point. Her fingers dig and hold. She hangs from his arm, her feet kicking against the slimy concrete. Levering hard, she pulls with all that she has.

There comes a scream: from within but, Jenny could swear, not just from her. Buried deep, carried for weeks. It flies from all around. Klaber too is screaming, the peal of the cry is so loud it has movement, it has colour; and the ice on the willow flashes for Jenny. The light is luminous.

With the scream, she feels his arm begin to give under her grip. Her shoulder pulls. The strain of his and her bodyweight hangs from her socket, but she is equal to this. It's her last stand.

And they both fall. Down, and down. The drain isn't more than six feet deep, but the fall lasts, and it's Klaber's face which is crumpled in shock. His feet follow, and he tips down on top of her, she hears the bang of metal, as the grate lands. The brick falls down after them. Heavy.

'No!' The scream belongs to them both. Voices lie atop of the other.

For a second, everything stills.

Braced for more, she feels him pin her, and with one gasp, his movement stops.

Klaber is heavy, and Jenny tries to push him off. She tries to haul him to the side so that she can reach Becky, make sure that she's not lying face down in water, which rushes through the drains.

But he is so heavy. The brick lies nearby, seeping its redness into the water: bloodied and guilty.

Stretching as far as she can, she finds Becky's fingers and she calls out, 'Can you hear me, Becky? He can't hurt us now. We just need to hold on. Can you hear me, Becky? I'm here. I'm not leaving you.'

Jenny's world dims. Drops of icy water hang from her, above her, all around – dripping like crystals onto the three of them, buried beneath. The morning light catches them, and they flash like lit beacons. There is fire in this ice. She knows she is going to pass out, the world swims around her, and she prays that the fire will light the way for someone to come.

They lie buried beneath the ground, with the vicious chill.

Klaber must not claim them.

80

Roads twist and tyres slide. Will grips, white-knuckled, to the car door and Maarten drives as he knows he shouldn't, keeping it only just under control... it could fly from his grasp at any second on a patch of ice. Fly out of his grasp as it had done in London, hitting that boy... It hadn't been his fault, but it is his burden – the boy had run into the road during a chase, not dead, but holding that body while they had waited for the ambulance. Fragile breath.

The car now could tip and then what would Becky do? How would he face Nic? What use would he be? He presses the brake, angry with himself, the roads, the dark.

Skidding to a halt at the roadside parking near the Watermill Café, where the river runs to meet the lake; the tyres slip as Maarten flings open his door and runs, leaving the hinge to bounce and strain. Will's footsteps sound behind him. The snow makes running hard, but most of the path is beaten down: it's slippery but not too deep.

'Jenny!' Will is shouting behind him, over and over. 'Jenny! Jen!'

The moon is full. It's easy to see the lake. Running, he scans left, right.

'Fucking hell!' Will powers past him, swerving right.

Following, Maarten looks ahead, in the direction of Will's stride. There is clearly something lying at the side of the lake, where the edge curves round close to the path and children persist in feeding ducks bread, despite all the signs telling them not to. Lit by the moon, he sees Will run.

'Jenny!' Will is screaming now.

Maarten, lengthening his stride, is faster. He reaches the mound before Will. And yet there is nothing, except scuffed, muddied snow, and a shoe.

'Oh my God.' Will crumples next to him, picking up the shoe. 'This is hers. This belongs to her.' His eyes lift and he scans the lake, looking for any sign.

The eerie stillness, like a painting, is laid out in faded moonlight. There is no one here. No sound at all. Backup is on the way. There is no point them diving in.

'But it's not just here, not just the lake,' Maarten says, gathering himself. 'Come on.'

Running, he moves to the willow, lying on the other side of the path round the lake. It looks like a beast in the dark, and he plunges in, where the ground is drier, into the heart.

'Becky? Jenny?' he shouts. She had said there had been the sound of rushing water. If she was holding a glimpse of something in her brain, then he cannot discount any of it. He needs to follow the clues. Klaber must have had somewhere to hide, to hide these girls quickly, even as a temporary measure. He must have had somewhere to run close by. It can't have been long since they were near the lake – the shoe is wet.

He moves forward, through to the other side of the willow. Behind it lies a fence from where a farm opens up: fields, grass.

Pausing, he listens. His heart beats heavily, he feels dizzy with exhaustion.

But beneath it all, he can hear it. Rushing water. It's silent in the park now. It had been night when she had first been here. That's why they can hear it.

Where is it? What is he looking for? He crouches low, sweeping his hands over the ground, and finds a long metal bar, and, flat on the floor, a large grate; it lies just before the fence, beyond the willow, by the clump of trees.

'Will, help me!' Pushing at the ground he finds the edge of the grate and tries to lift. But it's both slippery and heavy. Grabbing his torch, he switches it on to see a storm drain. It spans about three feet in diameter, and is based near the bottom of the field, which rises upwards from behind the fence. An inlet from the river runs through the field, feeding the lake.

'Here!'

Will follows his shout, and between them, they heave it across, using the bar. Their fingers slipping on the cold, the wet. The blackness of the night split by the torch beam.

Where is the backup? Maarten thinks about chasing but time is pressing. Instead, with a heave, they manage to slide it across.

Below, the dark is absolute after the glare of the torch, and he leans down, balancing his body along the earth, holding his torch low, swinging it left and right.

And there they are.

Jenny Brennan, from what he can see beneath a body lying across her, she's a sliver of her former self, lying flat in the water. Her head almost touching the back of the concrete wall. Drenched, pale. Her eyes are closed; her body so still it makes his heart race.

In her hand lies the hand of a child. He can hardly see in the dark, but it has to be Becky Dorrington. He can't tell from here whether either is alive.

'Jenny,' he says. 'Jenny, can you hear me?'

81

Jenny hears her name.

She doesn't feel cold. Finally some warm settles within her. And she feels light-headed, as though she's thick with wine. She tries to open her eyes, but the lids are too heavy. Her lips are sealed shut. She doesn't recognise the voice, and then she hears it again, and this time it's Will: Will. He's come.

The weight is heavy on her. The water is rising, and she can't see Becky. Her tongue, despite all the wetness, is dry and sticking, and she musters strength to open her mouth to croak out her name, but it's only partially complete. She only hears the last falling syllable: 'ky'.

Pushing hard, she manages to roll the weight a little, but it falls back. And then the darkness closes in.

The sound of her name becomes faint.

Then nothing.

82

Maarten lands with a splash; the water flies up and he sees Will leaning down, arms outstretched.

Klaber lies on top of Jenny. There is only her head and shoulder visible, and the water in the drain is constantly rushing, slowly rising. Scanning for Becky, he can see her on the other side of the two bodies.

'Is she alive?' Will's shout is frantic.

But Maarten reaches Becky first – she's the child, and he bends down, flinching at the chill on her flesh.

'Here!' he shouts, and cursing because he knows that moving her could be entirely the wrong thing to do, if she's fallen badly, if she's had a blow to the head. But he can't leave her in this water; if she is to live, then it's her only option. He lifts her high, gently. She is the prize. Children: life's finest prize. And Will scoops her up.

In the distance, Maarten can hear the siren of the ambulance, the backup arriving, and he turns his attention to Jenny.

Looking down at Klaber, anger grips. But he pushes him

off Jenny, forcing himself to focus on her, on what he can save rather than rage.

The water has begun flowing higher than her hairline, and runs across her brow. Kneeling, he lowers his cheek to her mouth, and tilts her head up and back. There is the faintest of breath, but her pulse is slow.

'She's alive, Will,' he says, and lifting her too, raising her above him, she is passed up and out.

And all he can do now, is pray.

83

Jenny can hear the sirens. They're getting closer. She can feel the sleepiness taking over. The cold, so cold, but she's stopped feeling it. Stopped feeling. But Will is here, and his hand is warm. His voice, babbling: '*Sorry, I love you, sorry, stay alive, hold on, stay with me.*' His wishes land softly, a caress, a warmth.

Jenny looks at his face and reaches out, trying to stroke his cheek. Her hand is heavy, her strength fading. '*Please, Jen, don't leave me. Stay with me.*'

His cheek feels how it did when they had first got together, after a night out at the very beginning: unwashed, rough, close.

84

The ambulance doors bang a distance away. Maarten holds Becky's hand like it's made of glass. She's still breathing, and it won't be long before they're here, to look after her, to make her whole. He lays his jacket over her, but doesn't want to press too tight. To break her.

He had lifted Klaber out. He lies sprawled in the snow.

Already the sounds of running feet are behind him. And yet there's a second before anyone will catch up with him, and he wonders whether Klaber will see the streets outside of jail again. Will he ever reach the full justice of the law? But the man lies broken before him. The fall into the drain, the angle of his body… He stares at him, Seb Klaber, Seb: bleeding at the side of his head, and the sight takes his breath away. He's nothing now.

Seb Klaber, broken, twisted. His good looks, his grace. He looks so innocent. Blood darkening his pale skin. Insubstantial.

What lurks beneath, blood so easily spilled. He had always thought they were a perfect couple: both a story of such success, coming from instability, broken homes; so contained, so driven. But so different. Imogen, vigilant with the law, tenacious. Yet, hidden in plain sight, here lay the gritty truth of human frailty, its violence and its fear: the demons and the knives.

'Thank you,' he says, lifting his eyes upwards, to the air, across the ripples, thinking of the girl who has almost been lost, and of the daughter mourned by the city. And whatever forces beyond his fingertips had saved her.

He looks to Jenny, Will bent over her, crying, stroking her brow. 'Thank you,' he says, almost silently. And his voice disappears into the wind.

85

The Dorringtons have arrived, and sit in the ambulance, listening to the paramedics reassure them about Becky: cold incapacitation and the beginnings of hypothermia, but her body temperature hasn't dropped dangerously low, and she's responding well, even now. Her eyes had opened, for the briefest of moments. And she had seen her mother.

Maarten listens, heart still beating at breakneck speed.

The phone lights and it's Adrika. She speaks quickly, in the hushed tones of the hospital, 'They're all here, sir. All at the hospital. The extended family of the Dorringtons waiting, almost celebrating. But the Hoardes are here too, just standing at the side. I spoke to them, told them how sorry we are. The father said he wanted to come, to see that it was over. But it's not over for them. I don't think it will ever be. Pickles is still unconscious, do I need to…?'

'It's Christmas Day. He's not going anywhere, Adrika. The others are still in custody, aren't they? Get someone to charge them. They should feel it. But not John, not today.' If those men hadn't spurred him into this. If those girls hadn't bullied her in the first place, then maybe she'd never have crossed his path. Hopefully Tim Pickles will pull through, and then John need only deal with his grief, to try to survive it.

But the lights on the ambulance begin to flash, and they're almost ready to leave. He rings off.

He moves to his car. Becky deserves an escort.

86

The ambulance doors are open, framing the lake, waiting to leave. She's cold, shivering, but conscious. Immersion hypothermia they had said. Concern, but she's in good hands. Antibiotics, staying still until her body regulates. Cuts seem mainly superficial. They will need to X-ray her cheek. But the cold had saved her, slowed her body functions down, stopped them collapsing; she had listened as they had explained to Will, who fussed around her, guarded her.

She lies still now, thinking of Finn, of holding him. Her arms crave him. It is the lack of him that will lead her to collapse. It's him she needs.

The liquid midnight blue of the lake is empty. Well, almost. She blinks, and before her eyes appears the young woman. She smiles. And her features blur slightly, adjusting to those of a face she recognises from her dreams, the photographs: her own face.

'Mum,' she whispers. The black hair in the lake; the green eyes. It had never been Leigh, or Becky. Always her mother, the memory of her lying in wait, locked away. Opened with

Finn, when she needed her mother the most. And in following the lake, Jenny had been able to save someone; the lake hadn't claimed them all.

Jenny mistrusts death, ever present, the imprint of a life surely never leaves the ground, the lake, it is soaked up, waiting to find a release. It has always been her mum, waiting for her. This new memory, the nearness, the water: she flows through Jenny.

If she had to decide where it all started, she still couldn't stick a pin in a timeline. Time has changed. Its softness, its malleability has pulled apart her ability to make sense of a day. In its fluency, it mocks the dead. It seems they can peek around the corners of the future, and fade back into the past. Her mother stands before her now, years after her death. The sense of her, the sound of her urgent voice: '*Jenny! Jenny!*'

And without any shock, or sense of surprise, she can remember. She can remember seeing her mother, struggling; feeling her clothes cling to her body as she hid in the willow tree, crying and watching her mother flailing, fighting. Water had made her socks soggy, and in her shoes she had balled her toes as she had screamed: '*Mummy!*' And her mother must have heard her, as the arms, waving, had swung high in the air, calling her name, grasping: '*Jenny! Jenny!*'

As quickly as the form appears, it melts from where it came. The urgency has lifted. And into the water, to find a final peace without dreams.

Black hair, bloated garments aslant, floating on the lake. If Jenny were to reach out her hand, in the night, when the world sleeps and time bends itself through half-consciousness, through dreams, what would she touch?

Epilogue

New Year's Eve

Jenny wakes suddenly, uneasy, in a skim of sweat. Has he stirred? She leans to look for Finn, and his breath, warm and milk-scented, blows against her cheek. But it is nothing, a fragment of a dream that slipped in and out as she woke; the heat is heavy in hospital, and there is little to do other than nap. Finn's buggy is wheeled up against her bed, and Will sits beside them, dozing in the chair. He hasn't moved for the week.

The light from the huge window glows violet as the bright sunlight dims and night dips over the tiny city. Jenny relaxes back into her pillow, watching the colours shift, the smooth shades of evening deepening, ready to let in the new year. The breeze from the vent is fresh, cold. The snow has slowed, and has begun melting, seeping away; a carpet of early snowdrops lies around the verge of the hospital.

They have said she can go home tonight, before New Year's Eve takes hold. The matron, often so busy, so brisk, had put her hand on Jenny's after check-up that morning: 'No place to be at new year, not after what you've been through.

You deserve the night back at home. Plucky, that's what you've been. And that lovely husband of yours. I've never seen anyone so committed. He'll take proper care of you, no doubt.'

Home. The sound of the word had rushed at her, like an embrace. And Matron was right – Will had not left her side. He had brought Finn in every day, from the first chime of visiting hours. He had quietly shooed away his parents and had managed her father well, who had been shaken to the core, addled with the weight of his revelations, with his hesitancy.

Her dad leaked a tear that morning, when she had hugged him, he had felt older, more fragile. 'Jenny, pet,' he had said, as he had kissed the top of her head. But it isn't his fault. And the city isn't spooked for her. If anything, her mother feels more real than she has ever been.

Jenny is feeling better. She is feeling real, present: *herself*. For the first time in quite some time.

The door opens, and Will stirs but doesn't wake, as Maarten Jansen steps in quietly.

'Jenny.' He smiles. 'I hear you're out tonight?'

'Yes, and Becky?'

'Not tonight, but in the next few days. I wanted to come to say good luck. Becky is doing well. She was terrified in that stable, but he kept her fed and watered, and until the night he brought her to the lake he never touched her. We think he abducted her to keep her quiet about Leigh. According to his records, Becky was the next child he saw after Leigh. I have no doubt he would have repeated this pattern if he hadn't been stopped. He said these were children who needed him, but I think once he started, any child would be a potential victim. He might reason to himself he was helping him... Deep down he must have known he'd have to kill Becky eventually, but he couldn't bring himself to do it until things got desperate. Nic and Sanne are visiting in there now.'

Jenny thinks of Becky. Jess Dorrington had been to visit, and had held Jenny in a wordless embrace. She had felt her tears slide down her neck, and they had both cried. 'Thank you,' had been all she'd managed.

'And then that's it? It's over?' Jenny says.

'For you, and Becky,' Maarten says. 'For both of you.'

There's a pause. And Jenny thinks of Leigh, of her family. And there had been the teacher who was recovering, but he would be OK. He is only young. Collateral damage from an assault, an act of hubris. An evil.

'How's DI Deacon?' she asks.

'She's got a lot to deal with. She didn't know... I haven't really seen her. There were police interviews, procedures...' His face is impassive, and Jenny knows him now, knows that this precise tone – the clarity in delivery – belies his empathy rather than denoting a lack.

'His death...' Maarten begins. 'It finishes things, doesn't it; it's cleaner.'

'It's more than he deserves,' she says. But she doesn't know – how long would jail have held him for? To have him back on the streets at any point would have been too soon. Imogen Deacon will have her own peace to find.

Jenny can't think of anything to say. Do you ever really know someone?

'Happy New Year, Jenny,' Jansen says, voice just above a whisper, and he smiles.

He is right. For them, it is over. And for that, she can be eternally thankful.

'Happy New Year to you too,' she says, and it is. The

ghosts of the night, the limberings in her brain, the figures in her mind – there is peace.

For Jenny at least, it is a happy new year.

It really is.

Acknowledgements

I am grateful to my brilliant agent Eve White and her assistant Ludo. I'd be nowhere without them. And huge thanks to all at Head of Zeus, in particular my editor Laura Palmer. She understood the novel exactly as I hoped it might be understood.

I'd be lost without my CBC writing group and my book club. Ella deserves a thank you in lights for reading every version of this novel in its entirety.

Thank you to my friends who have lived this one with me. There are lots of you, but for the reads and advice big thanks to Rachael, Imogen, Vic, Marielle, Cathy and Emma.

Not least, thanks to St Albans, both the real one, and the slightly blurred one I've created here.

And finally, a huge thanks to my parents and sister, who are endlessly supportive, and my amazing husband and two children.

A letter from the publisher

We hope you enjoyed this book. We are an independent publisher dedicated to discovering brilliant books, new authors and great storytelling. If you want to hear more, why not join our community of book-lovers at:

www.headofzeus.com

We'll keep you up-to-date with our latest books, author blogs, tempting offers, chances to win signed editions, events across the UK and much more.

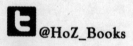 @HoZ_Books

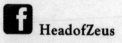 HeadofZeus

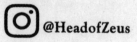 @HeadofZeus

🦉 HEAD *of* ZEUS